The Nativity

Seth Sjostrom

 *wolfprint*Media

wolfprint, LLC
P.O. Box 801
Camas, WA,
98607

For information, contact wolfprintMedia.

The Nativity / by Seth Sjostrom. - 1st wolfprintMedia edition

Trade Paperback KDP

ISBN-13: 978-1-7350236-2-5

1. Ryan Talley (Fictitious character)-Fiction. 2. Allison Tancredi (Fictitious character)-Fiction 3. Romance-Holiday-General- Fiction.

First wolfprintMedia Digital edition 2020. wolfprintMedia is a

tademark of wolfprint, LLC.

For information regarding bulk purchases, please contact wolfprint, LLC at wolfprint@hotmail.com.

United States of America

Acknowledgements

Kathi Sjostom for helping me find the right path on my walk and doing her best to keep me on it.

To small businesses and entrepreneurs everywhere, especially my writing haunts in Camas, Washington – thank you Jody, Allie and Britney of Caffe Piccolo.

Tom and Linda Sjostrom for their eternal support and belief in me.

All of my friends from Grace Church who help me to learn and grow in the light.

Hayden, my eternal inspiration.

One

Allison reached up, trying to find the nail she had left for the star last year. The November breeze buffeted the tall ornament as she stretched. With a third attempt, she pushed up from her toes, teetering precariously, she found the head of the nail. With a slight tug, she confirmed that she had rung the hook. The star in place, she let go in triumph. Her victory was short-lived. As she pulled back, she lost her balance. Flailing wildly, Allison plummeted backward towards the sidewalk.

Wincing as she anticipated the impact with the hard concrete below, she was surprised to feel a pair of arms instead. Her heart in her stomach, she cocked her head to see the face of a strange man smiling at her. "Barely December and Christmas miracles are in the air," the man said and gently set Allison on her feet. "Literally."

Blushing as she smoothed out her sweater, Allison gasped, "I'm…I'm grateful for you being there, thank you."

The man looked up at the star and tilted his head, "It's a little crooked." Glancing at the wobbly step ladder he added, "Do you mind?"

Still embarrassed, Allison motioned her reluctant okay with a flip of her hand. She watched as the stranger balanced on the ladder, reached up and straightened the star. Climbing down, the man admired his handiwork. "Well, there you go. Merry Christmas!"

Still a bit stunned from the experience, Allison mumbled a feeble "Merry Christmas" in return. She watched as the man continued on his way down the sidewalk.

"The manger is coming along nicely," a voice said from the storefront next to hers.

Allison looked up and beamed, "Thank you, Mr. Haverstein! Almost lost the star again!"

"I saw. Who was that young man?" Mr. Haverstein asked.

"I don't know, glad he was there, I guess," Allison shrugged.

"I told you that you need a new ladder, this one…this one is rubbish," the deli owner gave the rickety ladder a quick shake.

"I know," Allison conceded, "I just need to pinch my pennies a bit longer. Maybe after this season."

"Ah, it's been tight for all of us. You hang in there, you'll make it," Haverstein assured and retreated into his deli.

Allison sighed, looking up at her star for inspiration. Shaking off a chill, she set off to find baby Jesus to complete the scene.

Ryan Talley leaned against the wall. His notepad flipped open. He could almost write the article before the Twin Springs mayor spoke his first words. The politicians he covered never really shared anything more profound than the superficial rhetoric they served to the masses. Their mouths moved, but their voices carried the dialogue harkening the indistinguishable speech of an adult in a Charlie Brown cartoon.

Clearing his throat, the Mayor placed his hands on either side of the podium. "Just outside our hall, work has begun on the Twin Springs Art Walk. I know this project was met with challenges, our hardworking local businesses shouldering the bulk of the financial burden, but we expect dividends from this new attraction," Mayor Faslee declared.

One reporter raised their hand, "Mayor Faslee, was this initiative on the official ballot?"

The mayor played with the tie around his neck, "Well, we have a special provision process that allows initiatives to become proxy via majority signature."

"How many signatures did this initiative wring in?"

"Enough to satisfy the clause," Faslee replied.

"Who, Mr. Mayor, pushed this initiative?" Ryan asked from the back of the room.

"Uh, that would have been Elizabeth Faslee."

"Your daughter, sir?"

The mayor nodded.

"What forum did the local businesses have since they would be the ones shouldering this load?" Ryan asked.

"Well, you see, the way these signature initiatives work, they assume… well, they can write their own initiative next election," the mayor shared.

"If they're still in business," a voice from the doorway remarked. Mr. Haverstein closed the door behind him.

"If the businesses are worth remaining, they will still be there," the woman behind the mayor snapped. "This town needs an injection. An injection of culture, excitement. Those shops that don't survive will be replaced by boutiques and galleries that draw even more people into Twin Springs."

"Bring people in, Ms. Faslee? What about stores that serve those who are already here?" Haverstein pressed.

"What we're talking about is real money. A bigger circle on the map, not the tiny dot that Twin Springs is today."

"Who is asking for the larger dot?" the deli owner pressed.

"The signatures on the initiative," Elizabeth Faslee snapped.

The mayor put his hands up, "Okay, okay. We are getting a little ahead of ourselves. Today, we are talking about an art walk, not transforming the very fabric of our town. With the efforts of my daughter and like-minded citizens, we are accepting nominations for pieces to be displayed. Art will represent our town moving forward. Lizzie will collect the nominations and have photos available for voting and judging here at City Hall. We will finalize the first three pieces one week before Christmas."

In an effort to end any further back and forth from the audience, the mayor thanked the attendees and turned away from the podium. Kissing his daughter on the cheek, he hustled down the hall and into his office.

Lizzie Faslee stood tall on the little stage, looking at the small group that had gathered. Drifting towards the reporter pool, her eyes lit on a young man who did not fit in with the rest. He appeared a bit rugged, less refined than Lizzie's usual taste, but appealing just the same. Making a beeline for the stranger, Lizzie held out her hand, ignoring the local reporter as she brushed by.

"I'm Liz Faslee, the creator of the Art Walk project. I don't believe we have met. You are…"

Ryan slipped his note pad in his coat pocket, "Ryan Talley, I'm just here to report on the town meeting."

"Well, Mr. Talley, perhaps you would like to take me to coffee, and I can fill you in on more details of the project."

The reporter eyed the politician's daughter for a moment and then nodded, holding his arm out for her. With a wry grin, Lizzie Faslee slipped her arm into his.

Instantly met with the biting cool breeze, they instinctively inched closer to one another. "Sounds like you have some big plans for your little town," Ryan said.

Lizzie's eyes twinkled, "Oh, yes. I want to attract first-rate businesses to Twin Springs. This place has barely changed in twenty years, its due for a little overhaul. If I have my way, we'll replace the drab little shops with amazing boutiques. We can become a destination for people instead of a place just to settle down and hide from the world."

"I don't know. I think Twin Springs is kind of quaint," Ryan smiled.

Lizzie looked aghast, "That's just the problem! Quaint! Quaint is for old people. Quaint is for those without dreams, the unworldly. This place needs to wake up, or it will wither and die!"

Ryan stifled a chuckle at the young woman's outrage. As they strolled down the sidewalk, the writer soaked in the rather active downtown, "It seems as though things are going well enough."

"It's not the quantity of the people, Mr. Talley, but rather...the caliber," Lizzie insisted.

Ryan feigned understanding and nodded his head, "I see."

An older couple walked hand in hand in front of them. A family browsed outside the candy store window as the children took turns, pointing out what they would like. A young man ran around his car to open the door for his girlfriend. Ryan struggled to see how the people in the town weren't actually of exceptional character just as they were.

As they approached the cafe, Ryan glanced across the street at the little gift shop. The star he had helped to center was shining in the fading light. A sweet little nativity had been assembled below the star. Lizzie followed Ryan's eyes and scowled.

"That Allison Tancredi and her silly nativity. We have been after her for years to stop setting that out. I mean really, such a shabby display. It interferes with the town's decorations. It clashes with Christmas! We have the lit trees, have bows on the lamp posts…what more do we need?" Lizzie snapped.

A Salvation Army collector had just set up his station and opened the door to the coffee shop for them. Lizzie just brushed past without as much as a glance in the man's direction. Ryan nodded and thanked the man as Lizzie burst into another tirade, "And don't get me started about those panhandlers. How is begging for change and clanging an annoying bell going to get anyone into the Christmas spirit?"

Turning from the reporter, Lizzie faced the grinning barista at the register.

"Hi," the barista beamed, "May I interest you in our seasonal favorite, an egg nog latte?"

Lizzie looked horrified, her face twisted in displeasure, "Ew, that's disgusting. No, I'll have a skinny, half chai, two-pump vanilla, soy milk, 185-degree latte…light on the chai."

The barista stared at the elegant woman for a moment. Her expression completely wiped blank before returning to a bubbly grin, "Ok. And for you, sir?"

"Coffee of the day for me, though I may be back for one of those egg nog lattes," Ryan said, offering a smile to the young girl.

"See, that's what I mean," Lizzie snapped as they walked away from the counter and found a seat. "Even the coffee shop is so cheesy this time of year. Can't it just stay elegant? I mean, what is that playing?"

Instinctively, Ryan looked up at the coffee shop's speakers. "That's the Peanuts song, I think."

"That's a cartoon, right?"

"Yes, the dog Snoopy and the little bird Wood…" Ryan began.

"Simple piano music would be fine, how about George Winston. I like George Winston."

"He…uhh…Winston is good," Ryan started to tell her the version being played was by George Winston, but then thought otherwise and just nodded. Hearing their order called, he excused himself to retrieve their coffees.

"Thank you," Lizzie said, sipping her coffee.

"So, your plans for Twin Springs," Ryan prodded.

Lizzie's eyes lit up, "Yes! Oh my gosh, it will be so beautiful. A French Brasserie, an updated jewelry store, without all that fake gem stuff, high-end clothing boutiques, and a wine bar. Can't you just imagine it? The Art Walk is just the start of the transformation. We want to replace the fascia of all the shops, tie them into a central theme reflecting the new aura of the town. The shop owners will have to pay for their store's part, but it will be worth it to them. Those that can't, well, let's just say they won't be given any favors to keep their business."

"Very ambitious. You mentioned 'we' a lot. You have many of the shop owners bought into this transformation?"

Lizzie looked confounded, "Well, no. Not just yet. My committee, of course, is on board."

"Committee?"

"Only the most influential homeowners in Twin Springs. Tiffany, Annabeth, and myself," Lizzie replied.

"Auspicious voices for the town, to be sure," Ryan remarked.

Lizzie stared at him a moment, unsure of how to react. Finally, she let out a wry smile. "You're mocking me a little."

Ryan grinned and nodded, "A little."

"Fair enough. Perhaps I have work to do to get the rest of these people on board," Lizzie conceded. Placing her hand on his, "And that is where you come in."

Ryan pulled back, casting a suspicious eye, "Oh?"

"Yes! You write wonderful articles about The Art Walk and the plans we have. You help garner support from the community and pique the interest of the surrounding area."

"I see," Ryan mused. "I suppose I can see what I can do. They'll be promo pieces, I don't have a dog in the fight, so anything I write will not be my opinion."

"Oh, who cares? As long as they're good!" Lizzie replied.

"Well, with the business done and cups empty, I should probably be on my way."

"Walk me back?" Lizzie asked, a mischievous grin across her lips.

"Of course," Ryan agreed as he slid out from his chair.

Once more into the cold, Ryan and Lizzie huddled as they walked.

"How long have you lived in Twin Springs?" Ryan asked.

"All my life," Lizzie laughed, letting out a breathy laugh as she replied. "Except when I went to college at Strasbourg in France...I loved it there. Never thought I'd leave." Her head glanced at the stars.

"My mother died not long after I graduated. I was worried about my father, so I came back," Lizzie confided.

Ryan cocked his head and looked at the spoiled girl with a breath of new appreciation, "That's actually...sweet."

"Who said I wasn't sweet?" Lizzie protested in horror.

Ryan paused as he thought of a response and yielded to a shrug and a grin, hoping he wouldn't be too obvious in the darkening evening.

Admiring the star that he had helped straighten earlier that afternoon, Ryan caught the shop owner watching him as she straightened under the window display. Passing under the colonial-style street lamp, he offered her a smile. For a moment, he was met with a return glance before she quickly shrank away from the window.

On the cool night, under an umbrella of stars and bathed in the soft glow from the street lamps, Ryan thought the town looked fantastic. Everything was sweet and charming, a slice of forgotten Americana. He could imagine its charm only intensifying when completely decorated for the holidays.

Returning to the steps of City Hall, they paused. "How soon can you get to work?" Lizzie spat in excitement.

Shrugging, Ryan replied, "As soon as I get home, I can do a write up on the Art Walk art contest."

Clapping her hands in front of her chin, she delighted, "Wonderful. In a little over a week, we will have a committee meeting. I want you to be there. I'll send you an invite."

Nodding, Ryan waved her goodbye and headed for his car, not entirely sure what he had gotten himself into.

Two

The Humble Beginnings Giftshop was quickly turning into a miniature of Santa's Workshop. Allison stretched evergreen garland across the top of the display cabinets. "Maddie, can you tell me if the little elf village looks right?" she asked one of her clerks as she clenched the garland in her teeth so she could point to a cabinet.

"Allison, everything looks great," Maddie replied.

The door swung open, and her other clerk, Candace, bobbed in. "Reporting for duty, ma'am."

Allison smiled, "Candace, could you get some cider going?"

"Sure, but do you want to wait and see what kind of turn out we get today?" she shrugged.

"Nope, if we have one or one hundred, they are our guests," Allison answered.

Nodding, Candace complied, "That's why you're the boss."

"That and it's my life savings poured into this place," Allison grinned.

The door swung open again. Allison hopped down from her step stool, confident the garland would stay. "Hi Janice, did you bring more paintings in?"

The artist shuffled, "Well, no. I was actually going to take a few back. Things are selling a bit better in the city. You know how it is, I've got to go where the business is."

"Of course, I'm happy you're doing well no matter where they're sold," Allison conceded.

Grabbing a stack of painted plaques, Janice turned and asked, "Say, I was thinking about entering a painting in the Art Walk contest, what do you think?"

Stifling a grimace, Allison smiled. "If anyone's art deserved to grace our sidewalks, it's yours, Janice."

"Thank you, dear, you always brighten my day," the painter gushed, "Let me know if I sell any!"

As quickly as the artist entered the shop, she whisked away with an armload of paintings.

"Really?" Maddie cried.

"What?" Allison and Candace called in unison.

"She took all the best ones - the beach scene, the Springs...oh wait...we do have "Guy Holding Fish", that's a seller," Maddie retorted.

Allison laughed, "It's okay. They are hers. We'll just have to find a customer who remembers their grandfather taking them to the river for the first time. See? There's a buyer for everything."

"You're so good, Allison," Maddie exclaimed.

"How's job searching?" Allison asked.

Maddie chewed on her lip, "Not good. One interview says he's overqualified, next says not enough. There was one, but he would have to travel to the city each week. I don't know. We might have to take that one. Things are pretty tight."

Allison stopped and looked at her clerk, "Is there anything I can do for you?"

"No...," Maddie chewed on her lip again. Looking up through watery eyes, she admitted, "If I could grab my check a little early…it might help hold us until Mike finds something."

"Of course, Maddie," Allison crooned, "You know, let me take care of that right now in case we get busy."

The shop owner disappeared into her office. Standing in front of her desk, she lifted her checkbook. Underneath, she stared at the stack of bills. Glancing at the calendar with a date circled in red marker. The word "Lease" scrawled on that date. "Another day," she muttered to herself and scribbled a paycheck in her book for Maddie.

Three

Ryan Talley parked his worn little Jeep on the edge of town. He liked to take in the settings he wrote about as much as possible. The day was chilly, but sunny - a perfect time to stroll through the little hamlet of Twin Springs. From his vantage, he could see nearly the length of Main Street. Two rows of businesses flanked either side of the boulevard, all the way down to the City Hall, where Main Street ended at a little fountain in front of the town meeting place's steps. Looming over City Hall was a tall, rolling hill covered in trees, their branches nearly bare. The unspoiled leaves at the base of the trees still gave the hillside a warm mosaic of late autumn oranges, browns, and garnets.

Along either sidewalk, evenly spaced poplar trees leapfrogged by lampposts created a magnificent image of a historic colonial burg. Ryan, with hands in his pockets, admired the town. Most of the morning traffic was heading to or leaving the coffee shop. He figured that was good enough a place to start for him as well.

Ryan found the shop festive, Christmas music that surely would have annoyed Lizzie, played in the background. The pastry case overflowed with pumpkin and cranberry treats displayed alongside confections with elf, snowman, and reindeer icing. The same barista was behind the bar, offering him a broad, almost too large, cheery smile.

Her big, round brown eyes centered on him. "Back for that egg nog latte?"

Ryan smiled back, "You know, I think I will. Thank you for remembering. "

As Ryan stepped back into the crisp air, he sipped his latte. Glancing over the edge of the cup, he looked at the gift shop. With a few minutes to kill, he decided to check out the store a little closer. Parked in front was a little van. The shop owner and one of her assistants were studying the hatch and making unsuccessful attempts to lift something out of it.

Walking up, the reporter smiled at the two frustrated women. Nestled in the back of the car was a large armoire that barely fit inside the minivan. "Need some help?"

Allison and Maddie spun, each a little startled by the sudden voice.

"Uhm, we can...you know, yes, actually, " Allison admitted defeatedly.

Studying the car for a moment, Ryan suggested, "Why don't you two tag team the end, I'll walk it out from inside."

Opening the side door, he crawled behind the cabinet and lifted it. Following the ladies by hobbling on his knees in the back of the van until the armoire crested the tailgate. From there, they rested the armoire on the street while Ryan crawled out of the van.

Repositioning himself, he leaned the armoire back, "Ready?"

With Allison and Maddie on one side and Ryan on the other, they walked the cabinet toward the shop.

Mr. Haverstein, who was looking out his deli window, came rushing out to open the gift shop door for them. "Right against the back of the check stand," Allison grunted.

"You sell furniture too?" Ryan asked.

Allison twisted as she shook out her strained muscles, "No...I mean, probably would if the price was right. It is for smaller gift items. Twin Springs has been hit hard with the economy. I found some lower priced items and some stuff kids can buy their parents or their brothers and sisters without very much money. I just didn't have anything to display them in. I thought this might work nicely."

"And some poor television is relegated homeless for the holidays," Ryan shook his head in mock sadness.

"A worthy sacrifice," Allison replied. "So, are you going to keep saving me all season long, or are you trying to get on the payroll?" Allison quipped.

"Just passing through at the right time," Ryan shrugged, "Again."

Allison blushed slightly, "Well, I'm glad you did."

A glance at his watch told Ryan that he was about to be late. With a quick grin, he declared, "I'll be back through in a couple of hours if you need me." Not expecting or waiting for a reply, he turned and excused himself.

Mr. Haverstein and Maddie watched the scene unfold in silence. Mr. Haverstein wore a knowing grin while Maddie looked disturbed.

"Quite the gentleman," Haverstein declared.

"Or stalker," Maddie spat, and then her eyes narrowed, "Or worse, a spy for Lizzie Faslee."

Allison looked cross, "Stop it, both of you. People can just be nice."

Haverstein looked shocked, "That is all I said."

"But not all you implied," Allison's stern look melted into a grin.

"Hmmph," Maddie crossed her arm in front of her chest and watched the reporter walk down the street towards town hall. "He has been cozy with her."

Ryan paced the hallway, double-checking to see if he had gotten the room right. He was pretty sure he was where Lizzie had instructed they meet.

Hearing voices down the hall, the reporter took a few steps forward. Ryan recognized the voice of Mayor Faslee deep in conversation with another man.

"I gotta tell you, Faslee, things aren't good. The town loves you, but housing prices are down. Household incomes are down. Businesses are struggling; three have closed this year, and others are teetering. Of course, all of this means revenue for the city through property taxes are also down," the other voice declared.

"Got any good news?" Faslee asked.

"Maybe," the mayor's consultant responded. "Lizzie's Artwalk and Twin Springs Transformation projects might actually be of some help."

"I was a little nervous about them, myself," Faslee admitted. "Not exactly how I have managed the town through most of my tenure."

"Understandable. These are tough times. We need to bring new business here. We need higher-income families. They will have a positive impact, give you something to work with."

The conversation paused for a moment. Finally, Faslee asked, "What about the businesses and families that are already here?"

"That's a tough one, Faslee, but sometimes you need to let go of those that bring the system down to favor those that will help it prosper. It's a simple math equation."

"I'm not saying we bail them out. I am a free enterprise guy too. I just want to avoid levying things that are going to place an even greater burden. No reason to make their lives harder," Faslee argued.

"We focus on the positives of Lizzie's plans. The challenges of it stay in the background. You win, the most influential families of Twin Springs win. The town comes out stronger," the man said.

Faslee grumbled, "I'll take it under advisement, I know Lizzie would be happy."

"You're wise to consider all angles. I'll be in touch," the man said.

While not hovering too close to the mayor's office, Ryan instinctively backed away.

Just as the man visiting Faslee spun out of the room, Lizzie and her two committee members appeared on the other end of the hallway.

"Oh, hi, Ryan, I'm glad you made it," Lizzie called. Seeing the man exiting her father's office, she squealed, "Hello Eric. Getting my father going the right direction?"

The man replied, "Lizzie, my dear, you know your father is great at what he does. But yes, I do think he is beginning to envision the next era for Twin Springs." He walked up and planted a kiss on her cheek.

"And who is this?" the man asked.

"Eric, this is Ryan Talley. He is a writer from the city. He is helping us create a positive PR campaign," Lizzie replied.

"Wonderful," Eric reached and shook Ryan's hand vigorously. "If you need facts or figures on how we tend to turn this little speck into a thriving suburb of the metropolis, let me know."

Lizzie turned to Ryan, "Eric is an advisor to my dad as well as an amazing real estate guru."

"Oh, I don't know about guru, but I do own a half-billion-dollar book of business," Eric beamed. Then spinning towards the exit, he exclaimed, "Gotta go. I got wind of a little restaurant missing their second loan payment. I think I can scoop that property up from them. It's a great location. I can turn a quick profit on that one. See you soon, Ms. Faslee."

Lizzie and her friends watched the debonair young man hustle down the hall.

When he was out of sight, Lizzie turned to Ryan, "Shall we?"

Settling into the conference room, Lizzie, Tiffany, and Annabeth immediately launched into a tirade of the town. "I can't believe she put that atrocious barnyard scene up," Tiffany complained.

"Oh, I know. It is so drab," Annabeth agreed.

"You mean the manger?" Ryan queried to deaf ears.

"And what's with the cheesy seventies garland?" Lizzie added.

Laughing, Annabeth nodded, "I know. Is it any wonder this area is struggling?"

"Well, just even more why we need to clean the town up," Tiffany added.

"One step at a time," counseled Lizzie. "First, Art Walk. We got some "local art", but really, most of it belongs on a mother's fridge, not as the jewel of our town. So, I have some coming in from the city, California and New York."

Annabeth and Tiffany squealed and clapped. "I can't wait to see them!" Tiffany cried.

"They'll be here next week," Lizzie informed her friends.

Ryan looked confused, "Isn't the draw supposed to be Twin Springs specific. You know, come to Twin Springs and see the work of the local artisans?"

Lizzie's face twisted in a knot. "As our culture grows, we will attract more artists," she explained. "And then Twin Springs can claim them."

"Here is what your article should say," Lizzie turned to Ryan, "'Local artisans and artisans with ties to Twin Springs will be considered.'"

"Ties?" Ryan asked.

Lizzie beamed, "Yes! They will all have visited my family's estate."

"You're brilliant, Lizzie!" Annabeth cooed.

"We'll have to close off Main, the space by City Hall is what we will use for the staging area," Lizzie continued.

"What about those tacky decorations?" Tiffany asked.

Lizzie grinned, "I have a plan for that. Since this is a town event, separation of church and state and all that."

"Uhm, not sure that applies to their private space," Ryan interjected. "And the separation of church and state was to protect churches…"

"Whose side are you on?" Annabeth snapped." Anyway, I'll handle the gift shop girl and the others."

Lizzie's eyes brightened as she addressed the group, "And, I'm going to get Daddy to make the businesses to help out. After all, for those that survive and pretty themselves up to standard will benefit."

"Now, for you, writer man, you need to write it up in a way that serves notice on the city and the world that Twin Springs is coming on the map. You also have to write to get the community on board, you know, how it will help out even the shabby little boutique and that deli," Lizzie ordered. "Until it doesn't, of course."

Ryan stared blankly at her for a moment and then responded, "I'll see what I can do."

For a final moment, Lizzie addressed her friends, "Ladies, we get to create our own town. Our Sedona, our Jackson Hole, our Manhattan Beach."

Tiffany and Annabeth drank in and relished the thought and erupted with giddy glee.

Ryan took the moment to excuse himself, "I think I have everything I need to put together the articles. Ladies."

He couldn't wait to get out of the building and leave the women to their scheming. The fresh air was especially cleansing after the steaminess of the conference room.

As he retreated through the town, he noticed how quiet the downtown strip was. He imagined, as he walked, how challenging it must be to keep a business running in an environment like that. Yet, having visited most of the shops, he could tell that owners ran their businesses because they genuinely loved what they did, what they offered to their community. None of them, he guessed, would have opened their shops with the intent of becoming rich. Just make a living and be part of the town.

He waved at Allison and her crew as he passed. He considered sticking his head in and teasing Allison, but he wasn't sure how it would be perceived. There was something about the little gift shop owner that impressed him. A positive of Lizzie Faslee's scheming, he would have further opportunities to figure out what that little something was.

Many towns struggle to grasp the moment to stake their foundation, their future in the face of uncertain times. Twin Springs is one such town that is setting their own path. Making their own rules to guide them into better days.

Under the leadership of long time Mayor Faslee, and the spirited ambition of his daughter, Elizabeth Faslee, Twin Springs is embarking on a town-wide reformation. The quaint town is resetting itself from a quiet village, thwarting the pull of the city to an attraction that will draw from the city.

Twin Springs is announcing the groundbreaking of the Twin Springs Art Walk, a celebration of art and style that will become the heart of the town's culture and pulse as they move into a new era. They have broadcast a casting call for works that inspire and invoke dreams of the future to represent the inaugural Art Walk unveiling scheduled for late December.

Local artists and those from as far away as New York and Pairs with ties to Twin Springs are already submitting their entries, vying to be among the first honored in the new town attraction.

"This next year will bring new shops, bistros, and galleries to Twin Springs," Elizabeth Faslee reported. "The Art Walk is the beginning of something amazing that is bringing the town together."

Mayor Faslee is encouraged the Art Walk project will be an injection into the town's economy. "Twin Springs has always been independent of the metropolitan economy, and we feel this new direction for our town will surely enable us to maintain that autonomy."

A bold move for a humble town. The passion Twin Springs readily exudes was magnified by the coming together on the project and the town's future.

Four

The holiday shopping season officially underway, Allison had the shop fully staffed. Customer traffic had picked up a bit, mainly with her regulars and locals window shopping for Christmas present ideas. She watched Maddie and Candace do as much as they could around the shop. She was pretty sure it was the cleanest the store had ever been. It was clear that the flow of traffic was not commensurate with the store's sales.

Prudent business practice would have dictated that she send one of them home with the lighter traffic. She couldn't bear to take away hours that she knew were so sorely needed.

Mr. Haverstein walked in with a plate of sufganiyot, little fried donuts popular at Hanukkah, for the girls. "Happy Hanukkah, Mr. Haverstein."

"How's business?" Haverstein asked.

"It's picking up," Allison said cheerily. "I got in the chocolate gelt coins and the ornate tzedakah family charity boxes you helped me pick out."

Haverstein's eyes lit up, "You did? Let me see, let me see."

Allison led him to the section near the front dedicated to Hanukkah specific gifts. Her neighbor's expression reminded her of a child opening a present.

Haverstein excitedly snatched up a Hamsa charm and inspected it. He glided his hand across one of the charity boxes, feeling the craftsman details in the design. "Nicely done, Allison. I will let all of my Kosher customers know and send them over.

Allison hugged the elderly deli owner. "Thank you, Mr. Haverstein. You are always so good to me."

"Pish," Haverstein barked, "Good people take care of good people. You, my dear, are good people. Now I better get back, it is almost lunchtime."

"Thanks for the sufganiyot," Maddie and Candace called as the old man hurried back next door.

The afternoon wore on, with as many customers as the store had staff. Sitting at her desk, deciding which bills she could pay that week, Allison noticed how quickly her lease payment was coming. As much as she hated the idea, she couldn't help but to contemplate reducing hours. Slumping against her hands as she collapsed on top of her desk. Hearing the backroom door squeak, she quickly lifted her head.

"Hi, Candace. Hey, I've been meaning to ask you how the semester went," Allison queried.

Candace shrugged and nodded her head, "Good. I think I did pass all my finals."

"Duh, you're like a 4.0."

"3.85," Candace corrected. Wrinkling her nose, she added, "I might take next semester off though, kind of catch up for a bit."

Allison looked concerned. "Catch up. You mean money?"

Candace nodded.

"This is our busy season. I'm sure I'll have plenty of hours for you," Allison assured.

"Are you sure Allie, I mean we haven't exactly had our door beaten down...," Candace protested.

Allison nodded, "Absolutely. We've got the Art Walk thing, Hanukkah and Christmas..."

Candace frowned, "You mean Lizzie Faslee's thing? I don't trust that woman."

"We'll be good," Allison promised.

"Alright, let's go scare up some customers," Candace said, pushing her way back onto the selling floor.

Allison flipped her stack of bills over and followed her friend into the store. Just as she did, Ryan Talley and his grinning face pushed his way in from the sidewalk.

"Need any large, heavy things moved or women falling from the sky to catch?" the reporter asked.

Allison smirked, "I appreciate the notion, but I think my two very capable associates and I have everything handled."

"Alright," Ryan smiled, his dimples cutting deep into his cheeks. "Just couldn't pass by without saying 'hi'."

"I appreciate you stopping in," Allison responded.

Maddie jumped in, "Say, since you're here, we can help you get some of your Christmas shopping done. Let's see, who should we start with? Your wife or girlfriend?"

Ryan grinned at the sly inquisition, "Nope. The only woman in my life is my mom. You know what? I will take you up on that. I never know what to get her."

"Do you get along...I mean, what sorts of things does she like?" Maddie asked.

"Yeah, love Mom. That's part of the problem. I like to get her something special. Something that makes her reflect. On the year, her life, raising hyper little brats like me..."

Candace snapped her fingers, "I have just the thing." Running to the big tree, she selected a beautiful angel ornament. "These are gorgeous."

Ryan admired the ornament, holding up in his hand, nodding as the strung Christmas lights twinkled in the ornament's reflection.

"Make it even better and solve your problem for years to come," Allison added, "We've got these great boxes to put them in. Sharpie the date on the bottom and add a photo or note that is reflective of something you shared with her over the past year. It becomes a tradition that she will cherish, and you know what to get her next year, just with a little personalized homework."

The writer looked impressed, "Wow, you guys. That is brilliant."

"I'll ring you up," Candace said, heading to the cash register.

Allison very carefully began packaging the ornament in the decorative box. "You're around quite a bit lately," she said, looking up from her packaging for a moment.

"Yeah," Ryan nodded, "I'm not sure where this Art Walk stuff is going, but I've been asked to cover it."

"How's it going?"

Ryan shrugged, "Guess we'll find out."

"Well, here's your present. Don't forget your homework," Allison pointed at Ryan and handed the package over.

"I won't. Thank you, ladies."

As soon as the door closed, the girls let out a pent-up burst of the giggles. "Alright, I have to admit, he is pretty cute," Maddie said.

"And those dimples!" Candace gushed.

"Stop it you two. I know where you are going with this. I thought we covered it," Allison began.

"He's just nice," they all cried in unison and burst out laughing.

Five

R yan leaned against the back wall of the council room. Mayor Faslee sat at a table with Lizzie, five council members, and Eric, the real estate broker he had met his last visit.

"So, let's have the artists blinded for the contest, that way, we'll have less heat if we don't have some of the local amateurs' stuff in there," one of the council members suggested.

Mayor Faslee looked around at the gathering, "Or we can try and focus on local artists, we have such great talent right here in Twin Springs."

Lizzie gave Eric a look. The broker got the message and interjected, "We discussed that. This Art Walk must be a draw. Bring people in who wouldn't otherwise come to Twin Springs. For that, we need big-name artists. Maybe we can mix in some local color…but the focus has to be highlighting art that people will travel to see."

The mayor started to object but quickly realized he was alone in his sentiment. "Very well," he sighed.

With an apathetic approval, they moved on to the next agenda item, preparing the town for the big event.

After a pregnant pause followed by a sharp rap of her papers against the council room table, Lizzie addressed the council. "The Nativity thing. It's time we are done with it once and for all. It has to be gone for the Art Walk. A lot of the people we have coming in aren't into the whole religious thing."

"We do get a few complaints. We quit saying prayer before town meetings. The high school football coach was made to stop praying before games as well," the mayor sighed, rubbing his face. "I guess so."

"Any objections?" Lizzie asked, casting a stern look as she panned from council member to council member. "Good." Move her eyes to her father, she looked steadily upon him, urging him to make the final motion.

"So be it. The Nativity is hereby banned from being displayed outside in Twin Springs," the mayor ordered, his voice showing his reluctance at the decree.

Ryan was remised in the back of the room, squirming at the idea and, moreover, how Allison would take it. But what came out next nearly made him choke, as one of the council members suggested an additional step.

"All city entities and participating businesses must say Happy Holidays, if anything at all. Merry Christmas may be offensive to some. If we are wooing them to do business here, it's just best to avoid religious references altogether."

"Hear, hear. I think it is time we banned all religious references made in public settings," another council member added.

The mayor looked flummoxed. "Hold on. Are we sure about this? Bill, how are you going to address the pastor this Sunday? Martha, you have led carolers on the wassail tour for years. Is that going to banned too?"

"Oh, Mayor Faslee. We can make the order, giving us the ability to enforce the items that we genuinely find objectionable," the councilwoman named Martha scoffed.

"I don't believe that is how government should work," the mayor pleaded.

"Fine. We'll start with the dreadful Nativity at the gift shop and make all city sites, and workers comply with the "no Christmas" policy. That is fair, isn't it?" Martha offered. "After all, isn't that what separation of church and state is all about?"

Ryan coughed and began to correct the councilwoman, but was cut down by Lizzie glare.

"Enough! I think we have the path for now, before we get too carried away. Father, would you agree?"

After another deep sigh, the mayor said, "Very well. All in favor, say 'aye'." Noting that all but one councilman consented other than himself, he declared the motion passed.

Ryan himself sighed quietly to himself. If this is the direction the council and Lizzie were going, his articles were going to be decidedly harder to write.

After the meeting, Liz Faslee caught up with Ryan. She was very excited. "Things are finally progressing! I have been trying to get this town out of the 1900's for years. All that Santa Clause and wise men stuff were fun as a kid, but they just have no place in business and politics. I mean, do you want Muslims wishing you a Happy Rosh Hashana or African Americans Happy Kwanzaa? You aren't a part of those cultures. Why have it forced on you?"

Ryan looked at her. "I think if somebody wished me a happy anything, I would gladly accept it. If they want to make me a part of their celebration, I'm fine with that. Why wouldn't I?"

"Oh, you're taking this far too seriously, just relax," Liz chided him.

"Articles. I'll do a few more articles promoting the town and the Art Walk, but I think I'll leave the sensitive stuff out," Ryan said.

Lizzie nodded, "Good idea. Besides, you're really doing promotion, not news anyway."

"Yeah," Ryan agreed. "I guess I am."

"I'm going to get a group together for drinks. You want to come?"

"Maybe next time. I have some things I need to do."

"Okay, but you're going to owe me a makeup drink then," Lizzie said.

Hands in his coat pockets, he walked away. His Faslee experiences were becoming less and less pleasant. Pulling his collar up to his chin, he fended off the icy breeze that was slicing at any exposed skin.

The drive home saw the first snowflakes of the season drifting down in front of Ryan's headlights. Cycling through his playlist, he found a mix of Christmas songs. The tunes fit the mood as the reporter made his way home through the flurry.

Parking outside his small house, he felt it needed a little something for the season. Passing a tree lot a few blocks away, Ryan decided to see what they might have. Unlike the quiet streets of Twin Springs, the roads and sidewalks of the city were very much still very active.

The tree lot still had its lights on, and a few people, mostly couples admiring the selection, trying to find just the right one for their homes. A father and his two children milled about, looking at tree after tree. The kids excitedly bounced up to each one, eyes wide, calling their parents over. Eyeing a stand of wreaths, Ryan made his way over and studied the various styles.

A couple giggled as they held each other close, strolling through the lot for what Ryan picked up from overhearing them, their first tree together.

A little further down, Ryan could hear the squeal of the children, "This one, this one, Daddy!" From his vantage, Ryan could see the man inspecting the tag carefully and pointing to a smaller tree a little further down. The boy leaped on to his father's leg as his sister grabbed him by the hand and pulled him back. The man inspected the tag once more, shuffling nervously as an attendant walking by hoisted the tree over his should and the led the family to the cash stand.

Ryan returned his focus and pulled at his chin, deciding between a beautiful blue bow accented wreath and a classic red. Grinning, the reporter grabbed the classic. Maybe it was the effect of the little town he was writing about, but a traditional Christmas seemed to fit his mood. Lifting the wreath, he made his way to the check-out stand.

While the tree the family had selected was being wrapped in twine for the trip home, the father fumbled through his pockets, sheepishly counting bills as the man behind the register waited. With a small stack of bills in one hand, he patted each of his pockets with the other, returning to a couple more than once, hoping that the second try would yield a different result. The man glanced nervously form his children to the tree to the man who was growing impatient behind the counter.

The lot attendant made a motion to the attendant who was preparing the tree to stop.

Nodding to himself, Ryan understood the issue. Pulling a twenty out of his pocket, he stepped forward. Reading the father's concerned expression, Ryan held the money out in front of him, "I think you dropped this as you pulled your wallet out."

The man's eyes questioned Ryan's statement, but relented when Ryan put the money on the counter and stepped back in line. The cashier made a swirling motion with hand to the lot attendant, signaling him to finish prepping the tree and put the money into the register. The father paused to look at Ryan, his face still expressing doubt.

"Merry Christmas, that's a nice tree your kids picked out there," Ryan smiled, stepping up to the register with his wreath.

Biting his lip for a moment, the man nodded, "Thank you. These guys are everything to me. I want to be able to give them the Christmas they deserve."

Eying to the two children who had pasted themselves to their dad's sides, Ryan responded, "It looks like being with you makes them pretty happy enough."

Nodding, the man led his children to the man waiting with the tree and hoisted it up onto his shoulders, a little hand grasping either side of his jacket.

As the cashier took his money and handed Ryan his change back, the reporter watched as the little family walked down the sidewalk. The kids skipped along as excitedly as if their dad had given them a new puppy.

Six

Ryan admired the wreath he hung on his door as he left for the day. A light dusting of snow had fallen, but the streets were clear. Checking his watch, he had a bit of time before he had to be in Twin Springs.

Straightening the bow on the wreath, he headed down his steps and the sidewalk towards his local coffee shop. He liked the way his feet crunched on the thin layer of snow. No matter how old he got, he always enjoyed snow. It made the hectic world seem a little less hectic. Some of the time, at least.

At a crosswalk, an older woman tested the snowy patch just off of the sidewalk. Ryan could hear a man inside his BMW cursing at the woman as he had to wait. Ryan jogged up and stood beside the woman, placing him between her and the car.

"Fun to have a little snow," Ryan smiled at her as he slowed to her pace.

"It is nice. I would just hate to slip."

"That just makes you very sensible," Ryan replied. Glancing over at the driver who was inching forward, the reporter glared into the windshield of the sedan.

Reaching the other side of the street, Ryan called, "Merry Christmas."

Smiling back, the woman replied, "Merry Christmas to you."

Surprising her, Ryan spun and faced the crosswalk they had just navigated. The woman watched him for a moment, smiled once more, and went on her way.

When the light turned, Ryan endured his own set of impatient drivers, despite him jogging across.

Once more on the safety of the sidewalk, he turned down the block and headed for the coffee shop. Pausing as he saw City Hall up ahead. He looked at the large evergreen standing vigil in the ample, circular space out front. This was the second year that the tree was bare of decorations. A group had protested any notion of Christmas on the city government's property. What was once a wonderful tradition of the community coming together to share a moment, singing together, reminding one another of common aspirations of peace on earth, had given way to political correctness. A loud squeaky wheel that wasn't even representative of 10 percent of the city's population, but the politicians feared the threatened lawsuit.

Ryan shook his head and pressed on. Outside of the coffee shop, a bell ringer for the Salvation Army stood guard over a collection bucket. Tossing a dollar in, the reporter pushed his way into the shop. Unlike the cafe in Twin Springs, this one had not been decorated for Christmas. A few snowman decorations were adorned to the walls and on the counter, and a sign in blue letters, dressed in icicles hung behind the bar citing "It's the Season." Noting the décor, Ryan had to wonder what season it was they were referring.

As the door opened, the song of the bell wafted through. "Looks like we have to call the police again. I thought we took care of those people last year," the barista behind the counter snarled.

"I'll call. I can't stand them. So annoying," a girl huffed on the other end of the bar.

"What can I get you?" the first barista asked. "Do you want it in a seasonal cup?"

"Seasonal cup?" Ryan asked.

"Yeah, you now…like winter and stuff," the girl replied.

"And stuff," Ryan glanced around the shop. "Do you mean Christmas?"

"Well, no. We can't do Christmas. It is just the winter season for whatever."

"I see. Surprise me. And make it two," Ryan added.

The girl rolled her eyes and began making Ryan's coffees.

Picking them up at the end of the counter, Ryan backed his way out of the shop and onto the sidewalk. Holding out a cup, he handed a coffee to the Salvation Army ringer.

"Thanks," the young man nodded. "People haven't really gotten a hold of the spirit just yet." He glanced at the pot with Ryan's lonely dollar at the bottom of it.

"It will come," Ryan assured him. "It always does."

Glancing at the two patrolmen coming down the block, Ryan eyed the ringer, "You might want to move about a step or two that way. I have no doubt that the Salvation Army has the city ordinances in check, but those additional three feet will keep you well clear of the shop owners' reach for complaints."

Seeing the patrolmen as well, the man grinned, sliding his stand over a few feet. "Thanks, man!"

Ryan grinned as he passed the patrolmen, "Merry Christmas!"

The patrolmen eyed the reporter suspiciously as they walked by. "Officers," Ryan nodded.

Once out of town, Ryan's spirits lifted. There was a certain appeal that he had visiting Twin Springs. It was almost a step back in time. A simpler time. A time when the streets were a bit less crowded, people knew each other and could depend on one another. He thought of Lizzie Faslee and her initiatives. He wasn't so sure her plans were

really what was best for the town, what the town
actually wanted.

Ryan laughed to himself. At the core of it, he
wondered the truth behind Lizzie Faslee.
Desperately eager to get out, yet she came back and
stayed. Maybe it was her confliction that drove her
to demand the town change. She wanted so badly to
live a different life, and here she finds herself stuck
in her little small town with her little small-town
mayor father.

There were moments in his interactions with
Lizzie, where she actually seemed sweet. In direct
contrast to the pompous, opinionated snob that she
so well portrayed. Ryan sighed. It was best to keep
her at arm's length. It was the times when she was
not so sweet he feared she might chew his arm right
off.

Allison Tancredi arrived at her shop just in
time to see the city worker tape the notice to her
front door. The worker, seeing her in the door's
reflection, turned and offered an apologetic shrug
before shuffling off as quickly as he could.

Snatching the note from the door, Allison
read it to herself, "As of this date, December 2nd,
the religious display must be removed from the
dates of December 3rd through December 24th. City
Mandate BOL12120. Failure to comply may result in
fines, store closure, or forcible removal of referenced
artifacts." Allison snarled a scream of disgust and
balled the paper in her hand. "That Lizzie Faslee
and her little circle of witches!"

Unlocking her door, Allison pushed her way into the store and tossed the note in the direction of the cashier stand. Flipping on the Christmas lights and blasting the Christmas station, she focused on getting her store ready to open.

When Maddie came in, it took her no time to see that something was off. Casting a questioning raise of her eyebrow at her boss, she asked, "What is it, Allie?"

"Oh, nothing. The city wants me to take down the Nativity. The note is somewhere on the floor by the check stand."

"What? Tell them to kiss it," Maddie said, searching for the little ball of paper. Finding it, she smoothed it and read it. "They can't..."

"I don't think so. I'm not taking it down."

"Good for you, boss. I got your back," Maddie declared.

For the first time that morning, Allison smiled, "I know you do."

Before Ryan had even gotten out of his Jeep, Lizzie Faslee was standing outside of his window. A big grin escaped the hooded confines of her fur-lined parka. Ryan opened the door cautiously.

Lizzie's grin widened, "You are going to take me for a ride."

"I am, huh?" Ryan replied through a furrowed brow.

"Yes!" Lizzie cried and declared, "I even brought cocoa!"

Ryan wasn't sure what to make of this side of Lizzie. He wasn't a hundred percent sure he trusted it. Just the same, he grabbed her arm and gently guided her to the passenger side of the Jeep and let her into the seat.

Back behind the wheel, Ryan queried, "Alright. Where am I taking you?"

"Just head down Main, and I will direct you from there," Lizzie said confidently.

Complying, Ryan brought the little SUV to life and shifted into reverse. Heading back the way he came, he took in the town. It's soft dusting of snow making it look even more perfect. "Your little town is even more striking in white."

"I can't argue, I do love it here when it snows," Lizzie admitted. As Ryan past the last of the shops on the primary corridor into the heart of Twin Springs, Lizzie had him turn. "Right up this road. This thing has four-wheel drive, right?" Lizzie directed.

"Of course," Ryan replied and urged the Jeep up the hill.

The further up the hill and away from town, the thicker the snow. Ryan watched the thermometer on his mirror drop with every mile.

"I really appreciate your help with the Art Walk. It means a lot to me."

"I'll do what I can. The online article was read 67,000 times. Who knows with the print version," Ryan informed her.

"That's great! You are going to help me put Twin Springs on the map!"

"It is on the map," Ryan argued.

"But such a small dot! I want a big, luxurious dot!"

"Take away Atlanta, Buckhead is a small dot. Merilee Hills without L.A. is a modest dot. It isn't the size…"

"It's the median home price! The allure of wonderful shops and valet parking. It is French pastries and Italian espresso. It is a chalet with a huge fireplace and cups of Belgian hot chocolate. It is a place for artisans to express themselves and find their audience!" Lizzie's voice was impassioned.

"You really want this."

"Yes!"

"But, is it right for Twin Springs?" Ryan asked.

"Why not? The sleepy little town is dying. I can help change that. I want to do that for my father," Lizzie declared. Seeing a turn coming ahead, she pointed excitedly, "Ooh, turn here."

Ryan downshifted and popped the SUV into four-wheel as he plowed the Jeep through a thick berm of snow.

"Follow this windy little trail to the end," Lizzie instructed.

The Jeep didn't struggle much as it labored its way around several switchbacks before arriving at a large meadow.

"Can it make it out to the edge?" Lizzie asked.

Ryan shrugged, "I guess we'll find out. How are you at shoveling?"

Lizzie's disapproving look was response enough, causing Ryan to chuckle.

Shifting another gear lower, Ryan guided the Jeep to a little wooden fence. The view was spectacular. High above Twin Springs, they sat on the edge of a meadow that looked out over the valley. Rolling hills shrouded the town, with the most significant hills looming over the Town Hall.

"This is stunning," Ryan replied, drinking in the scene.

"This is our little town," Lizzie replied, pouring a cup of cocoa from her thermos and handing it to him.

"It is even more lovely from up here," Ryan said.

"This is one of my favorite spots. The Springs are, of course, beautiful, but everyone goes there," Lizzie said, pouring her own cup of hot chocolate. "My mother used to bring me up here. She said it reminded her of a little town in Austria in the wintertime. The hills, the cute little buildings all covered in white."

Looking over the hood of the Jeep, she pointed. "There's Town Hall, 'Hi Daddy'. There's Main and there…there is where the Art Walk will be. With any luck, those old shops right there will be converted into chic little boutiques, right outside the Art Walk."

"It's beautiful in either case," Ryan agreed.

"And there's my house. The one on the opposite hill. Daddy's little ranch. My horse lives just up above at the Twin Springs stables. Do you ride?" Lizzie asked.

"I have. Never owned a horse, and any more than a trot feels like I'm going to be flung off," Ryan admitted.

Lizzie laughed, "I'd like to see that!"

"Thanks," Ryan smirked.

Lizzie looked thoughtful for a moment. "I need to spend more time with Marie – that's the horse."

"You don't much? I bet it is fun to ride in the snow," Ryan said.

"Yeah, Marie loves it," Lizzie nodded. Over her cup of cocoa, her eyes focused on Ryan. "You are a little different than most of the guys I know around here."

Ryan looked curious, "What do you mean?"

"Most either suck up to me or ignore me thinking I'm a snot-nosed little witch," Lizzie replied. "You kind of don't do either of those things."

Ryan scrunched his nose, "We all have our good and bad points."

"And what do you see as my good points?"

"You're a very attractive woman, but that is easy. You are very passionate about what you want, if a bit zealous in your strides to get it. You obviously love your father very much. I think, I could be wrong, you kind of love your town, too," Ryan professed.

Lizzie smiled. "You got all that on me, huh? Not sure I want to learn what you think my bad points are, at least not today." Leaning on the console between them, Lizzie moved closer to Ryan. "You seem very sure of yourself. I like that."

Ryan shook his head. "I lose my way plenty. I try to make my direction simple. If confronted with a fork in the road, I try hard to listen to the advice within me. If the fork is too much about me, I realize it is usually the other path that I am supposed to take."

Lizzie pursed her lips, "That is a little deep. What does that all even mean?"

"Respond to the leading of the holy spirit. Some call it their conscience. You only really know when you truly listen and welcome it into your life, into your being," Ryan replied.

"You're not like a religious nut, are you?" Lizzie asked.

Ryan laughed, "No. Not really. I have just learned along the way I don't always make the right decision when left on my own. The sanctuary of the church, the lessons that are taught – they provide a set of guidelines to follow, a path. Whatever your beliefs, they offer a new perspective on the trials of life and the opportunities. A little faith makes them even stronger. I find myself happier when I let go of my impulses and choose to walk in a way that I can help others."

Lizzie looked thoughtful for a moment. "I guess that's alright. I mean, don't most people do that anyway?"

"We'd like to think so. At the end of the day, it is a struggle. Human nature drives us towards self-preservation. Sometimes we need a little help," Ryan said.

Lizzie leaned back in her seat and sighed, "I like what you say, I wish just a little bit that you were a hair shallower under that beautiful face of yours."

"The best things are those that build over time. They tend to be the ones that last," Ryan said.

"More church talk?"

Ryan grinned, "Nope. My mom and dad. They've been happily married for half a century."

"Very well, Mr. Talley," Lizzie raised her mug of cocoa. "To slow burns for the greater good."

"To the good things, come what they may," Ryan hoisted his mug in reply.

Seven

Allison perked up when the sleigh bells she had tacked on her front door rang. A slow day for customers, she was excited for the chance to greet someone. Seeing the man come through with an armful of letters, she sighed before smiling, "Hi Frank!"

"Hi, Allison, store looks great," the mailman replied. "Here's your stack for the day."

"Thanks, Frank. Would you like a cup of cider or hot cocoa? Pretty chilly out there."

The mailman waved her off graciously, "Thanks, but gotta run. Have to run two trips from the main site this time of year."

"Alright. Feel free to stop by in between runs!" Allison urged.

"Will do," Frank replied and scurried off.

"Hey, Maddie," Allison called. "Grab one of those thermoses off the shelf and wash it if you would please. We'll surprise Frank with his own "to-go" cup on his next trip through."

Maddie nodded and walked to the front display and selected a travel mug for the mailman. As she lifted her head, she saw a Jeep drive by with Lizzie Faslee laughing in the passenger. Recognizing the driver, she huffed as she turned away. "Your writer friend sure is cozying it up with Lizzie. You know she was the one behind the letter on the Nativity."

Allison shrugged, "He has a job to do. Lizzie does too…I suppose. Even if she is a bit misguided."

"What about the Nativity?" Candace asked.

"Oh, I got a notice from the city that it "may offend someone" and with the dignitaries coming in for Art Walk, they want it taken down," Allison informed her co-worker.

"You know it was all Lizzie Faslee and her little heathen friends. They have been harping on Allison's Nativity for years," Maddie spat.

"It's so silly. I noticed at the grocery, everything was "Happy Holidays" and snowmen. Sure, they don't mind making money off Christmas, but heaven forbid anybody breathing the word," Candace added.

Allison looked a bit sad for a moment, "I don't get it either. We have always had traditions in this country and allowed others to uphold theirs."

"Halloween decorations are fine. The town even closes Main Street for Trick or Treating. But Christmas…It's so stupid," Candace recited.

"It's politics and stupid political correctness," Maddie replied. "The problem with religion is that it pulls people together. When people have a forum to pull together, a community that reaches out to help others in need, there is less need for the government. They don't want us to listen to our pastors, our priests, or our rabbis. They want us to listen to them."

"I don't care much about the politics. As long as I own this store, I will celebrate Christmas my way," Allie said defiantly.

"Amen, sister!" Maddie applauded, a wide grin across her lips.

As Ryan drove into town, Lizzie huffed when she saw the Nativity was still in place. "Why is that still there!" she cursed.

"Is it really that big of a deal?" Ryan asked.

Lizzie cast him an ugly glance, "The people from the city, they don't want to see that…that broken-down structure with fake farm animals. Really!"

"Uhm, the slightly decrepit state is part of the message that a baby was born in those conditions. That baby was…" Ryan began.

"I know the story!" Lizzie snapped. "It's not the point. Do we want to show that we are a progressive town worthy of their investment? Their kind of place?"

"I'm not so sure Twin Springs doesn't exude that kind of charm. You want investors to come in and add to the community, not replace it," Ryan said.

Lizzie stared at the reporter for several long moments, "You just don't get it. This town needs a vision. A new direction, and I am going to lead it."

Ryan just shook his head as he pulled into a space in front of Town Hall.

"Well, Madame Visionary, what's next," Ryan asked, tongue-in-cheek.

With a roll of her eyes, Lizzie replied, "We select the art, prepare the announcement and make sure the town is falling into line. Starting with that eyesore of a barn scene!"

Eight

Allison tried to avert her eyes off the pile of mail sitting on her desk. The colored paper showing through the window of the envelopes was only too familiar to her. She had three weeks to turn things around, or her days of being a shop owner were over. The realization made her stomach ache.

A knock on the office door caught her somewhere between glad for the interruption and hoping her grey expression wasn't too transparent as to her troubles.

"Hey, Allie," Candace began, "You're not going to like this." Handing her boss a notice, the second one from the city that day.

"City council emergency meeting approved a mandatory $500 fee per business along Main Street for updating decorations? What the...this is too much!" Allison tossed the paper on her desk and rubbed her face. "What updating?"

"That's what I asked when the letter was dropped off. Apparently, for the Art Walk, the city is ridding their usual strung lights and wreaths for snowflakes. The excuse was that the décor could be used all winter without having to be changed," Candace reported.

"And no inference to Christmas. Do we have to pay? This is Lizzie's doing!" Allison charged.

Pushing onto the showroom floor, Allison saw Mr. Haverstein enter the store. In his hands, he waved the letter. "You believe this, Ms. Allison?"

"I think the City Council is going too far. Maybe if we all band together and refuse to pay…" Allison began.

"They will only use that as an excuse to further pressure to move us all out," the deli owner interjected.

"How can they do this?" Allison asked.

"Because they don't care about us. They have all the power in their hands. They want us out. I'm not so sure we can beat them," Haverstein added.

"What are we going to do?" the shop owner asked.

"We keep doing what we do best, keep doing the right thing," Haverstein insisted.

Allison pushed her lips hard together and nodded, "You're right."

"You hang in there kiddo," Haverstein said and left to return to his shop.

As the deli owner opened the door, the smiling face of Ryan Talley held it open for him. "You're Mr. Haverstein, right?" Ryan asked.

"Yes."

"Your family has owned that deli since the end of World War II. You are famous in the city for your Bimuelos. Are you making them this year? Let me know, and I'll be sure to put in a big order. Oh…" Ryan glanced at the date on his watch, "Happy almost Hanukkah. Starts tomorrow, right?"

Mr. Haverstein smiled, "You are well versed. Yes, starting tomorrow and for the next week, we will make Bimuelos. From lunch until dinner. Best eaten right out of the batch."

"Bimuelos?" Candace asked.

"Fried honey puffs. I'm not much of a fried food eater, but these things are well worth the exception," Ryan said. "Mr. Haverstein, I'll see you tomorrow."

"What brings you in here, Mr. Talley?" Candace asked, "Errands for Lizzie Faslee?"

Ryan scrunched his face, "I don't do errands for Lizzie. I cover the town's story and proposed changes. The Art Walk is the primary focus of the magazine. Hopefully, it brings in customers for you all on Main Street."

"That would be good, and I am hopeful," Allison said.

"But…" Ryan pressed.

"But, I'm just not so sure. The way it is being put together, most of the activities will be at the far end of the street by City Hall. When we had the

Christmas tree lightings and the parades, we all did very well. But those were all shelved for the Art Walk. I'm just...I don't know," Allison admitted.

Ryan looked thoughtful, "Hmm. I wasn't aware that the committee's functions pre-empted those things. Lizzie never mentioned them."

"That's because she doesn't care about the families. Or the businesses for that matter. They aren't part of her circle. She wants a bunch of twenty-somethings and pretentious society types. Not the ones who make up the genuine core of Twin Springs," Candace argued.

"I'll see what I can do in my article to encourage attendees to check out the rest of Main Street while they are here. Don't fight it, work it to your advantage," Ryan insisted.

Allison smiled and pounded the counter with her fist, "You're right, Mr. Talley. We will just have to make the best of it."

"I'll make sure I put a listing of the shops in the margins of the article. Here's my card. Send me your logo and specs. I'll put anyone else who wants to be included in there too. The only condition is you have to start calling me Ryan instead of Mr. Talley."

"That's very nice of you, Mr...Ryan," Allison accepted his card graciously.

The town of Twin Springs is bustling more than usual this year. Vendors and artists are beginning to make their way to the pretty village nestled in the hills less than an hour's drive from the city.

The Twin Springs Art Walk is front and center of the activity. More submissions to adorn the exhibit's opening have poured in for tomorrow's big unveiling event. A mix of front name and local artists have made the final list. You can judge for yourself which works get crowned for the inaugural display. Unique paintings and sculptures will highlight the draw.

With a dusting of snow on the ground, the town's Main Street is exuding even more charm than its already strong appeal. The shops, cafes, and eateries offer a glimpse at the town's past as well as the direction that supporters of the Twin Springs Art Work hope the display will lead them.

The local café serves what only small-batch roasting and hand-operated espresso machines can provide. Authentic bimuelos are made fresh to order at the local delicatessen. I have personally found the perfect present at the local gift shop with the help of their exceptional staff and well-procured selection.

Having the pleasure to sit in with the event coordinators presiding over the Art Walk, Twin Springs will be a destination of choice this December. Can't make tomorrow evening's event? Make sure you have the Art Walk on your to-do list this December. Experience the blend of new and old-world charisma.

Elizabeth Faslee, the Art Walk chair, states that "Twin Springs will be a destination that will attract art lovers and shoppers from around the country. From around the world."

The Art Walk unveiling is the first of several phases of introductions to Twin Springs. Faslee assures that galleries, boutiques, and dining to suit any connoisseur's tastes will be satisfied in the once quiet hamlet of Twin Springs.

Ryan Talley, freelance writer

Nine

"Excellent story on Art Walk," Lizzie prided.

"Thank you. I think it looked very nice. Thanks for taking me up to the viewpoint. That made a great cover photo," Ryan admitted.

"Just not sure about adding that bit about the shops on Main. That Allison hasn't even taken down that hovel of a scene, and most of the shops haven't paid their fee," Lizzie said.

"Economy is tough. Did the council solicit their opinion before the edict was sent down?" Ryan argued.

"They don't know what is best for the town. They are tunnel-visioned with their own needs. We have the luxury of the grander view. That's where decisions are best made," Lizzie added.

"Perhaps."

"Well, today is the big day. We have caterers coming in. I have several wineries donating tastings. The strings section from the Philharmonic on loan from the city are going to play, that by the way, was thanks to them seeing your article," Lizzie replied proudly.

"I am very happy for you," Ryan said.

"This is our town's big moment. I need you to capture it all. In fact, I allowed the B&B to waive their decorating edict by getting you a room at a discount rate," Lizzie added.

Ryan tried to hide his sarcasm, "Very generous of you."

"Well, I have to run. Lots to do for the big event!"

Ryan watched the mayor's daughter hustle off excitedly. Shaking his head, he decided to see how the rest of the town was fairing in preparation for the event.

The sun shone through clear skies, but it did little to chase away the chill. Hands in his pockets, he made his way down Main Street. The street lamps had all been adorned in silver snowflakes. They were simple and elegant. All other décor had been taken down and scrapped. Ryan truthfully wasn't sure which he preferred.

Several of the shops had complied, stripped their storefronts of their traditional décor in favor of silver snowflakes. Street crews were busy cleaning and polishing everything that could shine. When he approached the gift shop, he was pleased to see the humble nativity scene still in place. Oddly enough, it looked even more attractive amidst the stylish if somewhat sterile silver snowflakes that surrounded it.

The further he moved away from the town hall, the more the shops adhered to their own themes and décor. The coffee shop adopted an odd blend. From the outside, the shop took on the ambiance more akin to the town's requests. On the inside, it held the traditional decorations. Christmas music still played, and the atmosphere was cheery. On the big chalkboard overhanging the baristas, a note welcoming the first day of Hanukkah scrawled across the lower margin.

Grabbing a cup of eggnog latte, he left the shop and continued his journey. Skirting along the sidewalk, he made way for the mailman. An overstuffed bag slung over his shoulder; the mailman waved a good morning as he sipped from a travel mug.

Allison was just turning the key in her front door when Ryan walked by.

"Good morning," the reporter called.

Looking up and dropping her keys on the sidewalk, Allison offered a sheepish smile. Grabbing her keys, she said, "Hello. Thank you for the mention in the article. We all appreciate that."

"I just hope it helps. The target audience for the Art Walk is…interesting," Ryan replied.

"We'll all do our best."

"Good luck," Ryan said as he continued on his way. He waved at Maddie, who was on her way to work, the store associate offering little more than a slight nod as she passed.

"What did he want?" Maddie asked her boss.

Allison looked up, "Who? Ryan? He was just walking by. Don't be so hard on him. He put our shop and some of the others in his article."

"Well, he is still working for the enemy. He is not to be trusted," Maddie stated defiantly. "I see Frank got his cup."

Allison beamed, "He was so happy. He never has time to stop, especially during the Christmas season."

"What's this?" Maddie tapped an envelope on the counter. "Final Notice" was stamped firmly on top. Sliding it slightly askew, she could see another with similar markings just under it.

"Oh, nothing. Just need to move some things around, you know, get money transferred into the right accounts. I'll handle it," Allison replied.

"How bad is it?" Maddie pressed.

Before Allison could utter a response, the front door flung open. Haverstein burst in, both hands grasping a basket covered in a towel. The smells that emanated out of it were terrific.

"Bimuelos or Loukomades as grandmother called them. Fresh. My first batch. I hope you don't mind being my guinea pigs," Haverstein announced.

"Oh my gosh! Those smell divine!" Maddie salivated.

Allison nodded in agreement, "They do smell wonderful."

"My grandmother's recipe. From Israel through Greece to Twin Springs," Haverstein grinned.

Through a mouthful of the honey dough ball, Maddie exclaimed, "Mr. H, they taste even better than they smell. I didn't think it possible."

"If it weren't for the whole Jesus disagreement, I would almost consider converting," Allison laughed.

"I settle for friendship, Ms. Allison."

"That you have," Allison hugged the deli owner.

"Well, back to work. I have to get yeast to rise for several batches," Haverstein shared, shuffling towards the door.

"We won't hold you up, but we will send as many people your way as we can," Allison offered.

As soon as Haverstein left, the door opened again. A very sheepish man bowed into the store. In his hand, a sheet of paper. "I'm sorry Ms. Tancredi. I'm just the messenger. My family likes the manger."

"It's alright, Tommy," Allison said, taking the paper. "Another notice on the Nativity. Well, if Lizzie wants it gone so bad, maybe she should have the guts to come down here and talk to me about it herself."

"Yes, ma'am," Tommy nodded.

Allison slapped her hand on his shoulder. "Don't you worry about it. I know you're just doing your job. Want some cider or cocoa?"

"No, we have lots to do for the night's festivities," Tommy answered.

"Alright. You bring Jenny and the kids in some time," Allison said.

Nodding, the city worker hurried out of the store.

Allison stared after him while Maddie and Candace studied her.

On the closed street alongside City Hall, giant lights stanchions were wheeled into place. More lights covered the walkway that would be part of the Art Walk. A television crew from the city installed a small stage erected in front of the veiled pieces.

Lizzie and her friends had taken the afternoon to be pampered at a spa and then whisked away to hair appointments. Ryan had taken the time to work on his notes and prepare the background for the unveiling article.

Leaning against a lamppost, he watched the scene grow to readiness. This one block of Twin Springs transformed into a trendy, overdone production that was more akin to a Hollywood launch than the quaint little town he had first visited. It was certainly the vision that Lizzie had sought after. Everything was shining and first class.

An invitation-only artist's reception was to follow the unveiling with dignitaries, investors, and gallery owners from all over the country would be treated to a gourmet meal, all funded by the fees the City Council had levied over the past year. Ryan scoffed for a moment. The townspeople who paid for the function weren't even able to partake in it. He shook his head.

At times, Lizzie could appear so sweet, thoughtful. Others, she was so belligerently cold-hearted and selfish. When he listened to her one on one, he could tell that she meant well. She saw Twin Springs as a town in trouble. She heard her father struggle with decreased tax income as a result of everyone else's economic suffering. She couldn't see how a sleepy little town like Twin Springs could pull out of it without action. She figured she would go where the money was – and bring that money to Twin Springs.

A simple conversation with her father, Ryan had learned through interviewing the mayor, had spun into this event, the catalyst for more significant change to downtown Twin Springs. With the help of her influential friends, Lizzie had the machine rolling. Here they were at the doorstep. The changing face of Twin Springs.

From his vantage, Ryan could see both sides. He had seen how the city had gone through growing pains. But it was the city. Fast-paced, progressive business and politics. It was what you expected in the town. Places like Twin Springs were little gems of respite from all of that. Occasionally those small towns within reach of the city got swept into its current. Twin Springs was in the riptide.

Ryan pondered his role in casting off the town's lines from its own mooring. He wondered if allowing it to float into the flow of the city and the rest of the world was the right thing. The demeanor of Allison and her staff stung Ryan's mind. Not everyone in Twin Springs appreciated the change.

As Ryan wandered around the town as it was frantically assembled into an event site, he was able to observe the dichotomy. Those with ties to the Faslees and Town Hall were excited and put themselves into positions to orchestra the making of the new Twin Springs.

The others. It was the others that gave Ryan so much pause. The Allisons, the Haversteins. The coffee shop owner. He debated whether both sides of the perspective could exist in the same small town. From his time in the council meetings. He had his doubts.

The busy day began to give way to an even more hectic evening.

Avoiding a pacing and anxious Lizzie Faslee, Ryan found a little spot in a little-used room on the second floor of City Hall to take in the scene. Snapping a few pictures of workers and volunteers preparing the final adjustments for the event through an open window, he had a perfect vantage for Art Walk.

As the start time drew nearer, the entire length of Main Street was closed as Lizzie had prescribed, and visitors began arriving. The artists were first. Ryan ran out to meet each, gathering notes on their works and from what galleries they hailed. A few of the artists were pleasant. A couple were so full of themselves, Ryan laughed to himself that Lizzie would find herself to be trumped by them.

The final artist rattled off a list of demands to Ryan – a perfectly heated espresso, a non-public washroom where he could clean up and a snack, preferably a French Brie. Ryan wrinkled his brow and replied half-heartedly, "Sure" with no intention of complying or passing along any of those items to anyone else.

Walking away, he nearly ran headlong into Lizzie. They both drew back, momentarily startled. Ryan had to admit, the spoiled Mayor's daughter was absolutely stunning. His golden-brown hair cascaded in ringlets out of a white and tan fur hat that matched her coat. Open in the front to reveal a foal tan silk blouse and a string of pearls around her neck. Along with elegant clothes, she also wore a look of desperation.

"Oh my gosh," she breathed as she held her chest.

Ryan smiled calmly, "You okay?"

"What? Yes. Just nervous I guess," Lizzie conceded.

"It's a big night. Just be confident and speak with your heart. I have learned from writing that you can't speak to please others. You can only declare from your perspective, your honesty. If you do that, you'll always sleep well at night. There will always be critics. People will always disagree with you," Ryan consoled.

Lizzie pursed her lips, "I've had plenty of those."

"You'll have more. Just make sure at the end of the day, you aren't one of them."

"Thanks."

"You'll do fine," Ryan assured and left for the sanctuary of the little second-floor room.

From his perch, Ryan could watch the stream of out of towners descending on the little town of Twin Springs. Laughing to himself, he admitted he had never seen so many BMWs in one place. The parking lot at City Hall and along the street was a sea of grey and silver sedans. People clad in trendy outerwear filtered into the event space. A wine garden was set up, and it held the capacity of attendees.

Snapping a few shots of the guests, he turned his attention to Lizzie and her friends who had gathered near the veiled displays. The young socialite seemed less tense than she had. It appeared as though she had orchestrated the event quite well.

A few news vans raised their transmission antennas, and reporters began taking positions to cover the proceedings. Massive searchlights cut through the night while strings of white Christmas lights lined either side of the walkway along the covered art pieces. Pedestals with propane fed flames dotted the space, providing much-needed warmth for the spectators and participants.

Moving his lens down the heart of Main Street, Ryan could see the downtown area away from the event was a different scene entirely. Scarcely a being meandered among the shops. A few people streamed from the coffee shop, but they quickly made beelines for the unveiling. The gift shop, the deli, and the other stores were starkly quiet.

Mayor Faslee walked from City Hall, waving and stopping to shake hands with attendees as he walked along the lit path to the small stage by the exhibits. Lizzie and her committee followed, taking up one side of the Mayor while the selected artists resided on the other. Ryan chuckled as his lens locked on one very grumpy artist who had realized his cravings were not going to be met.

The television news cameras were switched on and trained in the direction of the stage. Mayor Faslee addressed the audience and welcomed all who had come. He noted the residents, the businesses, and his staff. He greeted those who came in from the city and from out of town. Finally, he saluted the artists nominated for the first Art Walk displays.

Turning, he motioned with an outstretched hand to his daughter and her friends. "Only someone who had spent their whole lives in Twin Springs could understand the journey it has been on, could recognize our town's needs and could have the vision to create not only a beautiful display for our town – for it by itself would be a mere extravagance – but created a new direction. I am proud to present the vision of Lizzie Faslee, my daughter."

Lizzie took center stage and looked out upon the audience. She paused, holding an air of grace and calm as she patiently began her speech. "Twin Springs is a beautiful place. I loved growing up here. When my mother was alive, she taught me to see the beauty in everything. As an artist, the world around her was a subject for every canvas, every sculpture…and in the undulating hills and sweeping valleys of Twin Springs, what an amazing place to draw your inspiration.

Today, I give to Twin Springs and all of her people, a taste of tomorrow. A Twin Springs of the future – prosperous, elegant, refined. A place that draws people in from all over to admire the artists, sample decadent cuisine, celebrate themselves in spas among this beautiful setting."

Lizzie held a long pregnant pause, as if allowing her words to sink into the audience. "Today, I give you twelve incredible artists whose amazing work will call Twin Springs home!"

As she said home, the searchlights swept down and met one another square on the exhibits. At their point of contact, the tethers that held the Art Walk canvases under shroud released revealing the six art pieces. Two stone sculptures, two metal sculptures, one glass sculpture, and seven paintings, sealed in crystal clear acrylic gleamed in the powerful lights.

Lizzie dropped her arms, and the searchlights instantly went out, yielding to twinkling string lights that created an arbor-like netting over the entire Art Walk. She beamed as the audience erupted in clapping and the occasional cheer. "With the many thanks to all of those who put in so much hard work, my amazing committee, the artists and the city folks, I say cheers and enjoy Twin Springs Art Walk. There will be stations in the wine garden, in City Hall and for those who have been invited to the reception for any questions regarding real estate, creating commerce in Twin Springs and recreation offerings. Thank you so much. I look forward to being able to meet each and every one of you personally."

Ryan nodded up in his perch, "Not bad, Ms. Faslee. If only your vision were a shared one amongst the populous, might not be bad at all." Snapping a few final shots of the event and the first crowd members to follow the dignitaries and the artist through the walk, Ryan closed the door and packed up his gear.

Slipping his camera into a little holster and his note pad into the breast pocket of his jacket, the reporter, made his way out of the Town Hall building. From his vantage on the town hall steps, Ryan watched as people meandered through the displays, took "selfies" of themselves and their friends for being at the event, and circulating back towards the wine garden where several regional vintners waited to share their craftsmanship.

From across the crowd, Lizzie saw Ryan and flashed a smile and nonchalant thumbs up. Ryan nodded his approval, and Lizzie slipped back into the throng of "her people". As the crowd made their procession through the walk, many headed immediately for their cars, some towards the wine sampling and a few toward the rustic Community Center across the town halls western flank.

Despite closing the entire stretch of Main Street, save for a few who ran down for coffee, very little of the crowd ventured down Main. Ryan noticed an exception, a group of men in suits stuffed into overcoats walking down the center of the street, pointing out particular shops and then swinging their attention to buildings on the opposite side of the road. Ryan recognized the man who seemed to be guiding the group as Eric Farnham, one of Lizzie's confidants from her "Vision Team".

Shrugging, Ryan crossed over to the sidewalk, remembering he could get his honey puff from the Jewish Deli. Passing by the gift shop, he stopped and pushed through the door. All three workers stopped and watched him come in. "Quite the night," he said.

No one spoke for a moment. Maddie cast a disapproving glare before Allison replied softly, "I suppose it is."

"A little quiet on this end, huh," Ryan frowned.

"Yeah, no thanks to you and your girlfriend!" Maddie snapped.

Ryan flushed, taken aback, "Girlfriend? Who...Lizzie?" Ryan's face twisted. "No. She and I...no. Just the hired..."

"Hired gun!" Maddie interjected.

"Maddie!" Allison scolded.

"I was going to say hired writer," Ryan bit his lip thoughtfully. "This is worse with the rest of the town than I thought."

Candace took a step towards Ryan and squared up with him. Her tone was even placed somewhere between those of her friends, "Lizzie's ideas will cripple shop owners like Allie and Mr. Haverstein. Even the coffee shop will be booted because it isn't French enough or corporate enough...whatever Lizzie's sweeping changes are for Twin Springs."

Ryan leaned against the counter. "I see. I knew its popularity was split, wasn't my cup of tea either. Didn't know it was that bad."

"How many people from town do you suppose were invited to the "Reception"? Outside of the Mayor's backers and Lizzie's friends...and that creepy Eric guy, they are all investors and owners of stores in the city that want to expand to open boutiques here. They consider us their suburbs. We're not. We're nothing like the city on purpose. We are Twin Springs because we love Twin Springs, flaws and all," Candace posed.

"We are going through a tough time as a town to be sure, but we'll pull out of it because of who we are not because of a bunch of out of towners and one crazy local wants to come in and change everything," Maddie added.

Ryan nodded his head silently for a moment, casting a glance at Allison. Her eyes had a hint of gloss to them, and Ryan understood. "Beautifully put, both of you. This would be resounded by most of the shop owners?"

Allison nodded.

"I'm sorry if my writing for Lizzie has made any of this worse for you, for anybody," Ryan said.

"It didn't. Not really," Allison replied. Her glance cut Maddie off who had opened her mouth to speak. "I read all of your articles. They were fair, opinionless, and factual. You sold the Art Walk as an event, not as a cultural change for the town. In fact, I picked up a fondness for Twin Springs in your writing. You painted our home as a beautiful place regardless of the iteration."

Ryan almost looked stunned at Allison's assessment of his writing. "Thank you. I was asked to sell the concept, and I made it clear my job was not to sell or market "The Vision" but to merely cover it. I believe I held true to that."

"You did," Allison quickly. "Our troubles past or present are not yours or because of you."

Chewing his lip, Ryan looked at each one of the women. Finally, he let out a sheepish smile, "I love the passion you all have for the town, for your home, this store. I promise you. I bet very few in the city have an ounce of the caring that you do. They are awash in the swells, tossed in the current. The city is always changing, that is its culture. Change can be good. Sometimes it isn't…I mean, people wore bell-bottoms once…that wasn't good."

Wanting desperately to change the subject or leave or both, he offered with his thumb pointing to the wall, "I was just going next door for bimuelos. Did you guys want some?"

"We're fine. Thank you," Allison replied. "Mr. Haverstein has been waiting for you. He mentioned you today."

"The allure of bimuelos," Ryan smiled and waved his ado.

"Something like that..." Allison whispered. "Well, ladies, I don't think the upper crust down at the end of Main is going to sulk with the likes of us. What do you say we shut down early and go? My treat."

Ten

The deli was as quiet as the other shops in town. Mr. Haverstein was busy making dough to rise overnight. Hearing the bell ring as Ryan entered the shop, he craned his head to see who had come in. "Ah..., Mr. Talley, the writer. How are you this fine evening?"

Ryan chuckled at the man's exuberance. "Good. Better than business, I'm afraid."

"Ah, business come, business goes. We get ready for another day just the same," Haverstein said as he dried his hands on a towel. "You came for bimuelos, eh?"

Ryan nodded, "I've been anxious all day waiting for the chance."

"How was the event, lots of people?" the deli owner asked.

"I suppose. Mostly from the city, I would guess. The "Who's Who", artists, media, investors..."

"It went well?" Haverstein pressed.

"For what it was," Ryan shrugged. "Ms. Faslee's message was surprisingly well elocuted. The mayor was positive and brief."

Haverstein paused, eyeing the young reporter. "You seem guarded, it was your job to report on and market the event, yes?"

"It was. Doesn't necessarily mean I agree or even support the effort."

The shopkeeper laughed, "I read your articles. Fair and to the point. Informational without selling it. I like the way you write."

"Thank you, sir."

"Why write what you don't believe?" Haverstein asked, placing the last bimuelo into a little pastry box.

"Reporting versus propaganda. Journalism versus a column or personal writing. It's my job," Ryan replied. "Do you sell things in your deli that you don't like?"

Haverstein scanned his shop for a moment and grinned, "My grandmother would roll over, but...gefilte fish. Never could stand it. My mother used to warn me before holidays at Grandmother's not to make faces and play with my plate when it was served."

Ryan flashed a knowing smile as he played with a jar in hand. "And yet, gefilte fish. On sale, even."

"Touché Mr. Talley, touché," Haverstein laughed. Handing over the box, he waved Ryan off as he reached for his wallet.

"I insist, Mr. Haverstein. Intended or not, my efforts on Art Walk have not helped business."

"You come back again. Bring your friends. Drop the deli into an article," Haverstein pushed.

Ryan couldn't resist a chuckle, "Alright, you have my word on all the above." Pausing for one final moment, Ryan held out his hand. "Mer...Happy Hanukah."

Across the counter, Haverstein grasped the reporter's hand. "Pleasure, Mr. Talley."

As Ryan left the deli, Main Street had fallen even more silent. Most of the businesses had closed for the day. Ryan felt a bit lonely as he walked down the sidewalk. He wondered if the town's plans might just be the boost that it needed. Yet, he couldn't help to feel lifted as he walked by each storefront's façade. The classic Christmas décor brought back a flurry of memories from childhood that had transcended all the way through his life.

A few stores sparkled with more modern lights and images, but it was the classics that really drew Ryan in. He rubbed his chin as he walked, maybe that was the charm of the town. It was a sweet, safe piece of America that resembled the image that people had in their minds of what an American town should be.

Fulfilling his duty, he made his way to the Community Center, where the reception was winding down. Peering through the window, he could see a dwindling crowd of Lizzie's invitees corralled into little cliques around the banquet hall.

Mayor Faslee looked deep in conversation with one group who appeared to be regaled by his story. Of the mayor's talents, spinning tales and entertaining people was undoubtedly at the top.

Lizzie flittered from one group to the next, looking like a nervous hen as she tried to make her impact with each. Once engaged, her posture evolved very quickly into confident and composed. She adeptly addressed everyone in the room, working the crowd with grace and finesse.

The actual content of the discussions, Ryan could only imagine, but he was sure they revolved around the "vision" of the town. Lizzie was actively seeking suitors to invest and take up commercial residence in Twin Springs. The only question was who and what businesses to replace as collateral damage along the way.

For a long moment, Ryan toyed with the idea of infiltrating the gathering to glean quotes and notes for the article. Finally, he decided watching the high society affair from behind a frosted window was enough for him. Lizzie would surely fill him with rants and raves in the morning during their recap.

Straightening the collar on his coat, he turned away from the Community Center. The adjacent Art Walk remained lit in its sophisticated elegance. While beautiful, it seemed a bit out of its element. Twin Springs was a collection of colonial trappings, historical as well as modern iterations of the theme. The Art Walk lent more towards modern architecture shrouded in glass and gleaming metal facades. Charming in its own respect. In Twin Springs, it somehow didn't quite match.

As Ryan passed the display, he nearly ran right into one of the artists. The man was glued to his phone as he shuffled along the sidewalk. His path blocked by the reporter, he snapped his head up to identify his impediment. Suddenly the artist's eyes widened before settling into a glare of disdain. "You!" he pointed a stubby finger at Ryan. "I provided very specific instructions. Not one of them was met. Not one of them!"

"Yep, probably not. Not sure who you expected to fulfill your whim, I am definitely not that guy," Ryan declared. "I do hope you had a pleasant evening just the same."

"Ah!" the man threw his arms in the air to display his disgust. Ambling off, he launched into a mumbled tirade in some guttural language Ryan interpreted as French. Occasionally the words "American" and "Twin Springs" were decipherable amidst the torrent of what Ryan assumed to be cuss words.

"Probably just as well, I don't understand the little man," Ryan chuckled to himself.

Veering from Main Street, Ryan walked uphill a couple of blocks to find the Bed and Breakfast that was to be his home for the next couple of weeks. The old colonial house looked like it was right out of a Thomas Kincaide painting. It's wide, wrap-around porch, a candle in each window, and a wreath hung on the front door welcomed him.

Gingerly opening the door, he found the interior no less inviting. A warm fire was crackling in a reading room immediately off of the entry. The scent of spices and cider filled the air. A little table in the foyer held ornate bowls offering pomegranates, oranges, and apples. Hot water for tea or cocoa was set beside the warmed cider and coffee.

The stairs leading to the second floor were wrapped in evergreen garland woven in a long string of white lights. More twinkling lights drew attention to a beautiful tree that barely fit its angel top under the ceiling. Simple decorations of red bows and handcrafted ornaments dotted its branches.

Lost in the warm, inviting atmosphere, Ryan was almost startled when a singing-like voice called to him from the hallway.

"You must be Mr. Talley," a cheery woman in a gingham apron said, "We've been expecting you. Welcome to The Byrd's Nest Bed and Breakfast."

"Thank you. This place is...amazing," Ryan replied.

"Please feel at home. Anything you need, just let us know. Your room will be on the second floor, room 6. If you like, once you put your bag away, you are welcome to come down to the study. There are cocktails and tea by the fire," the woman said.

"Thank you, Mrs...."

"Byrd. Merilee Byrd. A pleasure to have you, Mr. Talley."

Ryan found the guest room no less charming. Decorated in colonial trimmings on par with the house and the town, the room felt perfect. A tiny foot tall Christmas tree sat on the dresser, an equally tiny string of lights wrapped around it. Stowing his duffel on the foot of the bed, Ryan decided to explore the rest of the house.

Descending the stairs, he found the room off the foyer with the tree. A cat circled on a wingback chair, flanking the fireplace and plopped down. In a mirroring chair, an older man sat sipping on a short glass of wine.

"Ah, Mr. Talley, I presume," the man beamed, as cheery as Merilee had been. "Name's Charlie Byrd, a faithful steward of the Byrd's Nest B&B and husband to the lovely Ms. Merilee."

"Nice to meet you, sir," Ryan responded.

"Have a seat. Pour you a glass of Port? Nice and warming on a cool winter's night," Charlie offered.

"Uhm...," not much of a drinker, Ryan hesitated, "Sure, a little one."

"That's the only kind with a good Port," Charlie boomed. Sliding what looked like a miniature wine glass into the center of the table, the hotelier poured half a glass of the ruby liquid.

Ryan raised it in the air, "Merry Christmas, Mr. Byrd."

"Charlie," the older man replied, returning the gesture. "So, you're the writer Lizzie Faslee brought in to cover her grand transformation."

Ryan wriggled in his seat. "Well, I suppose, yes."

"You seem uncomfortable…"

"It's just, I kind of like Twin Springs…the way it is," Ryan replied.

"What about the economy, progress?" Charlie asked, a sly smile creasing his lips.

"The way I see it, Twin Springs has been here a long time. Through depressions and recessions, it's still here," Ryan shrugged.

Charlie nodded, "Yes, it is. I agree with you, though we are one of the few businesses that appear to be unscathed in the big plan. Good thing, too. Merilee seems sweet, and she is, but you bristle her feathers and whew…look out."

"Here's to Merilee then," Ryan toasted as he took a sip of the Port.

"To Merilee."

Charlie took a sip from his glass and studied the reporter. "And how was the grand event this evening?"

"You didn't go?"

"Oh, we had considered, but we elected to tend to the needs of our guests," Charlie replied.

"It was…interesting. Lots of people from out of town. The Faslees seemed to enjoy the reception after it," Ryan offered.

Charlie looked over his glass and smiled, "But…"

"You know," Ryan sighed, "Many who attended were a bit like the display itself. They didn't quite seem to fit what I have come to perceive Twin Springs to be."

"Indeed." Charlie said softly.

A New Era for Art in Twin Springs

Twin Springs hosted artists, critics and connoisseurs from around the globe to launch what many in the town propose to be a new mecca for art and culture.

The inaugural works represent a full sampling of sculptures and paintings from Europe, New York, and California. Many of the artists are said to have ties with families in Twin Springs. Traditional and trendy styles are explored in the Art Walks initial showing.

Twin Springs own Mayor Faslee kicked off the event amid dancing searchlights which welcomed the art community. Faslee's words struck at Twin Springs past and enduring residents, many who stretch back for generations.

Only upstaged by the art itself, Elizabeth Faslee, the project's director, launched the Twin Springs Art Walk with a moving dedication of the project, the town, and the transformational vision that was officially kicked off that very evening.

In her own words, she channeled the spirit she carries on from her mother, "As an artist, the world around [her mother] was subject for every canvas, every sculpture…and in the undulating hills and sweeping valleys of Twin Springs, what an amazing place to draw your inspiration from."

Add Twin Springs and the Art Walk to your weekend's plans and come see what may inspire you.

Ryan Talley, freelance writer

Twelve

Ryan surprised himself by sleeping incredibly well in the feathery bed of the Byrd's Nest Bed and Breakfast. Dawn's light touched his face before he woke up. Startled, he glanced at his watch. Grumbling to himself, he knew he would have to hurry to be on time to meet Lizzie for the Art Walk recap. He took a bit of solace in the fact that she herself had rarely arrived on time to any of their meetings.

Grabbing his clothes and a quick shower, Ryan scrambled to get ready. Clambering down the stairs, he waved good morning to Merilee and pulled his coat on as he ran out of the hotel. The morning sun sparkled off of the world, which had been painted frosty silver and white. Ryan had to step carefully as he hurried along.

Rushing inside Town Hall, Ryan shook off the cold and headed for the conference room upstairs. Lizzie was there waiting for him. She was brooding over her tablet, her finger swiping like mad against the screen.

"Latte for you, just how you like it," Ryan sang, sliding into a chair across from her.

Lizzie grunted a 'thank you' but remained intent on the news she was reading.

"Well?" he asked.

Shaking herself from the social media, she looked across at the reporter. "It went great. The revealing and the reception were wonderful. Thank you for your help. Your write up was great," Lizzie said, her words a bit hollow.

"But…"

"I kept getting flack about the "conservative nature" of Twin Springs. The art community is quite progressive. They liked the Art Walk and the vision I laid out for the investors. They just weren't sure Twin Springs was the right place. It felt "old" and too "homey for them", whatever that means. And then the religious tones – that stupid Nativity, the deli, the carolers that passed through, ugh! We might as well have said we haven't changed in two hundred years," Lizzie intoned.

"And then, this stupid article on the Nativity popped up. It has gotten as many hits as Art Walk," she added.

"Oh?" Ryan looked surprised. "Maybe it's not so bad."

"Not so bad if we want this dump to stay stuck in the 1800s. This is our opportunity to leap forward. I am not going to let a bunch of nuts ruin it!" Lizzie spat. "I'm sorry. This was supposed to be my big moment, and it was, it's just been marred."

"The night went great. I thought your speech was inspiring," Ryan consoled.

"Thank you. You captured that very well for me. Eric has investors coming back tomorrow to look at some options. I should probably get going; I have some things to take care of. Let's connect later. I think we need another push or two to get them over the hump. I have a few marketing programs I would like to run by you," Lizzie instructed.

"Okay. I'll be around," Ryan replied.

"Thank you for the coffee."

Strolling back down Main Street, Ryan thought about the shops. He studied the little hardware store. Christmas trees lined the sidewalk out front. A mural of Santa swooping down the local hills on his sleigh filled the window in bright colors.

The antique store next door had a fantastic display of classic Christmas decorations, turning their front window display into a luxurious 1920's living room. The entire front of the store was a woven tale from Dickens' classics to Norman Rockwell idealism. A glimpse inside reminded Ryan of Christmas at his grandmother's house.

Passing by, the evergreen bough flocked marquee of the theater proudly listed showings of "It's a Wonderful Life" among the current movies. Even a classic movie poster showing George Bailey running down the streets of Bedford Falls adorned one of the frames that lined the entry.

When he looked across the street at the Nativity, it all just fit. He hadn't thought much about it when he was first assigned to cover the Town Meeting. But as he took the time soak in the sights, sounds, and smells of Twin Springs, he realized that the little town tugged at him. He felt warm each time he visited. Staying at the bed and breakfast felt more like home than it should.

Ryan wondered if the feeling would transcend to other towns that shared the same aura. Americana – solid, simple, sweet. The Town Hall's columns, the dormers shared by most of the downtown buildings and area homes alike, the mix of wood, stone, and classic brick. Streets lined with elm trees and traditional lamp posts. They weren't just pictures in a history book. They were the original infrastructure of America.

Almost ribbing himself for his sappy patriotism, but he knew with her flaws and all, he lived in the greatest country in the world. He didn't always like the changes that were forced upon her. He was sure some good changes were painful along the way. He was also sure some change was painful because the change was right. It didn't fit the heartbeat, the culture of America. He wondered which was befalling Twin Springs.

Allison looked at the rows of wrapping paper under the check stand. In years past, there would hardly have been any left. This year, only a few had been exhausted. Business had picked up, but she was afraid not to the degree that she needed. With heart heavy, she worried this might be the last year for her shop.

Seeing Tommy Tulia arrive outside the shop with a sheepish look and a letter in his hand, Allison exhaled a huge sigh and met him at the door. "Good morning Tommy," she managed pleasantly.

"Good morning Allison. Don't shoot the messenger. I think they are all a little nutty down there these days. Should have more important things to worry about," Tommy said, nervously fiddling with the city badge on his jacket.

"I know. How have the goings-on affected you guys?"

"A lot longer hours, that's for sure. Who knew a bunch of snobs…err, I'm sorry…society's elite could be such slobs. Cleaning up after the Art Walk event was an ordeal, not to mention the nit-picking in preparation for it," Tommy replied. "On the bright side, at least they pay me overtime. How are things here? Should have brought in some big business for you."

Allison wrinkled her nose, "Not really. Business has been okay, but in reality, the entire Art Walk extravaganza has deterred visitors down along the markets."

"Ah, it will pick up," Tommy said cheerily. "Well, gotta run. Yours isn't the only letter I have to deliver, and there's already been talk of another big deal to prepare for."

"Take care of yourself, Tommy and don't work too hard. Merry Christmas!" Allison called as the city worker left the shop and hurried down the block.

Prying a corner of the envelope with her thumb, Allison tore open the letter. The words "FINAL NOTICE" were spelled out in big block letters across the top on the official city letterhead. A list of fines, penalties, and legal action were neatly bullet-pointed for her amidst a page of legal citations.

The message just left Allison to shake her head. "The city is claiming the sidewalk, including the storefront easement as government property, and as such, shop owners had to remove any signage or religious displays," she read out loud. "What a load of..."

Seeing Maddie bounce towards the door, Allison stuffed the letter in the wastebasket under the check stand.

"Morning, boss! I brought you coffee!" Maddie called.

"You are a doll."

"I know. Remember that around raise time," winked Maddie.

"How goes the search?"

"Things have really dried up. There some interviews set up for January. Everything else has been put off for the sake of the holidays," Maddie replied.

"It will work out. He's a good man. Something good will come," Allison consoled.

Nodding, Maddie sighed, "I know. It's just so frustrating…so scary."

Well versed in worrying about bills, Allison glanced towards her office door. She knew behind it, was a stack of bills that would likely spell the last days of her gift shop.

Maddie placed her purse in the cabinet under the check stand. Seeing a pink piece of paper next to the wastebasket, she bent over and picked up to throw it away. Glancing as she slid it in the mouth of the trash can, she pulled it back out.

"Seriously, that witch…that Scrooge is threatening you?" Maddie cursed.

Allison stopped what she was doing and turned to her friend. "What? Oh…you found the notice. Yes. Nothing really new in it except they threaten sanctions, fines, and Christmassy stuff like that."

"How nice. Some say it was because her shoes were too tight," Maddie scoffed.

"Her head, not screwed on just right," Allison giggled.

"We all know her heart is really two sizes too small!" Maddie doubled over laughing, tears coming out of her eyes.

The front bell tingling did not deter them. "Ms. Lizzie, I take it?" Candace asked, eyeing her friends with knowing suspicion.

"You know it." Maddie raised the letter in the air. "More threats to take down the Nativity. It clashes with her fur-lined harlots," Maddie mocked with a superior ring to her voice.

Setting her hat and mittens on the counter, Candace shook her head. "What is wrong with people today? We're not infringing on anyone's right not to look. A poor baby in a manger and a loving mom and dad...pretty scary stuff." She laughed as she shook off a fake chill.

"If they don't like it, they don't have to shop here. If they really don't like it, they can move to a different country," Maddie scowled.

"Now, you're talking. Christmas has been celebrated here since the Pilgrims landed. All of a sudden, it is this horrible thing. Wishing people a happy, merry day. You should be ashamed," Candace chimed in.

The banter surprisingly caught Allison a little sad. She didn't know what had happened to the world. Christmas was such a happy, hopeful time. A time when people from all walks of life wished each other goodwill and peace. Somehow it had become some kind of slander.

"No," Allison called out to herself more than her co-workers. "The Nativity stays."

"You bet it stays!" Maddie added resolutely.

Most of the day had Ryan bouncing from meeting to meeting, trying to glean anything of interest to include in another battery of articles touting the Art Walk and the transformation of Twin Springs. He watched Mayor Faslee vacillate between a slow evolution of the town versus his daughter's and her committee's calls for quick action.

Eric Farnham caught Ryan's ear more than anyone else. Watching quietly, he could see Eric work the room with cunning aplomb. He would bolster the mayor's ego, painting him as the foundation of the town and its would-be savior. Then he would address the committee members who had ties to the town's business community. Pushing change and the collateral fall out as necessary for the longer-term prosperity of the town. Those who played ball with the new Twin Springs would bear the rewards that the future was set to bring.

Most of all, the property manager worked Lizzie Faslee. Gushing over her plans, lauding the quality people she had brought in for the unveiling and crowning her the de facto princess of Twin Springs.

When it came to the current business owners along Main Street, the pairing proved to be heartless. They wished those shop owners away and ignored policies that they knew would be problematic for them. Eric was careful enough to save details of their cleansing when the mayor was out of the room as he tended to veto any change that levied hardship on those who were already in place and working hard for success themselves.

"I already have it on good word that several of the businesses are struggling. We would love to save them, of course. But, most are beyond saving," he shrugged.

Most in the room agreed. Some eager to see the businesses fail, others merely nodding the inevitable was going to come anyway. Resolving to do what was best for the town, they arranged a special investor dinner. They would bring in those who expressed interest during the Art Walk reception and pitch that they pre-invest in the town's future, guaranteeing them a seat at the resurrected Twin Springs.

Ryan fought to keep his mouth shut. This committee was betting on failure. Now they were about to invest in it.

When the meeting adjourned, the room turned in to a big love fest of self-perceived heroes. "They'll thank us one day," Annabeth shouted above the crowd.

"Are you kidding, they're going to carve your faces on the hillside overlooking Twin Springs. What you are all working on is historic," Eric egged them on.

With coats on and the room cleared, the crowd had proposed a celebratory cocktail hour at the local tavern. "Imagine a year from now, we could go to a wine bar or a champagne lounge," Tiffany drooled.

Migrating down the steps, Lizzie separated from the group for a moment. Slinking to the back, she cozied against Ryan. "So, you going to join us?"

Ryan's head split in conflict. A large part of him wanted to get away from the ruthless band. The other side of him wanted to see what additional information he could gain as they fueled their mammoth egos with cocktails. The latter was too much to resist. Looking the elegant blonde in her expectant blue eyes, he nodded, "I'm in."

Slipping her arm into his, she grinned, "Excellent!"

Candace admired how the crystal snowflake she pulled out of its display box danced in the light. Hanging it on the tree on just the right limb so that it received the reflections in the shop just right. "So, who do you suppose wrote the article favoring the Nativity?" she asked.

"I was figuring it was you," Allison said and then swung an accusatory finger at Maddie, "Or you…"

Holding her hands up in front of her, Maddie shook her head. "Not me. You know I don't write that eloquently."

"I got a 'C' in Persuasive Writing," Candace admitted.

The three pondered for a moment before Allison snapped her fingers, "Pastor Dave."

Candace and Maddie nodded in unison, "That's who it was."

"Such a good guy. I'm glad we have him in Twin Springs," Allison said.

"He and Daphne do so much for this town," Maddie agreed.

"And who else could make as good an argument for the Nativity?" Candace stared thoughtfully at the gleaming snowflake ornament. "Makes me want to sign up for one of their Christmas mini-missions."

Maddie scrunched her nose, "Me too."

"Let's all do it together," Allison chimed in. Looking up at the clock, she added, "You know what, it's close enough to closing time. Let's wrap it up early. Appetizers on me, and we can look at which one we want to do." Setting the stack of Christmas linens she was folding on the counter, she ran the daily report while Maddie pulled the till.

In record time, the shop was closed, and they were singing "Deck the Halls" together, dancing arm in arm down the sidewalk. Giggling as they sashayed their way to the front door of the Mill Pub, the trio poured into the restaurant.

The near century-old tavern was unusually busy for a Tuesday evening. The lounge was buzzing with loud conversations and laughter. "Someone's having a good time in there," Candace said to her friends.

The three craned their necks around the corner as they waited for the hostess to take them to their table. Recognizing a lot of council members from City Hall, their curiosity satisfied. As Allison was pulling away, she subconsciously paused on one of the revelers.

Maddie noticed her friend's hesitation. Following Allison's eyes, she flowed from the mayor to a councilwoman to Lizzie Faslee to…the reporter. "Humph," she scoffed, watching Lizzie's arm drape around the man. They both laughed together at who only knew what.

Suddenly Ryan's eyes glanced away from his audience and lighted on the three spectators.

Landing a look squarely on Allison, he instinctively pulled away from Lizzie. Lizzie turned, glanced at the three women in the doorway, and returned to her conversation completely unmoved. Ryan's gaze remained constant for several long moments.

"Come on, girls," Candace tugged at her friends. "We have some do-gooding to do."

As Ryan walked into the foyer of the Bed and Breakfast, bathed in warmth, he paused as he used his back to push it shut. His mind was murky, but he wasn't sure why. His mental machinery was hard at work, whirring, and tabulating but not really providing any direction for his melancholy.

The reporter's affect must have been transparent. "Looks like you could stand to take a load off," Charlie Byrd called from his seat by the fire.

Ryan grinned. "Good evening Charlie."

"Come on in, Mr. Talley."

Ryan held his hands out as he sat in the wingback chair opposite of the innkeeper. "The fire is wonderful."

"I don't care how much technology has evolved. There's nothing like a good, classic fire in a fireplace to melt the chill off you on a winter's night," Charlie said. "Mrs. Byrd thought you might be coming. She made a pot of tea."

Ryan smiled, "That's perfect. Thank you."

"So," Charlie began in between sips of his tea, "What ails you?"

"What do you mean?" Ryan asked, an eyebrow raised.

"You looked perplexed, conflicted when you came in."

"Conflicted," Ryan nodded. "That might be it. Probably the battle for Twin Springs weighing me down."

Charlie laughed, "The battle raging, is it?"

Ryan sighed, "You wouldn't believe the power-grabbing behind the curtain."

"Oh, I believe it. It's politics and business. Sometimes it's not pretty. What is so inflammatory to cause you gloom?"

"It has less to do with what they are trying to bring in, more to do with what they are trying to push out," Ryan admitted.

"Hmm. Got to get rid of the old to make room for the new," Charlie shook his head.

"Yeah. Kind of an ugly business."

"Maybe it is time for renewal. Maybe the businesses they are aiming at moving on are ready to retire," Charlie shrugged, his eyes not bearing the nonchalance of his tenor.

Ryan eyed the innkeeper for a moment before responding. "I don't think so," Ryan impassioned. "I think those family-owned shops, the simple artisan-style, the honesty of it all…I think they all help to make up the charm of Twin Springs. The atmosphere of this town wouldn't exist without them. Take your hotel, for instance. You could drop in a Marriott or Hilton, but it wouldn't fit. Twin Springs exudes this colonial, familial vibe that much of our country has lost. So many would beg for their community to feel like this. Safe, warm, inviting- that's Twin Springs."

Ryan almost surprised himself with the words and passion behind them.

Charlie just smiled behind his glass.

Neither of the men noticed Merilee in the doorway. "That was beautiful, Mr. Talley. I can see why you are a talented writer."

Ryan spun towards her, "Mrs. Byrd. I guess after spending some time here. I have been able to really appreciate the town for what it is. Twin Springs is a gem. People just need to know about."

"Not too many," Merilee smiled.

"Just enough to keep the businesses that are already here going," Ryan grinned.

"What about the people, have you developed an appreciation for any of them?" Merilee prodded.

Ryan hesitated, a questioning look across his face.

"I mean, Lizzie is a beautiful young woman. Allison Tancredi is as adorable as they come. Her co-worker Candace is cute, if a bit young," Merilee pressed.

"Really, Ma, as if the lad doesn't have enough fingers poked at him in this town. This is his place of solace, not an inquisition room," Charlie scolded. "Yes, this room is a sanctuary," he added defiantly.

"I'm just saying, he's an attractive young man and Twin Springs has its share of lovely women," Merilee huffed and spun out of the room.

"Pay no mind to her, boy. She means well. Since we have no children of our own, she kind of takes on all under our roof as hers," Charlie said.

Ryan waved him off, "No worries, sir. I find Merilee quite lovely."

"That she is," Charlie leaned back in his chair. The two men enjoyed the peace of the parlor. The crackle of the fire and its warm glow, the twinkling lights of the Christmas tree, and warm beverages soothing their insides.

Finally, Charlie spoke, "So…have you?"

The first week of December brings with it the kick-off of so many traditions. Lights are strung, wreaths grace front doors, and trees are flocked.

Shoppers assemble thoughtful lists and tackle the markets to see those lists fulfilled. They return home burdened by attractively wrapped packages for those they love.

In the peaceful town of Twin Springs, a humble gift shop carries forth its own tradition. Their storefront adorns a display of the humblest of beginnings. Each year the shop owner puts up a manger scene harkening the first Nativity. Simple in its construct, it faithfully represents what the season is truly about, the birth of Jesus Christ in the town of Bethlehem.

Generations have enjoyed the display with little enhancement over the years. Rustic to some, yet only the more faithfully it represents what was intended.

Like the manger in Bethlehem, the humble display in front of the aptly named Humble Beginnings Giftshop yields to a bright, heart-warming treasure inside.

As the town of Twin Springs welcomes visitors with the new Art Walk project, the traditions of the town also beckon a well-warranted visit. Come for the Art Walk, come for the local shops that invoke the holiday spirit in ways your mind may have forgotten, but your heart will recall.

Blogpost, unsigned

Thirteen

Allison was in a good mood despite only having enough money to fill her gas tank halfway. She thought of her father every time the needle dipped in the wintertime. His voice was in her ear, warning her that if too low when it was cold out, the gas in her tank could freeze, and her car wouldn't start. She smiled at the thought of her father. He was always supportive of her. His positive comments frequently laced with concerned pearls of wisdom.

She wondered what he would have said about opening her shop and how things had gone this year. She doubted she would have a store in a month. Another of her father's mantras ran through her head. He would always tell her and her mother that you can regret the past, worry about tomorrow, but today was the only day that mattered. Make the best of today, and tomorrow will be a little better.

Thinking about her parents while Christmas carols blared in her small car boosted Allison's spirit. Singing along with the radio at the top of her lungs, she wheeled into the little alley behind her shop.

Still humming, she walked through the alley and to the front doors. Jiggling her key in the lock, she spied her reflection in the glass. Rolling her eyes at her lopsided hat, she straightened it and turned the key. Heaving the door open, the bell jingled overhead. All seemed as usual except....

She cocked her head, trying to think what was out of place to her. Then she realized, eyes wide, she spun towards the street. The Nativity...her Nativity was gone. Mary, Joseph, baby Jesus, the manger- all of it was gone!

Stunned, she dropped her purse and ran outside. Scanning the sidewalk. Footprints, drag marks in the snow, and a trail of straw and pine needles leading towards the curb told the tale. Someone had stolen the Nativity!

Wrestling her cellphone out of her pocket, she stared at the device. Unsure who to call. Then she noticed a little pink slip on the floor by the door. Rushing over, she snatched the paper and read it. It began "By Notice of the City of Twin Springs..." Allison balled her fists and screamed to herself. "That Lizzie! She stole my Nativity!"

Mr. Haverstein heard the commotion and put down the challah he was folding into the bowl. Wiping his floury hands on his apron, he hustled next door. Apron blowing in the cold breeze, he poked his head into the gift shop. "Is everything al...oh, you found the Nativity missing. I was looking for you to come in," Haverstein said.

"Yes!" Allison steamed. "I can't believe they just came and took it!"

"I cannot either," Haverstein agreed. "This business of changing Twin Springs is becoming nasty, my dear."

"They think I'll just give up. Well, I won't!"

Haverstein grinned, "I do not believe you will."

"Were you here?"

"No. When I arrived this morning, the city maintenance truck was driving away. I noticed the absence of your manger," the deli owner reported.

"Tommy Trulia. I am going to call him right now. And then I am going straight to Mayor Faslee."

"Good for you. Is there anything I can do to help?"

Allison shook her head. "No. I will handle it. Thank you, Mr. Haverstein, you are so sweet."

By the time Tommy arrived, Maddie and Candace were at the store and were fuming over the removal of the Nativity. Tommy had barely made it through the door before a three-way verbal assault unleashed on him. Seeing the man's face, Allison stopped her friends. "It's not Tommy's fault."

"Sorry, ladies," Tommy waved his hands out in front of him. He nervously avoided looking at

Maddie, who was still shooting icy daggers at him with her eyes. "I even tried to argue against it, but they made me."

"Who's 'they', exactly," Maddie demanded, her arms crossed in front of her.

"Townhall. Not that that means anything, they are just the adjudicator. Any committee or city…"

"Come on, Tommy, it was Lizzie!" Allison demanded.

"Well, the Art Walk and Business Development Committee, yes," Tommy admitted.

"That would be a 'yes', Lizzie Faslee was behind it," Maddie added.

The maintenance man nodded in silence.

"How do we get it back?" Allison asked.

Tommy looked wide-eyed and stuttered in response, "I, I don't think they will let you. At least not until after the investor reception they are having tomorrow."

"Oh, so that is what this is about. Lizzie is afraid her group of big-city developers will be afraid of a religious display in her sterile "cosmopolitan" town," Maddie snapped.

The expression on Tommy's face was enough to confirm their suspicions.

Allison smiled calmly and stepped closer. "Tommy, where did they have you take the Nativity?"

"The impound at the city garage. I moved it all inside, so it stays dry. I'm sorry, Allison."

"I know, Tommy," Allison replied.

"Go and bring it all back here right now!" Maddie demanded.

The city worker shrugged, "I wish I could. But they'll fire me if I don't follow their orders."

"Then we will just have to make sure that you get those orders to bring it back," Allison said defiantly.

Ryan glanced at his watch. Yawning, he couldn't believe he slept in. He never slept so well as he did at the Bed and Breakfast. Shaking his head as he stretched, he knew he would have to hustle to be on time to meet Lizzie.

Brushing his teeth while he showered to save time, he hurriedly dried off and slipped quickly into his clothes. In less than five minutes, he was hurrying down the stairs, waving good morning to the Byrd's, and bursting into the chilly morning.

Taking care not to slip on the frosty steps, Ryan hustled down the street. As he closed in on Main Street, he has a sudden moment of inspiration. He decided to grab coffee for him and Lizzie. If she showed up before him a latte might buy him a pardon. Swinging back behind the shops on Main Street, he cut through the alley and ducked into the coffee shop. Slipping in between rushes, Ryan was fortunate to walk right up to the counter. He frowned, trying to remember Lizzie's specifications.

"For Lizzie Faslee? I got it," the barista said, seeing Ryan's frustration.

Grateful, he stuffed a large tip into the jar and thanked the barista for her help. Pushing his way out on the street, two hot coffees in his hands, the reporter started towards City Hall.

As Ryan passed the gift shop on the other side of the street, something struck him. At first, he wasn't sure what was out of place. Then it dawned on him. The Nativity was missing.

Curious, Ryan crossed the street. He could see through the windows, the three ladies prepping for the day. He could also tell they were not in their usual spirits. Ryan frowned and rapped on the door. Maddie was closest and stared at him absently for a moment. From across the room, Allison strode over and flipped the lock.

In an exasperated tone, she breathed, "Good morning Ryan."

"Hi, hey…I noticed the manger was gone, did you…" he began.

"It was your girlfriend!" Maddie cursed, her eyes eviscerating him.

Ryan scowled, "She's not my girlfriend!" Turning to a considerably warmer and calmer Allison, he asked, "What's going on?"

"I arrived this morning to find the Nativity gone. The city had come early and taken it," Allison related the day's events.

"How can they do that? The space out front isn't even city property, is it?" the reporter asked.

Allison looked at him for a moment and swallowed. "Technically, the space in front of all of the leased spaces is an easement from the city. That way, they take care of the sidewalks, lampposts, and everything else."

"That still doesn't seem right that they can just come and take your personal property like that," Ryan mused thoughtfully.

"You are a part of it. You and that committee. Trying to push people like Allie out so those boutique snobs can move in!" Maddie ranted.

Ryan looked at the incensed woman and sighed, "There is some truth in that. But I don't agree with it, and I don't push for that in what I write."

"No, but you are helping them shape and sway an opinion. So, in a way, your writing is almost worse because people don't get the good or the bad, just your middle of the road Twin Springs is sweet, and the Art Walk is lovely banter," Maddie called the reporter out.

"I...I guess I hadn't thought of it that way," Ryan frowned. "Let me help..."

Maddie cut him off, "You have done enough! You coming here has fueled Lizzie to new heights of power, thank you very much, and now her daddy is on board with how successful it has gone so far. No, thank you, Mr. Talley. We'll just leave you to the biddings of your boss or girlfriend or whatever she is!"

Ryan looked at Allison, glanced at Candace and Maddie before landing back on Allison. She looked distraught and exhausted. He wished he could help. Even she looked at him with disdain, though he wasn't sure why.

Finally, Maddie eyed him with contempt, staring at the two coffees in his hands, "Lizzie's latte is going to be cold. That will not make her very happy."

Ryan looked down at the two cups and resigned that he was not going to make any headway with the women in the shop. "I'll...I'll see what I can do."

"I'm sure you will," Allison offered a weak smile as Ryan backed out of the shop.

Ryan was despondent as he walked down the sidewalk towards Town Hall. He was disappointed in Lizzie for taking that step against Allison. He knew his writing for the Art Walk committee was unpopular with the ladies at the gift shop, but he wasn't prepared for the level of animosity it had created.

The look in Allison's eyes haunted him. She had been so bright and cheery, welcoming to all who came into her store. Now, she looked lost, beaten. He wondered how much he had a hand in that. He was careful when he wrote that he encouraged Twin Springs as a place of tradition, simple beauty. He scribed the Art Walk as an event, not indicative of future change for the town. Refusing any of Lizzie's pressure, he did not levy for the transformation. He was careful not to.

When he entered the Town Hall, he found Lizzie tapping her foot impatiently. Glancing at her watch, she scolded, "We have lots to do. The investor reception is tomorrow. I need you to cover it. We will present you with a dossier on each of the attendees. I think putting them in the article will pressure them to act and encourage their competitors into action as well."

With scarcely a breath in between sentences, Lizzie glanced at the two coffees, "Oh, is one of those for me? Great." Taking a sip, she scowled, "It's kind of cold, oh well. I will get one later. Thanks for trying. So, work, work, work. The committee is upstairs, I need that article out immediately following the reception, yes?" Lizzie ranted, shoving the undrunk coffee cup into a trash can on her way to the meeting room.

Ryan frowned at Lizzie, wasting the coffee, but followed her up the steps. "The Nativity at the gift shop…"

Lizzie's eyes widened, "I know, isn't great? Finally, gone."

"Stealing a shop owner's personal property… a little rash, isn't it?" Ryan pressed.

"What? She should have complied with the notices. On a technicality, that space in front of the leased building is a shared easement with the city. Therefore, it falls within the city's auspices. I had daddy's lawyers verify it," Lizzie replied.

"Does your dad know?" Ryan asked.

"Why? I don't need to bother him with little things like that. You don't need to bother yourself with the little things, either. Trust me, that Nativity mess is a little thing. Now, I need you to focus. Investors Ryan, come on," Lizzie tugged at him as they reached the hall in front of the meeting room.

Fourteen

Throughout the course of the day, Ryan tried to find an angle on the Nativity issue. He carefully prodded for a sympathetic ear, but found none. Even testing the committee members, he realized he was not going to win with anyone there.

The broker Eric caught wind of Ryan's inquiries and laughed. "Look, the little shop isn't even going to be there in the new year. It is all part of the cleansing man. If she wants a religious shop, she can move somewhere in the south and set one up. You have to go where your customers are. Have you seen the place? Not exactly bursting the doors open with buyers, you know what I mean? Even in business, there is tough love. That's what this is. Freeing…uhh, whatshername to get out of that store's shadow and onto something more successful. Part of the process."

"I understand business and understand some fail. I just think people have the right to try and fail or be successful on their own terms," Ryan pressed.

"That's why I like you, Ryan. So....charmingly naïve," Erica said, slapping his hand on Ryan's shoulder. Being met with a disapproving glare, the developer added, "But you write a heck of an article, man."

Finally, when he was no longer needed, and Lizzie had thrust a handful of fliers into his arms, Ryan headed down the Town Hall steps. On the second floor, he turned. Hearing the mayor's voice, the reporter had one more stab to make for diplomacy.

Peering into the room, he found the secretary busy on the phone while digging through her desk drawer. Sneaking past, Ryan slipped into the mayor's office.

"Mayor Faslee?" Ryan called softly.

"Mr. Talley, good to see you. My daughter has said some very fine things about you," the mayor beamed. "Very fine indeed."

"Thank you, sir. I have grown quite fond of Twin Springs during my time here," Ryan said.

"Wonderful town, isn't it?" Faslee said proudly, gazing out his office window. "A lot of fond memories here. My wife, Ellie, she loved it here so much. The town, the landscape...inspiration for most of her art. That painting behind the sofa, that was my Ellie's."

Ryan walked over to admire the painting. It looked like it was done from the perspective of the viewpoint that Lizzie had taken him to. "It's beautiful. She was quite talented."

"Oh, that she was. She probably would have been even more successful if she tried harder to get into more galleries. She didn't care about any of that. She was content to stay close to Twin Springs," Faslee nodded.

"She must have really loved it here," Ryan said.

"She did," Faslee looked distant for a moment.

Hearing the secretary hang up the phone and warn the mayor that he was running late, Ryan sped up to his point for being there. "Mr. Mayor, the Nativity, was taken by the city from the little gift shop downtown. I was thinking from a community goodwill standpoint, mightn't it be better to put it back?"

"Wondered the same thing myself, to be honest. The committee is all concerned about the investors and religious references...the strip in front of that part of the building is partially city property. I didn't even know that. Anyway, the committee preached the whole separation of church and state yada yada. Anyhow, the shop owner could put it inside the store, but..." Faslee muttered.

"Inside? The scene wouldn't fit in the store, and if it did, it would take up selling space..." Ryan argued.

"I know. I don't think it to be a big deal, but today. Everything is changing," Faslee sighed. "I guess it is time for Twin Springs to change too."

Ryan caught Faslee, glancing at his wife's painting.

The mayor sighed. "I won't go behind the committee, but personally, if the stuff in the city impound found its way back, I guess I wouldn't be to upset about it."

Looking at his watch, Faslee said, "I'm sorry, Mr. Talley. I need to be off for my next meeting."

"Thank you for your time, sir," Ryan said, following the mayor out.

"Any time. Keep up the good work," Faslee called as he donned his overcoat and hurried out of his office after receiving a folder from the secretary the way a running back would from a quarterback.

As Ryan left Town Hall, he heard two of the committee members cackling about the town being scrubbed of the simpletons. He thought about the image of the painting in the mayor's office. The city captured exactly as Ryan pictured it. It was beautiful in its simplicity. He knew there was a craving for towns like this. For some reason, in the guise of political correctness and so-called progress, towns like this were scoffed at. Celebrating holidays, any reference to Christianity, even genuine patriotism made you some kind of bigot. He didn't understand it.

As he walked down the street, the setting sun shot pink and orange beams reflecting off of the snow-covered town. People waved to one another as they passed. Children peered in windows at Christmas displays and ornaments of shops that had been scrubbed of such décor on the outside. A few had subtle items in defiance – stars, candy canes, and presents wrapped in red and green. Most of Main Street, it was hard to tell if it was Christmas or just a winter's day. As charming as it was, Ryan could only imagine the coziness of the town painted in all its full holiday splendor.

Chewing his lip, he found himself marching to the gift shop. Pushing through the front door, he was prepared for the onslaught.

"What are you doing here? Going to steal our Christmas CDs and our tree now?" Maddie snapped from the back of the store.

Allison looked at her employee and then at the reporter. "Any luck at City Hall?" she asked, her voice pleasant.

Ryan dropped his head towards the floor, "No. I tried, but they are fixated on these investors they have coming in."

"Humph!" Maddie scoffed.

"I did try. I even spoke to Mayor Faslee. He seemed sympathetic, but I think he is a little defeated with all of this as well," Ryan admitted.

"So, what are you doing here?" Maddie asked curtly.

"I came to help."

Candace looked confused, "But you just said you couldn't."

"I said I didn't have any luck at City Hall," Ryan grinned.

Allison looked at the reporter with suspicion, "What do you have in mind?"

"Do you know where the Nativity is being stored" Ryan asked.

"Actually, yes. Why?" Allison asked, her head cocked in curiosity.

"I'm going to steal it back," Ryan replied.

The three ladies stared in silence at the grinning reporter.

"They don't have the legal ability to actually take your things. Not without an injunction and a hearing where you were present. The easement grants the shops access to display things in front of their buildings. The coffee shop has tables in front of theirs. The beauty shop has their sandwich board out. The hardware store moved their tree to the back, but they have snowblowers and shovels out front. To remove your display without a process to prove why it is not within code is unlawful. If they stole the stuff illegally, they can't really claim we are doing anything illegal if we steal it back!" Ryan beamed.

"A Nativity heist...I like it!" Maddie smiled for the first time at Ryan.

Allison shook her head. "I can't have you stealing things from the city for me."

"Well, really, it's kind of unstealing, isn't it?" Ryan asked, a mischievous eyebrow raised.

"I appreciate the gesture. But my problems with the city are not your fault. And I cannot have people committing crimes for me," Allison refused.

Candace wrinkled her nose, "Yeah, it will be kind of obvious when the display ends up back in front of Allison's shop."

"Blame it on elves...," Ryan quipped, and seeing Allison's disapproving glare, he smiled. "Imagine this headline, "City Council Steals Baby Jesus". I don't care how left-field they are, that is not the national publicity they want."

Allison crossed her arm, still very unsure about the plan. "Fine. But it is for my shop. I will be there with you."

"Count me in!" Candace squealed.

Maddie looked at Ryan with suspicion. "I'll go too. Someone's got to keep an eye on this one."

Fifteen

Clad all in black, the four Christmas marauders met outside of the gift shop. Ryan pulled his Jeep alongside, drafting a trailer behind it. Before he got out, Maddie hooked her arm in Allison's and poked her lips to the rim of her boss' parka.

"He is charming, even seems to have a good heart...but be careful. He does after all consort with the enemy," Maddie whispered.

Allison gave Maddie a sideways look, "He has done nothing wrong, to me or anyone else that I know. He has a job to do, and I do not hold malice towards him because of it."

"Allie, Lizzie...the town is trying to put you out of business," Maddie warned.

Giving a little laugh, "The store would be struggling regardless of the town."

Maddie crossed her arms as she flashed a wry smile at the approaching reporter. Quickly whispering her peace to Allison, she quipped, "Well, they aren't helping."

"Mr. Talley, I see you came quite prepared for our heist," Allison eyed the trailer and satchel full of tools slung around Ryan's shoulder.

"Good operations require good planning, good people, and the right equipment," Ryan grinned. "Are sure you all want to do this? I can do it…"

"I'm quite sure," Candace stated.

"Oh, I'm in," Maddie agreed.

Nodding, Allison slapped her gloved hands together, "I'm ready to go."

"Alright, hop in. We'll pull the Jeep alongside and get this done," Ryan said, escorting the women to his SUV. Pulling a few items from the bag, he tossed it in the back of the trailer. To each of his party of rogues, he handed a little black flashlight. "Their beam is red, so it doesn't shine super bright, but it also doesn't make a beacon to our adventure, either."

Climbing into the Jeep, Candace asked, "Do this kind of thing often?"

Ryan just grinned in silence as he slid into the driver's seat.

Wheeling the Jeep and trailer near the rear entrance of the Municipal Maintenance Department building, the foursome gathered just outside of the Jeep. Ryan looked at the crew and asked one last time, "You all sure about this?"

Receiving three nods, he proceeded. "Okay, Candace, can you stay here with the Jeep? Let us know if anyone comes. Maddie and Allison, come with me. Stand just outside of that main gate," the reporter directed.

"But...how are you going to get in?" Allison couldn't help but whisper. "You can't break and enter..."

Ryan smiled, "I have a plan."

Rolling her eyes, Allison shrugged and pulled Maddie along with her into position as Ryan has instructed.

Sneaking off to find a spot along the fence line shrouded in the shadow of the building, Ryan began scaling the fence. Grasping links with his hands and poking his toes through two more, he made his way up the side.

From Allison and Maddie's vantage, they could hear the metallic rattling of the fence as Ryan scurried over. Across the yard, they could see his figure arrive at the top and flip himself over. Hanging for a moment, he dangled before releasing and landing in the snow on the other side.

"He's crazy," Maddie whispered.

Allison looked on and nodded, a little smile creasing the corner of her lips. She followed Ryan's shadow as it crunched across the snow and disappeared behind the metal storage building.

Maddie cast a curious glance at Allison, who shrugged in reply.

In the cloud diffused moonlight, Allison could just make out a black form wiggle up a tall drainpipe on the corner of the building.

Legs wrapped around the pipe, Ryan hugged his arms tightly as he pushed his feet upward. Half a body's length at a time, the reporter shimmied his way up to the roofline. Releasing one hand from the drainpipe, Ryan stretched up to the metal edge of the roof. Grasping it in his fingers, he clamped down tightly.

With a big, deep breath, he released his other hand, reaching precariously trying to get a second grip. Doing so meant releasing his leg hold around the pipe. Just as he released his legs, he slapped with his hand, fighting to find the metal edge of the roof. His fingers grazed the edge, but failed to hold on.

For a moment, Ryan clung from the roof with a single hand. His legs wriggled as he tried to pull up with the one grip that he had. Finally, in a desperate lunge, he got just enough height to grab at the roof with his other hand. For a moment, he hung, happy to have a second grip. Calming his racing heart, he wriggled his body over the edge and squirmed up onto the roof.

Allison gasped as she watched. Ryan dangled from the roof with one arm, her heart fell to her stomach, afraid he was going to fall. She felt terrible that he was putting himself in danger for her stubbornness with the Nativity.

Suddenly, his second hand reached up, and he steadied himself before pulling his body on the roof. In moments, his full silhouette could be seen giving a quick relieved wave to his team at the gate.

A few minutes ticked before a faint buzz emitted from a little box just inside the fence and the gate jerked into motion. As the gate wheeled itself open, Allison could see Ryan emerge with the manger and baby Jesus in his arms hustling toward them. Holding the manger out, he handed it to the women.

"Here, take this to the trailer, I'll grab another load," Ryan panted.

Before the ladies could respond, he had wheeled around and sprinted back into the warehouse. By the time Allison and Maddie had reached the gate, Ryan had returned with another load from the scene. This time, he handed Mary to Allison and Joseph to Maddie. "I'll be back with more!" he grinned and once again streaked into the storage building.

Piece by piece, the set was removed from the building and loaded into the trailer. "Can you drive a stick?" Ryan asked, holding out his keys.

Allison stared back blankly. Reaching out, Maddie snatched the keys, "I can."

"Good. You guys get out of here. I'll put everything back in order and meet you behind the shop," Ryan said, once more disappearing into the building.

Allison and Maddie nodded and jogged back to Candace and the Jeep. The fence shook to life and closed behind them. Climbing into Ryan's car, Maddie slammed in the clutch and turned the ignition. Wasting no time, she slipped the Jeep into gear and wheeled away from the maintenance lot.

Ryan's cheeks were rosy from his hike to the gift shop from the maintenance yard. Allison had brewed a pot of coffee for the crew of rogues. Seeing the reporter slip in, she held up a mug for him.

Thanking her for the coffee, he grinned, "It is all as if we were never there…save for baby Jesus and family being back to their rightful owners."

"I can't believe you did all that," Allison gasped.

"You were like a little monkey," Candace giggled. "I thought you were going to lose it at the top of the roof."

"You saw that?" Ryan winced. "It was a little dicey. Weren't you supposed to be on lookout duty?"

Candace gushed, "I couldn't help it. I had to see what was going on."

"You were pretty good," Maddie admitted.

"Couldn't have done it without my accomplices," Ryan said.

"How did you get in?" Candace asked, her eyes wide.

Ryan grinned, "I can't give away all of my secrets."

"A delinquent in your youth?" Maddie mused.

"I really can't believe you did for that for us...for me," Allison said. Suddenly, she looked tired and distant. "Probably shouldn't have, we could get in real trouble for this."

"Don't you worry about that. I had some inside help. That would absolve of us any real wrongdoing," Ryan confessed.

Allison looked confused. "Inside help?"

"If you had inside help, why didn't they just open the door for you? You had to scale the fence, risk your neck on the roof and sneak inside the building," Maddie wondered.

Ryan looked sheepish and held out a key, "I ran into Tommy at City Hall this afternoon. He seemed to be a friendly ear, so he helped me conspire. His job was really the only thing at risk this evening."

"Other than your neck!" Allison scolded.

"Yeah," Ryan admitted. "I could have gone through the front door, but what would have been the fun in that?"

"Ugh!" Allison smacked Ryan on the arm, causing him to spill a little of his coffee. "I was scared to death!"

"It was pretty fun," Candace interjected.

"Yeah, it kinda was," Maddie admitted.

The room fell quiet. Allison melted Ryan a livid glare. The reporter squirmed under her silent condemnation.

Finally, she let out a soft laugh. "I guess it was fun. If a bit reckless."

The shop burst into laughter. Each raising their coffee mugs to cheer their successful heist.

A very tired Maddie had excused herself to return home to her husband. Candace fought an early exit, but Allison demanded she go home.

"You don't have to stay," Allison told Ryan, who pulled the last piece of the Nativity out of the trailer.

"I don't mind. Besides, you'll turn into an icicle trying to put all of this together yourself," Ryan said.

"It is really nice of you to do all of this."

Ryan put down the piece of stable he was carrying. Studying Allison's face for a moment. Her soft features accentuated by the streaks of rose painted on her cheeks. Despite being exhausted, her eyes still managed to sparkle. "I am happy to. You impress me, sticking to your ideals. I like that. You are a special woman. You are good for this town."

Allison's cheeks grew even rosier, "I don't know about all that. Just sad to see people lose what is important in Christmas, in our world."

"Even more so why your resilience is so impressive. So important to support," Ryan nodded and hoisted the stable piece up. "Sun will be up soon. We should probably hurry."

With all the pieces back in front of the shop, Allison began the process of configuring the scene. Ryan awaited instruction and helped put the set together.

They were alarmed to hear a jingling behind them. Spinning, they turned to see Mr. Haverstein dangling his keys out in front of his door. "You're up early...or late," he said to them. "I see you got your manger back."

Allison wrinkled her nose, "Yep. With the help of Mr. Talley."

"I didn't think they'd let you have it back after all the fuss," the deli owner said.

"Yeah...they didn't exactly offer it back..." Allison admitted.

Haverstein frowned. "Won't they just take it again?"

Allison sighed and nodded. "Probably."

Rubbing his chin for a minute, he suggested, "Why don't you slide it in this direction. The wall that separates our two shops also separates the buildings. If you place it just on the other side of your display window, angle it towards your shop...it will still be part of your scene, but my building's line."

"So...?" Allison questioned.

"So, I own my building. My easement is different than the leased buildings," Haverstein informed.

"So, they can't touch it there," Ryan grinned.

"That's sweet, Mr. Haverstein. But you don't have to..." Allison began.

Haverstein cut her off, "A Jewish shop hosting a Nativity? Your symbol of peace does not upset me. And half of my customers aren't Jewish themselves, those that are won't be bothered. You have Hanukkah gifts in your store, don't you?"

"Yes," Allison nodded.

"Well, there you go. It's settled," Haverstein said. "Now, I have to get my bread going, or it will never rise in time. You two hurry and get out of this cold."

"Thank you, Mr. Haverstein," Allison said.

With a tip of the brim of his hat, Haverstein inserted his key and disappeared into the deli. Allison and Ryan stared at each other before shrugging and going back to work. Moving the display to the other side of the shop, just within the margins that Haverstein had pointed out and set back to work.

When they were finished, they stepped back and admired their work. The stable roof had already begun to collect snow that had begun to drift down. Mary and Joseph kept vigil over the sleeping baby bundled and resting in the feed trough.

"It looks good," Ryan admired.

"Even better than before," Allison rasped. Ryan noticed she was shivering. Reaching out with his arm, he gently wrapped his hand around her shoulder and pulled her close. Allison leaned into him. "Quite a night."

"He would have done it for us," Ryan smiled.

Allison looked up at him questioningly. The reporter nodded toward the manger. Allison smiled in acknowledgment. "Yes. Yes, he would have."

Tucked away in the historic town of Twin Springs, a small gift shop finds itself in the throes of battle. The shopkeeper continuing her longstanding tradition of displaying a holiday Nativity while on the other side, a progressive government misconstruing the founding fathers' guidance of religious freedom.

Political and financial pressures have been levied to urge the shopkeeper to take down the display for fear it may offend someone, though no official inquiries of offense have been made. The town has gone so far as to try and have the Nativity forcibly removed, though not within their legal rights to do so.

We have seen this building for years. Political correctness and the vocal minority waging legal and social measures to stifle what has been at the core of America since her creation. America was settled from Europe to establish a country in which religious expression was genuinely free.

Proponents of de-Christianizing America, such as those lobbying to rid the town of Twin Springs of their Nativity scene and other overt references to Christ in Christmas, misuse Thomas Jefferson's letter on the separation of church and state that so many wrongly think to be a part of the Constitution.

Thomas Jefferson's stance had nothing to do with limiting religious expression in government domains but rather just the opposite- to prevent the government from tampering in the rights of churches. The very reason many settlers fled to America in the first place.

For those of you who grew up with Christmas being a time of communities coming together. Uniting in collective celebration and spreading words of joy to all, regardless of their specific religious affiliations. For those who miss the words "Merry Christmas" being declared publicly. For those where Christmas trees are still Christmas trees and not holiday trees.

I urge you to visit the town of Twin Springs. I urge you to visit the Humble Beginnings Gift Shop as well as its neighbors. Support this fading bastion of Americana. The fading light of Christmas celebration and custom that has been a part of our culture since our country's very beginnings.

Blog Entry, unsigned

Sixteen

"Send the police!" Lizzie screamed. Her nostrils flaring, as she paced around the City Hall boardroom. "Someone broke into the maintenance yard, that's theft!"

"We don't know that, Lizzie," Mayor Faslee inserted. "Tommy said there were no signs of anyone breaking in."

"Then how did it get back on Main Street?" Lizzie ranted.

Curling his way into the room, Ryan offered, "Angels?"

Crossing her arms, Lizzie glared at the reporter in a huff.

"The investors are coming today. We need that messy contraption out of there!" Lizzie demanded.

"You mean the scene with baby Jesus...contraption?" Ryan prodded.

"Ohh!" Lizzie pouted. "You know what I mean!"

"What's the plan?" Ryan asked.

"We'll have to send Tommy to take it back," Lizzie commanded.

"Hmm," Mayor Faslee addressed his daughter. "We can't."

"What do you mean, 'we can't'?" Lizzie fumed.

"It isn't on the leased part of the block."

"So?" Lizzie contested.

"The easement on private property doesn't allow for interjection without a court order," Mayor Faslee explained.

"Then, get a court order."

"It isn't that easy. Even if it is granted, it may take days or even weeks," the mayor replied.

"Ahh!" Lizzie screamed. Facing the wall, she breathed in deep. "Fine. We will just have to deal. We have more important things to concern ourselves with."

"That's the spirit!" Ryan cheered to a disgruntled eye roll from Lizzie.

"Just make sure you have the dossiers on the investors. Do a brief bio on each and write a piece that appeals to each, please," Lizzie said wearily.

As her father left the boardroom and Ryan turned to leave, Lizzie stopped him. "I'm sorry you had to see me...me..."

"Throw a tantrum?" Ryan offered.

Lizzie frowned, working her lips but not precisely knowing how to respond. Sighing, she relented, "Yes. Throw a tantrum. It's just that this is so difficult, and people fight me every step of the way. Don't they see that I'm trying to save this crummy little town?"

Ryan looked thoughtful for a moment. "No. No, they probably don't."

In a moment of calm, it felt as if the heavy air in the room had released. "I tell you what, when today's event is over, why don't I interview you. You can tell the town…the world in your own words."

Lizzie looked doubtful, almost fragile. "You think that will help?"

"I find people respond better when they understand the 'why'. Understanding intentions can be as important as the action you are trying to implement," the reporter replied.

Lizzie nodded, "Dad says that about politics all the time."

"Your father is a smart man."

"He is. A good man," Lizzie agreed. "Okay. Let's meet tomorrow, and you can interview me. I'll take you to lunch or something."

"Deal. Now, I'll take care of my end of the investor prep. Don't worry about things like the Nativity or how people decorate their stores. The town is more than its fascia, and if your investors don't realize that, then they aren't the right fit for Twin Springs," Ryan assured her.

"Thank you, Ryan."

Ryan sat in front of the fire at the Bed and Breakfast. A stack of folders in his lap, each profiling a business leader from the city, New York, and even one from Paris. As he read about the people, he looked up their businesses on his cellphone. Two ran exclusive clothing lines in major markets around the globe. One was a specialized diamond importer who served high-end jewelry stores. Another was a chef who was profiled on a television show for his knack for creating elite restaurant spots.

Folder after folder, Ryan read about people and businesses found primarily in high-end resort towns. He pictured Twin Springs turning into the Hamptons or Aspen. While neither was terrible, it just wasn't Twin Springs. The city had an accessible charm that permeated through it from the hardware store to Haverstein's deli.

Ryan flipped open one portfolio. A high-end resort developer was listed. He had expressed interest in the viewpoint that Lizzie had brought him to as well as a little lake just north of Town Hall. Ryan wondered what impact that would have on the century-old bed and breakfast.

As the reporter made his notations and his list of who he had to do a write up on, he was startled by a figure standing across from him. "Will I disturb your work if I sit here and read?" Charlie Byrd asked.

Ryan laid down the file he was reviewing. "No, not at all. In fact, I welcome the company."

"You seem hard at work," Charlie noticed.

"Yeah, a little. Not exactly riveting, but valuable information to delve into," Ryan replied.

"Oh? More work for Lizzie Faslee?"

Ryan nodded. "There is a group of investors she is bringing in today to survey the town and see what they want to build and who they want to take over, I guess."

"Progress is progress, I suppose."

"Not always," Ryan cautioned. "Sometimes, what can seem like progress only puts you in holes in other ways. Others, that progress comes with a cost. Sometimes that cost is worth it, sometimes not."

Charlie smiled, "Astute perspective."

"Take this one, for example. Big resort developer. Eyeing two pieces of land that are currently owned by Twin Springs Parks and Recreation. Right now, trails and viewpoints and water access are open to the public. Sold or given to a private investor, that land is lost. Now, if that is what the town wants, so be it. But the town needs to make the decision, and they need to understand the additional repercussions."

Ryan continued, "A big new resort, means new constraints on power, sewage and water. Transportation infrastructure would need to be updated to accommodate the extra traffic. Main Street may not be able to handle that new load, so a new road is built. Main Street is suddenly off the map. Anything on it dies. The services this new resort offers – lodging, dining, maybe even shopping and recreation – suddenly, all of that is drawn to the resort. They win, the town loses."

"But it brings visitors, high-end visitors. High-end visitors bring in much-needed wallets and purses," Byrd posed.

"True. But given the resort scenario, how much of that will come to you and Merilee? How about the quaint family-owned restaurant downtown? The independent coffee shop? Most of the businesses currently in Twin Springs…how much will any of those families get?" Ryan pressed.

"It sounds like you are against the very plan you are writing about," Byrd laughed.

"I suppose at the end of the day. I am not in favor or against it – if that is what the town wants as a whole. Personally, I kind of like the town the way it is. But to be fair, I make my living and home in the city," Ryan replied.

"So how do you write an article on something you don't necessarily believe in?" Byrd asked.

"Very carefully," Ryan laughed. "I remain on point and factual. I leave opinion out and flavor it with my observations, current and future. Let the readers come to their own conclusion about which path is the right one."

"I look forward to reading that article," Byrd said. "Say, I know a charming bed and breakfast you could write about."

"Way ahead of you. Already working on an article on Twin Springs not related to the Art Walk," Ryan smiled.

"You're a good man, Mr. Talley."

Shrugging Ryan replied, "I don't know about that. Just an opinionated small-time writer."

Ryan sensed Charlie was about to get up. "There is something else you should know. One of the properties the resort mapped out includes the Byrd's Nest."

"I see," Charlie said quietly, stroking his chin. "Merilee and I aren't getting again younger, maybe it is time."

While playing devil's advocate had been Ryan's new friend's method for creating revelations in their discussions, this one caught Ryan off guard.

"Everything you have built. The memories the Byrd's Nest has instilled in your guests. The ones who come back every year for Christmas, their anniversaries. The generations of guests who have made your Bed and Breakfast part of their family stories," Ryan protested.

"Alright, maybe that one was pushing it too far. Besides, Merilee has already made it clear that this is the last home on earth we will share," Charlie conceded.

Relieved, Ryan sunk back into his chair.

"Well, I've bent your ear enough. You have work to do. Perhaps I'll see you late this evening for a fireside nightcap," Charlie said.

"Perhaps you will," Ryan nodded at Charlie and picked up the next file. He watched the good-humored man amble out of the parlor. Ryan laughed to himself. The elderly innkeeper was a master at playing all sides of a discussion. Even though the reporter had a good idea where Mr. Byrd stood, there was always a little doubt levied in the questions the man delivered. "He would have made a good lawyer...or reporter," Ryan thought to himself.

The reception for the investors was a bourgeoisie affair. Ryan shook his head at the taxpayer-funded four-course meal – catered from a "brassiere" in the city. Even the passé ritual of wine at lunch was resurrected for Lizzie's guests. The investors nibbled on French hors d'oeuvres as they looked at photos of Twin Springs past and present. Rough sketched mock-ups of investors' concepts overlaid on local scenery.

Models of Twin Springs economy and future projections were displayed as posters, and Lizzie and her team danced around their audience, ensuring glasses and ears were filled.

Ryan leaned in a far corner of the ballroom and identified individuals he had read about from the dossiers he had studied. He watched them as they chatted with their hosts and fellow prospective investors. Eric Farnham was in form, working the room with precision. He avoided some of the less likely, less profitable boutique proprietors while focusing on the heavy hitters.

The reporter observed the business team from France inspect the appetizers and tentatively take small bites. Across the room, the television chef and two women that escorted him did the same.

The air in the room was so different than what he had come to know Twin Springs to represent.

There was no doubt, this was a collection of successful people. They had valuable stock in the images they represented. But as Ryan looked on, he could surmise that they had their brand to sell and could care less about what the town of Twin Springs thought- Lizzie Faslee included.

Occasionally, Ryan would circle the room. He would make small talk with the guests, asking a probing question or two as he passed. Moving by Lizzie, he offered her an encouraging smile as she struggled to maintain composure.

Curious, he stationed himself near Eric. He listened to him exalt the promise of the future Twin Springs. Often, he would belittle the town in its current state, branding the area putty for the investors to shape their own town. Ryan watched the real estate developer's eyes. He skillfully kept tabs on all his key targets. He would smile and nod in one conversation while deftly keeping tabs on another.

Ryan had to hand it to him. Eric was a skilled talker, making friends throughout the banquet. What Ryan didn't like, was the developer's knack at doing so in antipathy to Lizzie's team and the colloquial town.

At one point, Lizzie gathered the crowd, thanked them for coming, and assigned them to an ambassador made up of Lizzie or one of her team. Bundling up, the procession filtered out of the banquet hall and spilled into the streets of Twin Springs.

Tommy and his team had done a fantastic job of once more prepping the town. The roads and sidewalks were immaculately cleared of snow. Lizzie's winter theme sans anything reminiscent of Christmas, or Hanukkah was sparkling and in its proper place. Before the procession divided into their emissary led groups, Lizzie paraded them through the Art Walk. Some of the investors had a taste of it during its unveiling; many of the faces in the crowd were new.

Lizzie was on top of her game with the Art Walk. She spoke passionately about Twin Springs, celebrating art and how her team had handpicked from the entries that were inspirational for the town's future. Ryan found it was becoming easy to disagree with but respect the thoughts of Lizzie Faslee. The elegant woman concluded her piece on the walk and the transformation of Twin Springs.

Ensuring each guest had their time to appreciate the town's latest installment, she then had them disband into four groups. One led by her and each of her committee members and the last group headed up by Eric Farnham. Doing his best to be part of the background, Ryan elected to tag along with the previous group.

It was clear that Eric had hand-selected his troop. Each was an influential member of a large corporation, development firm, or otherwise deep pockets. From Ryan's studies, the financial holdings of Eric's guests were easily three-fold any other groups'. Ryan also noted to himself that not one of them had any ties to Twin Springs, most had scarcely any connection with the region.

Observing the route of all four groups, Ryan noticed Eric took his on a slightly different route. Lizzie did her best to manage Main Street while avoiding the gift shop and the deli. She, in perfect timing, drew her group's attention to the building opposite of Allison's and her nativity scene and kept their attention until they were well past.

Eric had no such reservation of taking his investors directly to that section of the block. "This building could be available at the turn of the year. Nearly every tenant has graciously bowed to progress. You could lease part or the whole, purchase outright, whatever suits your needs," the real estate broker shared.

One of the men frowned as he stared at the building, "If purchased, could we tear it down and rebuild?"

Eric nearly laughed, "If you buy it, it's yours to do with what you please."

"Why wouldn't you do that anyway? This colonial-style is so passé. It's gross," a scowling woman said.

Ryan struggled to tell whether she scowled due to the sun peeking through the clouds reflecting off the storefront window of the gift shop or if she was just really that unpleasant.

"We are thinking about that," Eric replied and then released a wry smile. "Then again, we do not expect it to be on the market for very long."

A Japanese man paused, looking in the window of the store. "Is it on the market, yes? It seems the businesses here are still well in operation."

"Not officially. We are holding many of the properties of Twin Springs aside for investors, such as yourselves. These locations are more than just lots and buildings. They are the future of Twin Springs. Your future. I mean, look at these tired businesses. These dinosaurs are gasping their last breaths. They have no place in this town's future. We don't want any buyer, we want the right, discriminating buyers," Eric told his audience.

The same Japanese businessman eyed the Nativity. "You hardly see these or anything of a holiday displayed anymore."

"Exactly. Main Street is no longer going to be the image of cobblestones and American history, but a gathering spot, a respite for society. Your investments won't be returned in nickel and dime plebian economy. No. The new Twin Springs will be an elite mecca. It is already starting. I hope it isn't too premature, but I have a major player who is dealing with the city to purchase an amazing resort to rival Amangani, The Montage, or The Broadmoor. That is the clientele that will stay, play and dine at your establishments," Eric grinned, his voice almost theatric as he spoke about his potential buyer.

The Japanese man looked confused, "Hmm. I would think you would embrace the colonial heritage and incorporate that into the new fascia."

Eric nodded, "Sure, sure. We looked at doing that. But that doesn't speak to the patrons we want to welcome. Art Walk is a magnificent example. Fresh, contemporary. It feels like a town in motion. It is a town in motion, forward motion. Come with us. You won't be sorry. Alright, let's move on to the end of what we now know of Main Street to an area set for expansion."

Hearing enough, Ryan held back, allowing the group to continue following Eric and listen to his spiel. Slipping into the gift shop, he was taken by the stark contrast of Lizzie and Eric's sterile world to the warmth of Allison's. The Christmas lights woven in with the evergreen bough garland, Bing Crosby crooning carols, and the smells of pine and apple and cinnamon gave his senses a rush of happiness, of memories, of the holiday.

"How's it going out there, master thief?" Allison asked.

Ryan scoffed, "Okay. Enough hot air and ego to inflate a Macy's Thanksgiving Day balloon."

Allison smiled, "That good. Glad our town is in such good hands."

"Yeah, about that. They are betting on you and the beauty shop next door and everyone else in a lease to fail," Ryan said, his voice fallen.

"I know that. That's why my lease keeps going up. It was annually, but then it got bumped again right around Halloween. They claim it is for renovations. I know it is to allow for businesses who can pay even higher leases. But what else can I do but try and make it," Allison confirmed. "Though with days like these, that seems a bit less likely. Another Lizzie big money day to frighten real customers away."

"It's been having that bad of an effect?" Ryan asked.

Allison shrugged, "Hasn't helped."

Changing the subject, Allison asked, "How did Lizzie react to the Nativity returning?"

"She blew a gasket. Surprised you didn't hear her from down here. She wanted to sick the sheriff, Tommy, her Dad…the IRS- anyone she could on you," Ryan laughed.

"I could have guessed," Allison grinned.

"I think they would have, too, had it not been for Mr. Haverstein. He was spot on with the easement difference," Ryan said.

"I'm glad they figured that out too."

Smiling wide, Ryan said, "A little bird planted the idea in Mayor Faslee's head."

"Nice work. You are the master at covert ops. Even infiltrating the nest of your foe and influencing them," Allison nudged him with her elbow.

"Where's your crew?" Ryan said, looking around.

"I told them to come in late or stay home today. They were pretty bushed after being out so late last night."

"How are you holding up?" Ryan asked.

"I'm on my third cup of coffee, and I have taken to singing Christmas carols out loud to stay awake. Since I have no customers to scare away, it has been a pretty good plan so far," Allison beamed.

"Don't stop on my account, wassail away," Ryan bowed.

Allison looked at him hard for a moment, "I am not sure I want to scare you away, either."

Ryan's eyes danced around hers, trying to interpret the full meaning of her statement. "I can't imagine anything you do would frighten away anyone," he finally said.

"You haven't heard me sing," she grinned. Then her eyes grew large, "Mr. Talley, would you like to go to church with me?"

"You know, Ms. Tancredi, I would love that," Ryan replied.

Allison looked serious, "Bright and early. Church starts at 9 a.m. sharp. You're at the Byrd's Nest Bed and Breakfast, right? I'll swing by around 8:45, and we can walk together."

"It's a date!" Ryan looked uncomfortable with how those words came out. "Well…a meeting…uhm...church…"

With a gleam in her eye, Allison corrected, "It's a date, Mr. Talley. 8:45. Now run along, I have work to do!" Waving her arms, she shooed him out of the store.

She watched from behind the check stand, standing tall and confident. As soon as Ryan was out of view, she collapsed on the counter. Shocked by her own forwardness, but very grateful for it as well.

Ryan was in front of the fire, tapping away on his tablet when the clink of glassware caught his attention. Mr. Byrd entered the parlor with a little tray holding a pair of glasses and a small bottle of Port.

Pushing the standby button on the device, he leaned it against the chair leg by his feet.

"Evening Charlie," Ryan called as the man settled into the chair opposite the reporter.

Setting the tray on the little table next to the chair, Charlie poured a glass for himself and gestured toward the other. Receiving a nod, he filled the second glass halfway with garnet liquid. "Salud, Mr. Talley."

"Skol," Ryan raised his glass.

"The town is buzzing about the big investor reception," the innkeeper said.

"I imagine. Quite the affair," Ryan acknowledged.

Charlie raised his eyebrows in curiosity, "And? Any revelations on the rebirth of Twin Springs?"

"As too frequently happens in business, a little shadiness here and there. Money over people. The new trumping the old," Ryan shared.

"Sounds exciting, and a bit ominous. Anything you can share?"

Ryan frowned, thinking, "Well, most of it is nothing you probably can't already surmise. The investors have no legacy in Twin Springs. Removing its face and slipping another on is as simple to them as a trip to a plastic surgeon. Which, I believe, a few have done on more than one occasion, incidentally. Who cares if it doesn't really function anymore, long as it fits the image."

"Hmm. What happens to the people and businesses already here?"

"That's the real rub. They don't really care. I suppose they assume people in town will be so grateful for a job that they will delight to be towel boys at the spa or maids at the posh resort. There is even talk of displacing one of the town's parks to accommodate an investor," Ryan said.

"Sounds insidious. And Mayor Faslee is okay with this?" Charlie asked.

"To be honest, I am sure he doesn't even realize," Ryan defended. "Even Lizzie, I think, is blind to the degree the flood gates of change will come once that stone is turned."

"The impact of many through the power of a few," Charlie mused.

"Be it government or too powerful a corporation, a bad design," Ryan agreed.

"So, what will your article say." Charlie looked interested.

"The facts. The who's, what Twin Springs is now, the interpretation of what is proposed," Ryan replied.

"You don't look happy about it."

Ryan looked through a slight scowl, "I don't think I am."

"So, what will you do?" Charlie prodded.

"My job," Ryan shrugged.

Charlie looked a bit confused, "And that's it? Let the chips fall?"

"What do you mean?" the look of confusion shifted to Ryan.

Charlie shifted excitedly in his seat. "You have a wonderful job. A powerful voice that few have. That levies your opportunity, and if you are honest with your inner self- duty."

"I still don't follow..."

"You are obligated to write about the proposed transformation of Twin Springs. That is only half the story...," Charlie replied.

Ryan was thoughtful. He slowly sipped on his Port, allowing his gaze to move from the innkeeper to the dancing flames of the fireplace. Turning back, he looked resolved, "You're right. I have said all along my job isn't to sell Lizzie's proposal, but to report on it. The story isn't the transformation...the story is the town."

Charlie grinned, "That it is."

All things change over time. Sometimes that change or prospective change is invited. The town of Twin Springs is in the process of studying their own destiny.

Starting with the Art Walk, Twin Springs has welcomed visitors to explore the town and its shaping of the future. The Art Walk opening was a large-scale success with visitors from across the country and even the globe taking part.

In the days and weeks following the event, investors have been invited to consider their image of what Twin Springs might become. Restaurateurs, resort developers, and retailers have begun to share their visions for what they would bring to Twin Springs.

The Art Walk and Business Development Committees have started crafting a new Twin Springs. Clean and modern, drawing a market for a new audience.

Economic packages have been put together that show a substantial increase in public and private revenues, further enticing the residents and officials of Twin Springs to consider the direction of change.

The first step of change is scary. Twin Springs has its proponents and its opponents for opening up to new development. Change is largely inevitable. You can invite it in. You can create it yourself. You can try and fend it off.

What change ultimately envelopes the town of Twin Springs will be something to watch.

Ryan Talley, freelance writer

A town is more than an expanse of land. It is more than its government and its rules. It is more than the economy that serves as its engine. More than anything, it is its people.

On the doorstep of change, the town of Twin Springs is struggling to understand and perhaps be true to its identity. A down economy makes giving into outside investors attractive. The politicians serving the people are desperate to turn the tide to prosperity. The people are caught in the motion of the tides.

The tides of change. Economic development. Giving investors the image of what is it they want to see. The acquiescence to that image forever changing the fabric of the historic community forever.

While some are caught in the currents, others are trying to remain steadfast to the ideals, make- up of the town they love, and have raised generations.

The heart of a town like Twin Springs isn't found in a bank statement, but in its people. It isn't found in a sheet of metal or glass, but the wood and stone stained with history.

While some see this resistance to change as short-sighted and sentimental, those with deep roots in Twin Springs understand that the town has endured for centuries through storms, wars and recessions. They did so as a community of families intent on caring for one another and providing for one another.

The opponents of Twin Springs are proud to be sure. But they aren't resistant to change itself, but rather the type of change that is being lobbied. They would suggest that growth in Twin Springs is one thing. A replacement of the fabric of Twin Springs is quite another.

Blog, unsigned

Seventeen

Ryan chewed his lip as he studied his meager wardrobe. He had only brought with him a handful of dress shirts and slacks. A benefit of being a writer, he could usually manage with street clothes. Knowing he could always run home and replenish his options, he grabbed his last dress shirt off its hanger.

Watching the time carefully, he put himself together. Checked himself on the way out of the bathroom, passing the bedroom mirror and once more just as he exited his room. Straightening the collar on his shirt, his suit jacket, and his overcoat, he marched down the hall.

Several guests were heading in for breakfast, passing a handful that had just finished. "It's brunch until one, Mr. Talley," Merilee sang from the dining room.

"Thank you, ma'am. I may be back, it smells wonderful!" Ryan called from the foyer.

"The best in town, I assure you!" she squealed. "Off to church, are you?"

"Yes."

"Charlie and I will see you there!" Merilee hurried off to their residential part of the grand house. Ryan assumed to get ready herself after prepping for brunch.

With a deep breath, Ryan checked his watch and opened the door. Standing tall and straight, wearing a beautiful smile, was Allison Tancredi. Her hair was partially held up by a bow. Bundled in a thick wool coat and a scarf that matched her bow, she looked like a character from a Christmas romance.

"Wow, you look…amazing," Ryan managed.

Allison accepted his arm, and they turned toward the steps. "You clean up pretty well yourself, Mr. Talley."

Pulling her closer, he replied, "If you are going to link arms with me, I insist you start calling me Ryan."

Allison looked up at him and smirked, "Hmm. That seems so personal, so racy. I don't know…"

Ryan scowled, "We have stolen baby Jesus together. I think we can manage a little less formal."

Allison scrunched her nose, "Don't put it that way. It sounds so wrong…especially since we are on our way to church."

"Yeah, you're right," Ryan agreed. "How about helped Jesus?"

"Still not right," Allison shook her head. "Let's just stick with 'got the Nativity back'."

"Ooh, that's good. Concise, factual. I like it," the writer agreed.

"You're a goof!" Allison chided, tucking her arm in his.

"You invited me."

Allison puffed her bottom lip, "I did, didn't I. You better behave."

"Yes, ma'am."

Only a few hundred yards from the bed and breakfast, the pair swung up the drive to the front of the church. In traditional colonial style, it had a tall steeple with a small bell alcove in its center. The body of the church was simple. All painted in white, with small windows adorned with neat, straight grids. Trees along the path were strung with Christmas lights, and a Nativity scene sat just outside the entrance.

Leaning over, Ryan whispered, "That one is pretty good."

"Just don't let Lizzie see it, she might take it!" Allison whispered back.

Ryan stopped her and looked straight into her eyes. "Any more negative quips before we go inside? You did say best behavior."

"Ugh, I guess you're right. I should model good behavior for you," Allison grinned. "Come on," she pulled him. "I want to get good seats."

As the church filled, Ryan was surprised to see how many people he recognized. Tommy was there with his family. One of the baristas from the coffee shop. The Byrds had made it in just after them. Maddie and her family were a few rows ahead of them. Almost to his surprise, Mayor Faslee and Lizzie Faslee streaked in just as the worship team concluded, and Pastor Dave Magdalen greeted the congregation.

"I love this time of year," the pastor said. "It always feels fresh. An excitement in the air. A time ripe for miracles." Slowly taking in the entire crowd with his eyes, he continued, "That is what I want to talk to you about today. Miracles. Large and small, they are all around us. They happen every day. Sometimes that happens when you most need them, desperately need them. Others, they are blessed upon you out of the blue.

Take Mary, when Gabriel came to speak to her. Betrothed to Joseph, trying to make ends meet, just living life, her very young adult life. And then, wham! Here comes this angel and says, this amazing, incredible, miraculous thing. She and her soon to be husband had been chosen, hand-picked by God to help bring his likeness to earth. His earthbound self.

I am pretty sure she was not hanging out, pining away for an immaculate child to be bestowed on her, within her womb. Yet, she was blessed. As all parents are blessed to bring their amazing children into this world, she was gifted with the King of kings.

Not all miracles are like Mary's. There are others. Families struggling to conceive, and the amazing happens. Loved ones fighting cancer, all medicine exhausted, and the amazing happens. Wonderful, amazing miracles. They happen.

I think what I love about this time of year, isn't that miracles happen more...I'm not sure they do. I think we are more willing to accept them as what they are this time of year. Christmas reminds us of the magic and beauty and wonder of the Nativity."

Ryan couldn't be sure, but he thought it appeared as Pastor Dave shot a glance at Lizzie in the last pew.

"Christmas, with all of its fervor over presents and traveling and visiting relatives or preparing to host them, reminds us of the magic that is around us. That is what we feel during the Christmas season. Take away Santa Clause and presents and even the decorations, I promise you...I promise you...that feeling will still be there. You will still feel just as electric, just as excited.

Look around at your neighbors and wish them Merry Christmas, would you? When you do, whether saying it or receiving it, how does that make you feel? Are you getting a present from them? You might...but that's not it. It isn't reindeer with flashy noses, saints in colorful red suits, trees that glow, or even mistletoe...well, maybe that last one a little bit.

It is that God loves us so much, he sent his only child, his son to us. He gave him to us. An

amazing, beautiful miracle. The season reminds us
of that miracle and all the others that we are blessed
to receive.

Some of you might be going through a tough
time. Hard economy, an illness, stress at
home...You might be asking, where's my miracle?"

Pastor Dave scanned the crowd, making eye
contact with as many in his congregation as he
could. "Sometimes, our prayers are answered as we
request them. More often than not, they come in far
more subtle ways. Sometimes the miracle isn't a gift
resolving a situation, our struggle. Often it is the
fuel that keeps us going. The answer, direction we
know to be the one we need to follow.

Many of you can look to your left or your
right, maybe both and understand an example of
what I am speaking about. One of the greatest
blessings bestowed on us, is the power of humanity
to love. When times are tough for me, I think about
my family. I shut my own mind up, stop my
whining, and look at my family and know that I am
blessed. Often, that is when my answers come.

Sometimes when I prepare the sermon or
when I am up here speaking to you, I begin to
recognize the miracles that have happened in my
life. So, when your car breaks down. When your
terrible boss fires you right before Christmas. When
your roof starts leaking, and you can't afford to fix
it. The miracle may not be a new car, a new job, or a
new roof. It may be the strength to keep forging on
until you can fix it. It may be the inspiration you
have needed to make a powerful change in your

life. It could be a simple cup of coffee offered by a stranger when you have had a bad day.

Or, it could be a visit from an angel or a star shining brighter than any other way up in the sky.

Whatever your miracle is, accept it. Know that God has a plan for you. Have faith that whether it is an obvious solution, or the strength to keep climbing that mountain, that miracle is a gift. Personally selected, wrapped, and delivered just for you, from God."

When the service was over, and the worshippers funneled down the aisles, Ryan and Allison waited for their turn to exit as well. Ryan was taken aback by how many people from Twin Springs recognized him and said hello. Lizzie offered a weak smile at the pair, and Mayor Faslee gave a hearty wave. The mayor seemed as if he were going to wait for them, but Lizzie tugged him out of the church by his sleeve.

Pastor Dave made his way through the crowd, greeting members as he moved. Reaching Allison and Ryan, he paused. Holding out his hand, he introduced himself to Ryan. "I'm Pastor Dave. I'm glad you were here today." Turning to Allison, he asked, "Ms. Tancredi, is this your doing?"

Allison smiled and shrugged, "It was."

"Nice work," Dave replied. "I see you got the Nativity back."

"We did. Thank you for your influence, by the way," Allison said.

Pastor Dave frowned, "What do you mean?"

"Your letter to the editor. It wasn't enough to keep the city from taking it, but it was nice to have the support," Allison acknowledged.

"Oh," the pastor nodded. "I read that. Very well written. But I must confess, I didn't write it."

Allison scowled. She looked at the minister questioningly. "But…then…"

Her eyes grew big. Turning to Ryan, she pointed an accusatory finger. "It was you. Should have known. It was quite well written."

Ryan just smiled.

Allison's jaw dropped. "It was you!"

Pastor Dave patted them gently and walked on, "I hope to see you for Christmas Eve service."

Allison looked at Ryan, her eyes inquisitive. "Why didn't you tell me?"

"I didn't do it for recognition. I just wanted to share my view. It obviously had little impact on the end result," Ryan admitted.

"But people did come into the store and mention it. A few that I had never been in before," Allison lauded.

"I'm glad it had a good effect in some way."

"It made me feel good," Allison beamed.

"Hey, the Byrd's invited us for brunch. Will you join me?" Ryan asked.

Allison paused, "I'd love to…but I have to get the shop open."

A voice perked up behind them. "I can open for you, Allie. I'll be there anyway."

Ryan and Allison turned to see Maddie, her husband, and their two children.

"Hello, Allie," Ryan said.

"Good morning. Ryan, this is my husband Joe, and our little toe heads Kali and Patrick," Maddie said. "Sorry to overhear, but…Allie, you haven't hardly taken any time for yourself since Halloween. Go. Enjoy a nice brunch. Take your time."

Allison hesitated. "Are you sure?"

Maddie looked perturbed, "Are you kidding me?"

"Okay, okay. I'll see you this afternoon."

"I hope not," Maddie quipped and led her family away.

"I guess I'm yours...for a few hours," Allison said, looking up at Ryan.

The writer grinned and pulled her close with his arm around her shoulders. "I'll take it."

Sunday Brunch at the Byrd's Nest was an impressive spread. Ryan wondered if Merilee was in charge of feeding the entire town on Sundays. A giant roast served as the centerpiece, neat folds partially sliced. Next to it was a brown glazed ham that met Ryan's nose as soon as he entered the room. Turkey, half a dozen salads, and heaping mashed potatoes glinted with garlic and bits of cheddar cheese rounded out the spread.

A large table was set in the dining room with so many chairs, Ryan couldn't figure out where they were stashed when not in use. On the table were beautiful evergreen centerpieces with flames dancing atop their candles. Full place settings with a broad assortment of forks, spoons, knives, and glassware that caused Ryan to take a quick inventory and pull from his mental database, which to use when.

Pastor Dave and his wife Meredith sat at one end where Charlie Byrd migrated. Leaving a space for Mrs. Byrd, the innkeeper called Ryan and Allison over with his hand. "Sit here you two. We're so glad you could be with us today."

"Wow, this is incredible. Does Merilee cook like this every Sunday?" Ryan gasped.

Charlie chuckled and patted his stomach, "Nearly. This is a little special, being the last Sunday before the holiday and all. Merilee likes to sneak in a celebration prior to folks heading off for their families' occasions. If every Sunday brunch were like this, I'd either have to stop eating the rest of the week or...exercise."

"We couldn't have that now, could we?" Mrs. Byrd chuckled from somewhere in the background.

In a whisper, Charlie bowed his head, "Woman has the ears of a fox!"

"Yes, I do, dear!" Merilee sang as she headed into the kitchen to grab the fresh-baked rolls.

"See?" Charlie shook his head.

Laughing, everyone prepared to sit. Ryan pulled out Allison's chair and handed her napkin. "Thank you, good sir," she said.

As Merilee arrived with the rolls, she paused. Having witnessed the young couple's interaction, she looked expectantly at Charlie.

"Sheesh!" Charlie quickly plunked his napkin on his plate and launched out of his chair to seat his wife. "With young couples around, I've got to be on my toes!"

"You always have to be on your toes, dear," Merilee said, her eyes twinkling.

With the Byrd's church friends seated, along with the inn's guests who accepted the invitation to brunch, Merilee looked at the minister. "Pastor Dave, would you do the honor?"

"Yes, ma'am." Everyone bowed their heads. The Byrd's held hands. "Dear Father, thank you for allowing us to gather as friends and family in this most glorious season. To live in your world of daily miracles, the miracle of all miracles, we prepare to celebrate. I pray you help us to keep our hearts and minds content, to reach out to one another in loving grace to honor you and the day you sent your Son to live among us. Lord, we are truly blessed, Amen."

"Amen," everyone cheered.

"Merilee, you continue to outdo yourself. Everything smells delicious," Pastor Dave said.

"When did you have time to do all of this?" Ryan asked. "And get ready for church. Truly amazing."

Merilee's eyes twinkled, "I look forward to this day every year. I usually can't sleep the night before and get started quite early." Addressing her guests, she added, "I hope I didn't wake anybody."

"I have never slept as good as I have here, Mrs. Byrd," Ryan admitted.

"Well, dear. You are welcome anytime. Charlie has rather enjoyed having you here, I think. Especially for your nightcap chats," Merilee said.

"Nightcap chats? That sounds exciting!" Allison exclaimed, eyeing both Ryan and Mr. Byrd.

"Oh, what happens fireside...well, it is all rather confidential," Ryan laughed.

"Hmm. Very mysterious," Allison raised her eyebrows. "Thank you so much for inviting me. This is all so lovely."

"Anytime, honey. You are such a wonderful fixture in town. Charlie and I have always adored you and your store. You have a beautiful spirit," Merilee confessed.

The table toasted with goblets of wine, water, milk, or juice held in the air.

Allison blushed.

"And the best Christmas spirit!" Pastor Dave added.

"She does, she does," the crowd agreed, causing Allison's cheeks to glow an even deeper crimson.

Seeing her twist under the spotlight, however beautiful she looked in her humility, Ryan stepped in to bail her out. "Perhaps rivaled by yours, Mrs. Byrd. From the moment I stepped in your inn. I was enveloped in the warmth that only home at Christmas can bring. I have to tell you. I haven't felt that in years!"

The crowd turned to toast Merilee, allowing Allison's cheeks to soften back to normal.

"So, Mr. Talley, how long do we get for before you head off for the holidays?" Meredith Magdalen asked.

Ryan almost looked confused for a moment. "I...I'm not really sure. My parents live in Minneapolis. I'm going to visit them in the New Year as soon as my assignment is over. And my sister's family, it's her in-laws' year for Christmas, so we'll all meet at Mom's the first weekend in January."

"Your assignment, about the Art Walk?" Pastor Dave asked.

"Well, I have that going on, but I have another one that I have been trying to finish up," Ryan shrugged.

"Ooh, what's that one about?" Mrs. Magdelan asked excitedly.

"Well, if it gets printed. I really shouldn't talk much about it – kind of a writer's jinx," Ryan said.

"A mystery," Allison in mocked splendor.

Pastor asked, "How are things with the Twin Springs Transformation going?"

Ryan was thoughtful in his response. "It has attracted quite a bit of attention," he finally said.

"Good or bad attention?" Mrs. Magdelan blurted.

Unfazed, Ryan replied, "Both, I think." He put down his fork and surveyed the room. "Twin Springs is a wonderful town. It is beautiful. It has amazing people in it. The Art Walk concept and the transformation concept and investments are…they're not bad. I just wonder if they are right."

"I see," the pastor said. "I think I might wonder the same."

"Take all of the fuss about the Nativity and the decorations around town, for example. It's like stripping the town of its history, its identity. Twin Springs just doesn't strike me as a politically correct, scrubbed down, sterile town for outsiders to come in and act like they do in the city. I like the two atmospheres myself. The city is there when you want certain things, and towns like Twin Springs, set a bit off on the periphery, are there for what they offer. I guess I'm not one for whitewashing everything," Ryan confided.

"It would bring in a lot of income for our little economy," the pastor suggested. His demeanor with the question reminded Ryan of his chats with Mr. Byrd in the parlor.

"It would…for someone. It won't be for Allison or the Byrd's or…Mr. Haverstein. It will help the municipal tax base if they aren't exhausted in credits to lure them here. But no, the local economy grows, it just doesn't necessarily grow for those who need it to," Ryan railed.

The pastor tried to stifle an impressed smile from cracking his lips. "I see. What about Lizzie Faslee?"

Ryan glanced at Allison and responded, "At the core of it, her heart is in the right place. Twin Springs is struggling. Her project will bring growth and change. The question is, how much of Twin Springs do you want changed?"

Meredith Magdalen pointed her glass in Ryan's direction, "I like this one." Glancing at Allison, who had remained conspicuously silent during the meal, she prodded, "He's a keeper."

Allison looked shocked, "Oh, we're…uh…we're not…" She pointed her finger back and forth between her and Ryan to suggest the word "together".

"Ah," Meredith cast a suspicious smile at the couple.

"Ok, these two are never coming back if we interrogate them," Charlie warned and then grinned, "That is later for the parlor!"

"Great," Ryan mumbled softly. "Better get my strength up. Fortunately, dinner is delicious!"

Allison nodded, "Mmm. May I have some more of those amazing Brussels sprouts?" She looked at Ryan, a look of exasperation dancing in her eyes.

Merilee accepted Allison's help cleaning up the brunch dishes but refused Ryan's. Effectively splitting up the women and the men, Ryan followed Charlie and Pastor Dave into the sitting room by the fireplace.

"Great meal, thank you, Charlie. You and Merilee are exceptional hosts," Ryan declared, accepting a small glass of Port from the innkeeper.

"She and I have been at it for nearly half a century. Pretty well-oiled machine by now," Charlie responded.

"And yet, you both seem like you genuinely love it," Ryan admired.

Charlie chuckled, "That's because we do. We get to work together, serve the town and be near our friends like Dave and Meredith, and meet interesting new friends such as yourself."

"To friends and happiness, then," Ryan raised his glass.

"I've been reading your articles, Ryan. You are quite good. I enjoy how you find a way to put a warm and personable spirit in them," Pastor Dave said.

Ryan nodded, "Thank you. I wouldn't have any fun writing if I weren't able to make it my own. I like to have a conversation with my readers."

"Am I to assume you were responsible for the Nativity article?" the pastor asked.

"I was," Ryan admitted.

Dave looked thoughtful for a moment. "I might have to borrow some of your words for my Christmas Eve sermon. Very heartfelt, logical take on sharing one's faith."

Ryan shrugged, "Why not? I can't fathom the harm of wishing peace and goodwill towards someone – in any language from any denomination."

"People forget what this country was founded on – religious freedom. Freedom of expression and freedom to worship how they wish," Charlie added. "I like you Mr. Talley. You are of sound character and seemingly sound mind."

"Thank you, sir. Coming from you, I take that as a high compliment."

"Ha. You don't know him that well then!" Dave chuckled, slapping a hand on Charlie's shoulder.

Glasses of Port drained and brunch evidence cleared, the Magdelans bid their farewell. Allison and Ryan offered their gratitude to the Byrd's, and Ryan walked Allison out. Bundling up against the cold, they huddled as they gingerly navigated the inn's steps.

Amidst little wisping snowflakes, they strolled along the sidewalk, making fresh footprints as they went. "Thank you for a wonderful day," Allison smiled, looking up at Ryan.

"It was a great day, wasn't it?"

"It really was," Allison's grin widened.

Ryan let out a sigh, "Under the scope for a bit."

"Wow, you are adept at changing the topic when you need to," Allison said.

"Years of training in covert ops, really paying off," Ryan smirked.

Allison spied the writer, suspiciously, "I wouldn't doubt it."

For a block or two, they walked in silence. Pulled in close to one another, they were content to enjoy the late afternoon. Glancing at her watch,

Allison scrunched her nose and asked, "Do you mind stopping by the shop?"

"Not at all."

"Thank you," Allison gushed. "Kind of an overzealous Mom, I guess."

"You've put yourself into it. And you care for Candace and Maddie."

"I do," Allison admitted. "The store and those two are kind of my family."

Ryan followed a snowflake from high in the grey sky, tracking it as it danced down until it joined its fellow snow on the ground in front of them. "You amaze me."

Allison shot a curious glance his way. "How so?"

"Through the struggle with the city, the Nativity…a slower than expected season…you never waiver. You stay positive and giving. That is pretty special," Ryan replied.

"Maybe when people are looking," Allison grinned. "What am I supposed to do?"

Ryan chuckled, giving her a light squeeze. "Freak out. Look perturbed. Turn pale. I don't know."

"I could…I have," Allison admitted. "It's just the town. My girls. I don't want to let any of them down." Her voice choked and sounded sad.

With a glance, Ryan saw a small glint of tear welling in her eyes.

"You won't fail them."

"How do you know?" Allison gasped, the glint turned full-fledged watery.

Ryan pulled her even tighter and offered a reassuring smile, "I just do."

They both grinned as they walked past the Nativity.

Allison continued in silence until they were just outside of her shop. "You're crazy."

"Yep," the writer nodded, holding the door open for her.

"Hello, boss!" Maddie called from behind the counter. The store was impeccable. Christmas music played softly in the background. The clerk leaned nonchalantly on the back of the check stand.

"How was the day?" Allison asked, a hopeful ring in her voice.

"Good," Maddie offered meekly.

Allison frowned, "Where's Candace?"

"I…uh. I sent her home," Maddie grimaced. "It was slow."

Allison took the information in, shrouding a reaction. "Oh," she nodded.

Maddie looked impish, "How was your day?"

"Nice. Excellent service at church and lunch with Pastor Magdalen and his wife.

"Oh," Maddie said, expecting more.

The two women stared at each other in silence for several moments before moving on.

"Well, get out of here. I can shut down, go see your family," Allison commanded.

Maddie studied her boss, "You get out of here. I've got it."

A second stare down launched between the two strong-willed women. Ryan squirmed out of the equation finding a trinket to suddenly take great interest in. "I should probably be going. I've got deadlines to hit and whatnot." Ryan said, letting the ladies off the hook.

The two women shifted their stares to him. After several long seconds, Allison responded, "I had a lovely time."

Ryan looked at her, intently, "So did I."

"Well, I'll see you…later…then," Allison said.

"Good evening, ladies," Ryan bid and made a hasty exit.

Watching the writer make his way out of the shop and out on to the streets of Twin Springs, Maddie waited until he was out of earshot. "Well? How did your date go?"

Allison frowned, "It wasn't a date!"

"Yes, it was," Maddie replied in defiance.

"It was church."

"For six hours? Pastor Dave is getting a little long-winded," Maddie said incredulously.

"And brunch," Allison defended.

"If you don't want to tell me…"

"Nothing happened!" Allison protested.

"Why not?" Maddie pleaded. "Allie, you have been single for what, two…three years? I had my qualms about Ryan, but…he is cute. And, as much as I hate to admit it. He seems like a great guy."

"I just don't have time right now to think about guys. I appreciate his help. I appreciate his friendship. Right now, I need to focus on keeping my business," Allison answered.

Maddie steamed, "What business? Allie, I love you, girl. But this is your last hurrah. I know what you have been going through. Candace and I, we appreciate what you have done for us. I also know you should have canned us months ago. The shop is so slow you could run it on your own, and you still wouldn't be in the black!"

"Maddie!" Allison fumed, her eyes burrowing into her friend's. Her face softened. "You're right. The shop...it's time is up. I should have talked to you two. I wanted to..."

"Allie. It's okay. Candace and I are big girls. We can take care of ourselves. We adore you and all you have done for us," Maddie walked up to her boss and squeezed her in a big hug.

Suddenly, breaking into tears, Allison choked, "I appreciate you two too!"

"Oh, girl, stop it. The store is a store. Your soul leaves with you. Wherever you land will be brilliant. If there is room for Candace and I, we would gladly follow. At the end of the day, you need to take care of yourself. I am going to look out for my family. Candace is just a baby. She'll land on her feet," Maddie said.

"I know. I just kept thinking somehow things would work out. That business would pick up," Allison sobbed.

"You always think of others…see the bright side. That is why you are so loved."

"So loved?" Allison scoffed. "By who?"

Maddie turned cross, "Oh no! You don't feel sorry for yourself. You are beautiful, big-hearted, and everyone…especially charming, possibly schmoozy writers adore you. Don't start the woe is me a bit. I don't buy it!"

"Okay, okay," Allison acquiesced. "I am blessed. Poor, but blessed. Happy?"

Maddie perked up and grinned, "Yes. Now, go be with your writer!"

Allison started for a moment towards the door and turned. "Get out of here. Be with your family. Or you're fired!"

"Hollow threat, but I give up. I will go see my family. Do you know how I got a family? I went on dates. Just saying…" Maddie scoffed and grabbed her purse. "Goodnight, boss."

"Goodnight, Maddie. Thank you."

Alone, in her solitude minus "O Holy Night" playing overhead, Allison locked the door to her shop and began closing it down.

Eighteen

Ryan's phone buzzed by his ear. Glancing at the call screen, he cleared his throat and sat up in bed. Seeing Lizzie Faslee's number, he hesitated before hitting the "Talk" button.

"Ryan, all of our work is paying off!" Lizzie squealed into the phone.

"Our work?" Ryan asked sleepily.

"Yes! One of the investors is coming back into town today and wants to discuss a property!" Lizzie said excitedly.

"Congratulations?" Ryan replied.

"So, I need you to meet us at City Hall. I want you to capture the first cog in the transformation of Twin Springs!" Lizzie sang.

"I can't wait. When do I meet you?" Ryan asked, his voice ringing in sarcasm.

"Can you come now?" Lizzie asked.

Swinging his legs over the bed, he answered, "I'm on my way."

A fresh layer of snow had fallen on the town. Everything looked bright and clean. Half the town was dressed for Christmas, a postcard for the season under the white blanket. The other half, relenting to the pressures from City Hall, was scrubbed bare. Still pretty in its wintry state, but felt like something was missing.

Ryan chuckled as he passed the Jewish Deli with the manger scene out front. The snow added a level of genuineness to the Nativity. The small shelter barely protected Joseph, Mary, and the newborn. Snow-covered the fringes of where the new parents knelt near their son. The star, still shining even in the day, was streaked with icicles.

Haverstein was gracious to share his space, and the union of Hanukkah and Christmas seemed to complement one another in a strangely beautiful way. Memories of grade school, learning about the two religions made the pairing fit somehow. He wondered if children even learned anything about the holidays anymore. He remembered plays on the Nativity and 'Twas the Night Before Christmas. He remembered playing with a dreidel and learning from his friends how they celebrated with their families.

Suddenly no tradition, certainly those brought to America by the founders, was acceptable to even mention. Studies in Middle East culture were fine. Alternative lifestyle curriculum was mandatory. Theories on global warming, presented by political figures, was welcome. But "God Bless America", "One Nation Under God" – they were stricken from the public's vocabulary.

If you were in the majority, you were somehow shamed. So what if your church or synagogue helped needy families across the country, brought water to distant lands that were thirsty? None of that mattered. Who cares if your family helped overcome segregation and fought for freedom for all? The country had turned on those who made it the country it is.

Ryan kicked at the snow as this flurry of thoughts danced around in his head as he walked towards City Hall. For centuries, America celebrated together. Peace on Earth. They celebrated miracles, together. Haverstein and Allison- read different stories, put up different décor, but share the same message. The nation had adored the message since its modern birth. Now, with programs like the Twin Springs Transformation, the message, the magical time, had a boot to its throat.

Walking into Town Hall, Ryan felt like a double agent. He listened, half-heartedly participated, and managed his role. His eyebrow fluttered under his new-found passion. The writer was not going to allow the project to be successful. Somehow, he had to make things right.

Lizzie was frantic, rushing from person to person in the boardroom, doling out final instructions as quickly as her lips would allow. Eric Farnham stood in the center of the chaos, a calm, cool mast. He casually flipped through his notes, stifling what Ryan knew to be a cocky grin under the man's charming demeanor.

"Oh, good, you're here!" Lizzie called when she saw him. Making a beeline through the small mass of people, she said, "The first investor wants to take a closer look at one of the buildings on Main Street. Its location is ideal for a medical building – spa, aesthetics, maybe even dental. He has this amazing vision. A new façade all in glass and architectural rock – it would reflect the mountains...can you imagine? Gutting the inside will take a bit of work, but it can be carved up into a medical suite. That is perfect!"

"I see," Ryan nodded and then furrowing his brow, he asked, "What is my role exactly today?"

Lizzie stared at him directly. "Sell it! It is the perfect image of what Twin Springs will grow into. Not everyone is going to be on board; in fact, a few people are probably going to be downright angry. Your job, my silky wordsmith, is to paint the concept in a way that makes sense to everyone. Bend those who are bendable to see the potential of what it is we are trying to do!"

"That's all? Convince a natural beauty that her life will be fairy tale perfect if she gets a nose job and butt implants. Got it," Ryan mocked.

"Oh, that's aesthetics humor...I get it," Lizzie waved him off and scurried away to command another committee member.

Ryan rubbed his chin and watched the chaos swirl around the boardroom. Eric Farnham had been eyeing him and sauntered over. "Lizzie is quite fond of your talents," he said, giving Ryan a smirk.

"Well, she is trying to affect major change. Without support, it would be an even more difficult job. I share her message," Ryan responded.

"Her message. You don't agree with it, do you?" Eric asked pointedly.

"It isn't my job to agree. It is my job to articulate the facts."

Eric studied the writer for a moment. "You know, I'm not sure anyone reads your words, and if so, how much they matter. Fact is, sometimes, major change is necessary, and it is better for people to live in the fruits of it rather than plead for their blessings."

Ryan smiled evenly, "And this committee is undoubtedly so wise, it can think for the rest of the simple people. At least those who stand to make a big paycheck and get to go back to wherever it is they came from will make out."

"It's not that simple. Some will be rewarded for their hard work. It is your choice to be part of that or not," Farnham said indignantly and walked away.

Ryan chewed his lip as he watched the broker storm off. He didn't trust him before. Now he knew he was not to be trusted.

There was no concealing the investor's presence when he arrived. He whisked in, an entourage in tow. Lizzie and her friends snapped nervously to attention. Ryan caught Eric Farnham take a deep breath and then puff out his chest, striding forward. "Mr. Marcel, this is an exciting day!"

The investor paused at Farnham's exuberant welcome. Finally, shaking the broker's hand, he responded, "Yes. So, let's see this property one more time. I want to make sure the mockups will work."

"Of course, we can go right now," Eric replied.

Lizzie bounced up, "You are going to love it! It will be right in the center of the new shopping district. Eric tells me you already have prospective tenants."

"Yes. I bring in clients who serve higher-end clients to their health and wellness clinics. None of that riffraff with bills that go unpaid. Aesthetics, spas…," Marcel gave Lizzie and glance over. "You know what I mean."

"It is ideal for the new Twin Springs!" Lizzie said excitedly, her eyes dancing around, trying to determine what the investor had inferred.

"Shall we?" Eric clapped his hands together.

Marcel waved him off, "It means nothing unless the building is empty. These…renters, they will be gone?"

Eric grinned, "Uh, yes, sir. I…"

The investor cut him off, "How soon? I don't want my money put into something just to have it sit."

"Not a problem," Eric assured. "Two have agreed to leave, and the other two, well, I have it good authority they will be leaving very soon."

Marcel stopped and looked at Eric squarely. "Good authority? You can write a check to good authority. I will invest, in fact. That is why they call it real estate."

"I hold the leases. They haven't paid, according to contract, they defaulted, and it stipulates their eviction process can be enacted," Eric stuttered.

Marcel smiled, "Then get your little process moving. Evict those hapless squatters."

"Yes, the paperwork is being filed as we speak," Eric assured, his thumb tapping away furiously at the cell phone by his side. "We can have them out in a week, two max."

Marcel looked thoughtful for a moment and then nodded.

Ryan cocked his head, "But it's Christmas," Ryan pointed out.

The investor looked at Ryan with indifference, "Right…." Ignoring the writer's pleas, he turned to Eric. "If we can get the paperwork done and the building cleared, I could have contractors here by New Year's."

Ryan was incensed at the nonchalance of the developer. "Seriously, what would a week or two matter? Let the families have their holiday before you shatter their dreams?"

"Who is this, man?" the developer snarled. Turning his nose up at Ryan, he scoffed, "You put your million dollars on hold for a few weeks, then maybe you would understand."

Eric slapped his hand on Marcel's shoulder, "You just keep scribbling on your little pad, we'll handle the business, Mr. Talley."

Lizzie nudged Ryan and shot him a look that pleaded for him to be quiet. Frowning, he followed them down the stairs and onto the sidewalk.

A woman with Marcel busily tapped away on a tablet as she followed each conversation Marcel had, especially when speaking with Eric. On the opposite side of the investor was a balding little man who was constantly scrolling web pages and spreadsheets on his phone.

The procession took Lizzie's obligatory path through the Art Walk, though Marcel indignantly walked around it, instead staring at the building ahead. Ryan followed the man's eyes and felt a pit in his stomach when he realized what the investor was staring at.

Ryan realized he shouldn't have been surprised to see which "hapless" tenants were due to be removed. His eyes fell squarely on Allison's shop. Catching a glance from Lizzie, she merely offered a shrug.

"I thought you got rid of that rubbish," Marcel waved his hand in the direction of Haverstein's deli.

"You mean the Nativity?" Ryan asked, his questions clearly floating away into the cold crisp air as is unheard.

"The building next door is privately owned, the ordinance..." Eric began.

Marcel shook him off, "Oh, save it. I can see that it has moved. Surely the Jew won't be putting it up next year. Maybe I'll have to buy his building too. No matter."

The woman with Marcel dashed in front of him, the tablet displaying a digital recreation of the street. The building looked nothing like the colonial that stood today. The building was square with gleaming exposed metal framing massive glass panels. Rock matching the hills shaped the foundation and lower edge of the fascia.

In and of itself, Ryan had to admit. It was a handsome building. He just thought it would look silly plunked down in the middle of Twin Springs. But he knew the plan was for the rest of the town to follow suit. Sterile aesthetics with a touch of natural elements to make the statement that they are in tune with the earth.

He watched Lizzie peer over Marcel's shoulder and converse with her friends. It was their vision of Twin Springs. Some glimpse of a town they had visited, on some trip that made them feel glamorous, important. They wanted that. They begged for that life to be brought to Twin Springs.

"Very well, write it up, Mr. Farnham," Marcel announced. "And get those tenants out of there!" With a snap of his finger, his two assistants, still nose deep in their electronics, about-faced and followed the investor back down the sidewalk.

Eric grinned at Lizzie. "Let's go celebrate! I have champagne on ice back at the boardroom."

"It's happening!" Lizzie squealed. Tiffany and Annabeth circled her as they danced with their arms joined together. "It's really happening!"

As a group, they walked back towards City Hall. Ryan peeled to the back. For a moment, Lizzie joined him. "This is really what you want?" Ryan asked.

"Yes! The building was beautiful. He will bring in doctors and aestheticians and world-class masseuses...what's not to love?" Lizzie squealed.

Ryan nodded in silence and let her rejoin the group. Stopping, he allowed them to continue without him. As they crossed the street heading to the town hall's steps, Lizzie glanced back just for a moment. She looked at Ryan, slightly hopeful, but unrelenting. Bouncing along, she carried on with the group to toast their first prominent new investor. The second cog in transforming Twin Springs was moving into place.

Ryan retreated to the coffee shop. Tapping away on his laptop, he did his best to perform his duty while being true to himself. He struggled to fall in line with the thought that the town needed to be transformed. More so, because most of the city was a spectator in the process. Lizzie and the real estate broker had the inside track. Mayor Faslee was still well-liked and trusted. He could put the town at ease when they were unsure or resisted. He could even talk them into adopting the political correctness that chipped away at the town's true identity.

Running his fingers through his hair, he sighed, trying to come up with the right words that told both stories in the same piece. He thought of the image on the tablet held up for the investor. The gleaming windows, stoic rock, and statement of gleaming metal slamming into the Rockwellian core of Main Street. Ryan laughed to himself. He would wake up from a dream finding the town a posh version of Pottersville at the hands of Lizzie, Eric, and that creep Marcel.

Chewing his lip, he began pressing the keys, putting thoughts into letters, words into images. The story of Twin Springs in its pivotal moment.

Nineteen

Allison smiled when the bell over the door jingled. "Merry Christmas, Sheriff Davis!"

The man looked sheepish as he strode up to the counter, "Merry Christmas, Allison."

"Come in to find your beautiful wife a present, or are you here to find something for your daughters?" Allison's eyes went wide, and she snapped her fingers. "Ooh, I have just the thing..."

Bolting out from behind the check stand, Allison darted to a display of dolls. "These are darling. And look...they're twins, just like Rebecca and Brittaney!"

Sheriff Davis eyed the dolls and nodded, "They're perfect."

Allison stopped and read the dour tenor of the man. "What is it? Everything alright?"

"It's just…," the sheriff bobbed his head around and kicked at the floor. "I have to give this. It is an eviction notice. They called it in this morning. I'm sorry."

Allison snatched the paper from the man, reading it and nodding. "It's not your fault. Been a tough year."

"Yeah, for all of us," Sheriff David nodded.

"Well, I guess that's that," Allison shrugged. She could feel Candace and Maddie closing in from behind her. "Take the dolls for Becky and Britt."

"I can't do that, here," the sheriff dug in his wallet for a few bills. "If there's anything I can do…"

"Thank you, Sheriff. Merry Christmas," Allison managed a smile as the officer left with his package.

She stared out the door, avoiding her employees. She knew as soon as she looked at her friends, she would lose it.

"Allie…" Candace called softly.

Allison was right. As soon as she turned to Candace, she burst into tears. Maddie and Candace converged, squeezing Allison into a sobbing sandwich.

"I knew it was coming," she choked. "I just wanted to get through the holiday."

"Why didn't you tell us it was this bad?" Maddie gasped. "We could have cut our hours. I would have come in for free. We would have worked something out."

"You two have your own stresses, I didn't need to add to that," Allison replied.

"Allie, we're friends before we are co-workers. We would have helped you," Candace scolded.

"It wouldn't have mattered. Not really. Things have been so off this year, I wasn't even close to making it," Allison argued.

Maddie plopped down on the counter. "So, what now?"

"I don't know…" Allison shook her head.

The girls had scarcely noticed the bell over the door. They certainly didn't see the man standing in front of the counter trying to find something to look at rather than stare directly at them.

"Ahem," he coughed softly.

"Ryan? Oh, I'm sorry, we…" Allison started.

Ryan waved her off. Concern clearly planted on his face. "What's going on?"

Allison wrinkled her nose and waved the notice, "I guess I'm done."

Ryan understood. "That broker. He's squeezing you on the lease."

Allison nodded, "I thought I had a little more time."

"Maybe you do. I had a feeling that might be the next step for them. I did a little digging. You can appeal. If you put in a notice of hardship, it will buy you a little more time," Ryan said.

"I don't know. It's not like it matters," Allison sighed, tossing the letter on the counter. "I might as well just give it up."

"Is that what you want to do? If it is..." Ryan asked.

"Well, no, but what can I do? The busiest season is nearly over, and I am way too far under. When the January lull hits, I'm dead anyway," Allison argued.

Ryan looked impish. "Why make it easy on them? It's not just you. It's the town. They expect everyone just to roll over and allow them to take over. Why not at least go out with a fight?"

Allison wiped her tears away and laughed, "I like the way you think, but according to this, if I don't catch up on November's payment, I have to be out in three days. I don't have it. We're not exactly pulling customers in by the busload."

"It's three days," Ryan shrugged. "You never know."

Allison eyed him suspiciously. "I guess it can't hurt to last it out. I have some customers picking up orders all this week anyway, and I need to call the artists that have stuff on consignment."

"Hang in there," Ryan urged.

"No other plans this week, might as well," Allison replied, her affect a bit vacant.

Maddie and Candace watched the conversation unfold. Maddie frowned, weighing the writer as if she were trying to see inside him.

"Well, I have a few things I need to get done before the sun sets. I should be off," Ryan said. Then with a turn, he asked abruptly, "Are you free for dinner tomorrow?"

Allison's cheeks glowed pink, "I...uhm...maybe a late one, after closing."

"Alright. I'll swing by and meet you here," Ryan said and, with a nod, smiled, "Ladies."

The three women watched the writer make his exit, a slight hop in his step.

Exhaling a laugh, Candace broke the silence. "He is pretty adorable."

"I don't know. He's hard not to like. I just still want to know that we can trust him," Maddie cautioned.

"He helped us rescue the Nativity, even risking getting arrested for breaking and entering," Candace defended.

Maddie screwed her face into a knot, "He admitted it was a setup, a nice dramatic touch to be sure, but he was never in any real danger of getting arrested."

"He risked his writing gig," Candace pressed.

"Maybe," Maddie said and then opened her eyes wide, "Unless he is a double agent. Being nice to Allison so that Lizzie and her cronies can get the inside track. Notice how he wasn't surprised that Allie was getting evicted?"

"Everyone could see that coming," Allison rolled her eyes.

"They got want they want. Why would he still be hanging around unless he thinks our Allie is cute, which she is," Candace cooed, leaning her head on Allison's shoulder.

"You guys are nutty," Allison giggled, wrapping her arms around both of them.

"So that's it then," Charlie said to Ryan as they sat in front of the fire.

"I encouraged Allison to hang in there. Let things play out to the very end," Ryan shared.

Charlie looked thoughtful. "Go out swinging," he said approvingly.

"Exactly. Besides, you never know what can happen."

"I think our town has gone to your head," Charlie laughed. "But, I like it."

"It is one thing to lose the battle. It is another to give up and let the victory be stolen from you. I think life takes people for a ride, sometimes entire towns, countries even. They get swept up into the motion to the point they think that is just how it is. They forget that they have a say in the direction of their future. They can take a stand for what they believe, for the town or country that they love," Ryan said. His words coming faster and faster into a crescendo.

Charlie smiled, "Well said, young Mr. Talley. The toils of those who have come before, we forget the weight that they had to bear and struggle when that yoke becomes our burden."

"Do we let the weight crush us, or do we straighten up. Make it ours, standing tall on wobbly legs until they are strong enough to no longer shake!" Ryan added.

Before Charlie could add to the dialogue, they were cut off by a voice in the doorway. "What on earth are you two talking yammering about?" Mrs. Byrd queried behind bewildered eyes.

"The town," Charlie spat.

"The Gift Shop," Ryan blurted.

"Are you sure you are even having the same conversation? My heavens, no more Port for the two of you," Mrs. Byrd scoffed and spun on her heel, leaving them to their folly.

The two men could merely laugh. Charlie held up his glass, Ryan reached across to complete the sentiment, clinking the two drinks together.

Twenty

Ryan groaned as he received his second urgent message from Lizzie in two days. Relenting, he followed the command and wrapped up his work to set out for City Hall. The morning sun was quickly warming the snow to slush. Ryan took care to avoid sloshing in pools as he navigated the sidewalks of Twin Springs.

He noticed the street and maintenance crews were busy toiling around the town. "Lizzie is expecting more guests, I see," Ryan muttered to himself.

Town Hall was a frenzy of Lizzie's committee members, the mayor, and several of the councilmen Ryan recognized from his first visit. He noted that several looked heated in hushed conversations. Part of him wanted to linger, but the figure of an irate and stressed Lizzie Faslee on the landing of the stairs leading to the boardroom beckoned.

She shot daggers at him as he climbed the steps. He eyed her with curiosity. "What's up?"

The young woman shook the newspaper in front of him, "The most beautiful thing in the gleaming glass and stone building would be its reflection- the town of Twin Springs as she stands in its gaze. Weathered against time, storms, and even wars. She is a piece of America, rich in tradition, history. Even more rich in her people. At the end of the day, the reflection of a town, a city, isn't its shops, galleries, restaurants. It is her people. When you set to debate the future of Twin Springs, what do you want her reflection to reveal?"

She lowered the paper and glowered at Ryan.

Grinning, he said, "I know. It sounds even better when you read it aloud."

Rolling her eyes and pursing her lips, she thrust it in Ryan's gut. "You captured Marcel's visit okay, if a little charitable on the current inhabitants. But what was all that "her people" stuff? It sounds like you're arguing against it."

Ryan shrugged, "To be frank, I am neither for nor against it. I am doing my job and representing the town."

"You're supposed to be representing me," Lizzie snapped. "Whatever. You are a good writer, just stay focused. We have bigger issues to undertake. We have another investor coming in tomorrow. Can you believe it? Anyway, they are adamant the town follows strict civil liberties protocols."

Ryan scrunched his face. "So, no stoning people we have differences with. That a big problem around here?"

"No religious stuff. You know, like that Nativity thing," Lizzie rolled her eyes again. "I know, we can't remove it again. But anything that is connected to the town itself must adhere. We are having an emergency town meeting to make sure we are consistent with such measures."

Ryan looked confused, "What do you mean?"

"You know. Christmas trees, wreaths, Santa Clause, Merry Christmas. They want to make sure we are modern in our approach to protecting its populace and not some bible-thumping backwoods Podunk town," Lizzie replied.

"I see. And you are okay with that?"

"Yeah," Lizzie was incredulous, "Why not? I mean, people can celebrate what they want in their homes, but why put it in other people's faces."

Ryan nodded, "Pander to the smallest percentile at the detriment to the vast majority. Makes sense."

Lizzie stopped cold in her tracks. "Are you going to be a problem?"

"I'm just saying if I was the three or four percent who didn't celebrate Christmas or Hanukkah, and that is being generous, I would either try to understand or go somewhere else,"

Ryan quipped. "I will write succinctly, factually and honestly as I always have."

"Good. I need you on this," Lizzie pleaded.

The afternoon consisted of frenzied preparations for the second investor. Proposed sites were designated. The streets were plowed, sidewalks swept.

Most of the day was spent corralling members of the City Council for the case of a godless civic identity. When they didn't respond in kind, a litany of rationale for courting new businesses and consumers to town were regurgitated. When those failed, the stakes rose dramatically. Support for re-election, reduced business alliances, and being painted as intolerant were all levied.

By the end of the day, a reluctant City Council was set and primed for their emergency town meeting. From Ryan's vantage, he was at least excited that covering this meeting was going to be a whole lot more exciting than the first he had attended.

Submitting the article he was working on, and closing the lid on the laptop, Ryan saw he only had one-half hour until the town meeting. Giving himself a once over and re-tucking in his shirt, he grabbed his coat and headed out the door.

Despite running a bit late, he decided to take the long way around the block toward Town Hall. Outside of the gift shop, he found Mr. Haverstein and Allison talking. Haverstein looked up and smiled, "How is our young writer today? Ooh, aren't you going to be late for the meeting? I was just convincing Ms. Tancredi to join me. Perhaps you will have better luck."

"I am not sure if I can handle any more this season," Allison admitted.

Ryan laughed, "I can understand that. But, Town Hall meetings aren't just listening. I think this one will be particularly vocal from the crowd."

"Ah, your inside track to privileged information," Allison ribbed Ryan.

"Come on, could be fun!" Ryan held out his arm for her.

Allison looked at both men and then sighed, "Alright. Let me lock up the store. Haven't had a lot of customers anyway."

Haverstein and Ryan waited and watched patiently as Allison secured the shop. "Gentlemen," she called as she offered her arms to her escorts.

"What treat are we in for this evening, Mr. Talley?" the deli owner prodded.

"The next step in the war on true religious freedom. To impress a potential suitor, Lizzie's committee has demanded the City Council scrub any reference of God out of the town's vocabulary," Ryan confided.

"Hmmm. My people remember how this sort of thing goes," Haverstein scoffed.

"Well, I don't think it is quite there yet," Ryan said and then admitted, "Though I get your point."

"Doesn't the Council have to agree?" Allison asked.

Ryan nodded knowingly, "Yes, they do."

"They didn't!" Allison gasped.

"They did," Ryan confirmed.

Allison looked astonished, "That Lizzie has been a busy little girl."

"I fully expect her to come down from a rooftop and warn you and your dog, Toto, off any minute," Haverstein joked.

"That is a perfect illustration, Mr. Haverstein," Allison agreed. "What about the mayor? Surely he couldn't have signed off on it?"

"You'll see," Ryan said. "He is adeptly playing both sides. Agreeing to a temporary measure in light of the mystery investor."

"Any insight into who that is?" Haverstein asked.

Ryan looked thoughtful for a moment, "If I were to pick a company off the dossiers I read, I would say it was the so-called "Green Resort" company. They profess to be environmentally friendly but then exhaust massive resources to build and maintain their resorts. Veiled in recycled materials and lovely natural elements, people buy into it."

Ryan chewed his lip for a moment, "Or the French Brasserie. The owner is renowned for being outspoken in removing religion from public centers and schools."

"That would explain a lot," Allison pursed her lips.

"Well, this is still our town," Haverstein stated defiantly.

When they arrived at the City Hall building, the meeting room was already bursting at the seams. Ryan excused himself to wriggle his way to steal a spot near the Council Members who all sat in a row behind a table dotted with microphones. Haverstein escorted Allison to a spot where they could lean along the back wall.

As the big clock in the back of the room hit 4:30, Mayor Faslee leaned into the microphone directly in front of him. He wore his usual friendly smile and approached the contentious audience as if he were about to kick off a bingo game. "Wow, what a turn out for our fair city of Twin Springs. I am always touched with how much you all- our friends and neighbors- care about this town. And that is why we have assembled today's meeting. I apologize for the short notice, and I can see many of you left your businesses to come, so thank you." The mayor paused and scanned the crowd, the smile etched in his cheeks.

"Twin Springs has received a wonderful opportunity. You all know what a success Art Walk is, and it is drawing some incredible attention to our town. Attention that can turn around our little recession, way ahead of other towns and cities, and around the country. We are accomplishing that through being proactive and bringing change here as opposed to waiting for it to take us over. For that, we have Lizzie Faslee, Eric Farnham, and the Art Walk/Twin Springs Transformation committee to thank," the mayor said, proudly nodding towards his daughter and the commercial broker.

"Thank you, Mr. Mayor," Eric Farnham spoke into the microphone. "I...we have been working tirelessly to find investors who believe in Twin Springs as much as you do. They are sharp and know how to bring money back into Twin Springs."

"In two days, we have had two major parties interested in making substantial investments that will improve the economy for everyone here. If you have been looking for work, they have it. If you have needed more customers, they will attract them here for you. At the inn, there will be guests. At the coffee shop, there will be more coffee drinkers than you can handle. This is an exciting time," Lizzie heralded. "There are a few things we need to do as a city. Our country has gone through growing pains and the realization that we need to be tolerant of all walks of life forces us, at least in our civic culture, to curtail our personal beliefs in favor of respecting others."

"You mean, like no Christmas!" someone shouted from the crowd.

"Yeah, or Allison's Nativity!" another voice called out.

Lizzie held out her hands in front of her, "Now, come on. Allison got her Nativity back. We have always loved it, but we also need to adhere to legal norms. No one can stop Christmas. It isn't a decoration, lights, or a tree."

"You're stealing Christmas anyways, Grinch!" someone yelled to the favor of the audience, which erupted in laughter.

"No one is stealing Christmas," Mayor Faslee assured. "While we have some sensitivities to manage to accommodate guests in our town, no one is saying these changes will necessarily remain in effect forever. But, with the advice of the esteemed City Council, I am approving their conclusion to remove religious references for the time being."

The crowd burst into a frenzy of questions and shouting.

"Alright, hold on now," the Mayor tried to calm the crowd. "I have heard some of the questions. The most common one, I think, is what does that mean. Simply, it means no group prayer before the session. It means any remaining decorations specific to Christmas...or Hanukkah...will be removed from Town Hall and any other government building. The town tree, which is on city property, will be undecorated."

"That's been up for over a century!"

"I know, I know. I feel much the same way. This is a temporary order that we will come together as a town to work out after the holiday," Mayor Faslee declared.

The audience was undeterred by his assurance, and the volume in the room rose to nearly painful levels.

In an attempt to paint the discussion in a way that displaced fault away from his office and the council, he once more got the town's attention. "I am not in favor of many of these changes either. Pastor Magdalen and I were talking about this at church just last Sunday. But towns have been sued around the country for such practices. There is a certain sensitivity to our melting pot country that, as a public entity, we need to remain constant and welcoming to all faiths or those who choose their own direction."

"Tolerance?" a man from the center of the room called out, "How about tolerating Christian values, or is tolerance only reserved for things non-Christian?"

"Uhm, we are rarely tolerated," Haverstein offered up from the back of the room.

"Right, sorry, Haverstein. Christians and Jews are absolved from concern and protection?" the man corrected.

Lizzie interjected, "Politics and religion do not mix. Separation of church and state..."

"But they do mix," Ryan stepped forward. "It is in our Constitution, our Pledge, even our currency. America, as it was developed, was marked by Christianity, Catholicism...Jewish and Mormon faiths. The root of all them- be kind to others. Love one another. Wish me a Merry anything, and I will say thank you. Who is possibly offended by someone wishing you peace, goodwill."

Lizzie scowled at Ryan, "It isn't the message, it is the religious reference, like the manger thing." She pointed randomly across the room.

"Okay...then who is so deeply offended by a baby?" Ryan said, causing the room to burst into laughter.

Lizzie got cross, "You know it is not about babies and sweet messages and peace on earth. What about the people who feel excluded or shut out because they don't celebrate Christmas or whatever?" Lizzie pondered. "What about them?"

"So, they can't reasonably accept a simple Merry Christmas or Happy Hanukkah?" Ryan looked incredulous. "So, if they sneeze and we say 'bless you', will we get fined? Bless you means "good health" or "long life", by the way, which is where the saying originated. Or is their ignorance valued more than our supposed ignorance?"

"It isn't about messages of goodwill or good health. It is about religion and government crossing lines. It is about the future of our town. We need this. The rest of the country has already enacted these simple things, leave your religion in your home, in your church...or synagogue." She received a nod from Haverstein.

Pastor Dave stepped forward to speak, but the mayor, seeing the debate shift to his daughter, and the minister was not going to be well perceived. "This is about following current trends in government," he said quickly, relieved when Pastor Dave calmly retreated to his spot. "We are talking removing overt singularly focused religious tomes from our government halls. Halls that are to represent all people. We aren't removing mistletoe or stockings or traditions from your homes."

"You seriously want us to dispose of the town Christmas tree? Where does this stop?" a voice in the crowd bellowed.

Haverstein grumbled nervously in the back.

Mayor Faslee looked calm and steady in front of the crowd, his voice never wavering or rising. "We are merely suggesting we are respectful to those courting our town. I don't have to tell you the challenges we face at the municipal level, as well as how so many of you are struggling. This is a chance to dramatically improve our economy."

"What about the respect for those who have been here for generations, don't we matter anymore?" a woman asked.

"Of course," Faslee beamed. "You are who we are doing this for. Is it reasonable to make this brief exception? We can address the tree and other issues after the New Year. I look forward to a friendly discussion on all of these issues at our regularly scheduled meeting in January. For now, we must push forward. Businesses, if you own your space, the committee asks for your respect in welcoming new visitors, but you are not obligated. Government entities by this temporary decree will hereby be managed per stipulation."

The crowd stirred in a restless groan, but as the mayor, the council members, and the committee rose from their chairs and scampered into the hall behind the stage, the audience knew the discussion was over. From Ryan's vantage, very few in the town seemed to favor the changes, even if temporary, in any way.

He overheard one man telling his neighbor, "This is how it starts. It's just temporary…until it's not."

"And then they slam the next thing in. Put on a smile, say it's all for us, and push it through. If it were really for us, wouldn't we have a voice in it?"

"Should, but 'the people' can't think for themselves," the man sneered mockingly.

Ryan let out a breath as he observed the audience making their way out of the meeting room. He felt the mayor handled it the best he could, but that was one politician in a real hot seat.

Ryan skated through the crowd and met back up with Allison and Mr. Haverstein, who had been joined by Charlie Byrd and Pastor Magdalen. "Aren't you supposed to be meeting with Lizzie's team to prepare for tomorrow's event?"

Ryan wrinkled his nose, "I think I just got myself fired…or quit."

"You were pretty good in there. I thought poor Lizzie was going to explode," Allison couldn't help but to giggle.

"You bring logic into an emotional debate," Haverstein agreed.

"It's funny, while the faithful are attacked for not being science and logic-based, it is the arguments of the anti-crowd that generally are fueled by emotion and lack substance," Ryan shrugged.

"You keep this up, you will be in the pulpit for me one of these Sundays," Pastor Dave warned.

"Honored, but unworthy, Pastor Dave. My relationship is still very immature, though I learn and grow a little closer every day," Ryan smiled.

"Nonsense. Your strongest connection is with your heart, not your mind. And there, my boy, you have got it very well together," Charlie insisted.

Ryan gushed under the praise, "Thank you."

"What do we do now?" Allison asked.

"We remain steady in the season of miracles," Ryan smiled. "I need to send the story in, are we still on for this evening?"

Allison blushed, "We are."

Waiting for her to unlock the doors, he waved goodbye and nodded, "Gentlemen."

When Ryan showed up, he wore a funny expression on his face. Allison looked at him with suspicion. "What?"

"If you don't mind, I wanted to see if we could delay our date for about an hour to exact a little mischief," Ryan said, looking a bit sheepish.

Allison's look of expression intensified, "Mischief? What are you planning now?"

"Just had a little decorating in mind," Ryan said nonchalantly and led her to his Jeep.

Glancing in the back as Ryan helped her in, she noticed several full shopping bags an assortment of hardware. "What are we decorating?"

"You'll see!" he grinned and shut the door behind her.

Running over the driver's side, he slipped the Jeep in gear and wheeled it in a U-turn away from town.

"I'm not being kidnapped, am I?" Allison teased.

"We won't leave City Limits," Ryan promised and pressed the Jeep up a snowy hill.

"Where are we…ohh! So that's your plan? Hmm. The Robin hood of Christmas strikes again!" Allison's eyes grew as wide as her grin. "Are we decorating trees?"

"Better," Ryan replied as he wheeled into the pullout for the overlook.

Climbing out, he opened the rear hatch and began pulling plastic totes out of the Jeep.

"What do you want me to do?" Allison bounced alongside excitedly.

"Would you take these over to that little hill over there?" Ryan pointed to a berm just to the right of the split rail fence that marked the safety buffer for the viewpoint.

"Will do, boss!" Allison giggled and grabbed a tote in her hands, and marched it over to the hill.

With several totes pulled out of the SUV, Ryan began sliding an armload of planks out onto then snowy ground. Maneuvering around Allison, who returned for a second load herself, Ryan made his way over to the berm. Quickly, he began hammering the boards into a triangle, the angle facing town stood 90 degrees straight up.

As Allison plopped the final tote near him, she admired. "Wow, far more industrious than I had imagined."

The triangle erected into a sturdy base. Ryan walked the tallest plank over. "Would you mind holding this for me?"

"Sure," Allison nodded and grasped the board, pressing it against the flat edge of the triangle, which stood over the town of Twin Springs. "Like this?"

"Perfect," Ryan said as he closed in behind her and reached up to fasten the boards together with a series of nails.

Allison took her eyes off of the board for a moment to steal a glimpse of Ryan, concentrating on his work. His eyebrows dipped slightly, and his tongue creased the edge of his lips as he focused. She smiled at this man who had burst into action to take a stand for the little town of Twin Springs.

Not noticing Allison's study of him, he backed away. "One more," he sang, "Here, hold this upright about…here." With a horizontal board, he hammered it into position while Allison held it into place.

"Nice work, Mr. Talley," Allison admired. In the faint moonlight that escaped the tyranny of the clouds, the wooden cross loomed overhead, almost beautiful in its rough simplicity.

"We're not done yet," Ryan answered, studying the cross. Opening one of the tubs, he pulled out a large string of white LED lights. Out of another, he began unscrewing the ends of a pole. Sliding it out, he extended several sections.

"Telescopic pole, you are a clever boy," Allison noted.

"Thought about having the cross pre-strung, but the Jeep is too small," Ryan shrugged, hooking the end of the lights onto the v-shaped end of the pole. Tying a loop in the end of the light string, he maneuvered it up the tallest plank and gingerly slung the loop he had created around a nail he had set into the top of the plank.

"Should have had this when I was trying to put up my star," Allison said.

Ryan took his eyes off of his work and looked at her. Several moments passed as he looked like he was trying to calculate something. "But," he finally said, "Then maybe we wouldn't have met."

The simple statement took both of them aback for a moment. They looked into each other's eyes. Searching to read the mind of the other, they looked both hesitant, almost expectant. The thought of not being on top of a snowy hill, miles from the city, erecting a cross with this very woman suddenly seemed so foreign to Ryan. He felt he was right where he was supposed to be.

"Well, when you put it that way," Allison whispered back, her lips hovering close to his. "I should be grateful for rickety ladders…"

Ryan was lost in the moment. Allison's eyes danced in the moonlight, mere inches from his own. Her breath cut through the cold night air, making their connection intimately real and human. He wanted to, he thought about...Ryan shook himself back to their unfinished project, the end of the light string waving erratically in the air, clanging wildly against the cross.

"Oh," he exclaimed, leveraging the pole with his forearms to complete the task of stringing each arm of the cross. Laying the pole down, he knelt in the snow and angled in a nail at the base. Lacing the light string down the post, he snaked the cord onto the inside of the triangle, on the plank resting horizontally on the ground.

Suddenly, Allison frowned at the scene. "Uhm, I hope you brought a really long extension cord."

Ryan glanced towards town, "Yeah, you don't mind plugging it in real quick, do you?"

Allison shot a feigned scowl at him.

"I have a secret weapon," Ryan exclaimed, "Let's see what's in box number three." Unfastening the lid of the final tote, he slid it to the inside of the triangle next to the light string. Placing the string into the plastic tote, he connected it to the box that held a car battery.

"You are full of surprises," Allison admired.

"I have another battery charged and ready to go in the Jeep. Should last a couple of days each," Ryan replied.

"Well, until the town comes up and rips it all away," Allison muttered.

"It will make a statement for as long as it stands," Ryan replied. Taking a step back, he appreciated their handiwork. "Ready for a sneak peek?"

"Yeah!" Allison squealed, clapping her hands.

Ryan flipped a switch, and they were bathed in brilliant light.

"Aaaahh!!" Allison sang.

Walking to her side, he studied the cross. It was stunning. Almost too bright to look at from where they stood, but he knew it would be perfect from town.

Allison gave him a squeeze, wrapping her arm around him. Looking up at him, she marveled, "How did you come to bless this town…me?"

"An evil queen lured me here, or so you seem to have thought," Ryan quipped.

"I did think," Allison nodded. Slowly she added, "But I realize that was not the case. You have come from an entirely different path. His path." Pushing up on her tiptoes, she kissed him on the cheek.

Closing his eyes, he drank the affection in. A simple peck on his cheek flooded him with a warmth that spun him dizzy. Afraid to become lost in the moment's grasp, he smiled, "I think you might be right." Pulling himself free, he said, "We should probably get these off for now. Don't want the surprise taken away before its proper debut." As he walked over and flipped the switch off, he took a moment outside of Allison's view and let out a sigh. He tried in vain to collect himself, but a part of him was still swooning by her side, her lips pressed against his cheek.

Covering the tote back closed, he placed the hammer and nails in an empty one and began carrying it towards the Jeep. "Shall we complete our date in town?"

"We should," Allison sighed. "I kind of like it here, though. It is peaceful. Under the moonlight, the shadow of the cross, the twinkling lights of Twin Springs below…you. I like it here. I like you here."

Ryan set the tote he was carrying down and made his way over to her. Wrapping her in his arms, he hugged her tight.

"I'm so grateful for you being here and all you have done," Allison said.

"I haven't done anything. Not really."

"Yes, you have. You have given a broken girl hope. That's something no earthbound being has offered me in quite some time," Allison said.

"If you do the right thing, good things will happen. That is the mantra I have lived by. No matter how tough things get, I just keep being me. Having faith in God's path for me. Things can get pretty rough, but they always work out," Ryan said.

"I like that. It can be hard to stay positive sometimes," Allison said.

Ryan nodded, "I know. I've been down to my last dollar. I turned down corporate jobs because I knew it wasn't my path. You question, wonder if you are wrong or aren't interpreting His plan properly."

"What do you do?" Allison asked.

Ryan chuckled. "Pray. I knew for me. I was sitting in church one day. It hit me. Something was missing in my heart. I wasn't following my path. I like to write. I like to collect stories, give me people a medium to share theirs. Sure, I take jobs like Lizzie's to pay the bills, but then I get to freelance and find my own. Whether it is writing to share a charity group's project or just a story that I feel needs to be told."

"Like a tiny little gift shop fighting to keep a shabby little Nativity display?" Allison prodded.

"Allegedly. I believe the author of that one was "Anonymous"," Ryan shrugged.

Allison slapped him on the arm, "I know it was you, silly."

"I'll never tell," Ryan grinned. "Come on. I should probably feed you dinner."

Ryan led her to the Jeep and opened the door for her. Stowing the totes in the back of the Jeep, he started it up, took one last look at the cross, and headed back for town.

Skipping a formal meal, Ryan and Allison elected to stop at the coffee shop for cocoa to shake off the chill from their nighttime mission. Staring at Ryan over the steam rising from her cup, she eyed him mischievously.

Frowning, Ryan shuffled behind his own mug, "What?"

"I was wondering," Allison's eyes twinkled, "How many nighttime clandestine acts we are going to take part in."

Ryan looked thoughtful, "Well, I guess that depends on how far we have to go to overthrow the Faslee regime. The people must be freed."

"And then what? When the peace is brought to the land of Twin Springs...do you just move on?" Allison asked, suddenly struck that the question had very forward implications. "You don't have to answer that. I was just..."

Ryan was calm across the table. "I don't know. These past few weeks in Twin Springs, I've become pretty attached to this place."

Allison looked relieved by his response. "I think the town has become pretty attached to you. In such a short time, you have become part of the community. I think you have even created enemies. Impressive."

"No enemies," Ryan corrected. "Friends who don't realize it yet, that's all. Not sure about that Eric guy, though."

Allison giggled, "You have a very positive attitude. And, he's not really from here."

Ryan shrugged, "Control the things you can, don't sweat the ones you can't."

"You should start writing the little notes inside of fortune cookies," Allison said.

"More of a Hallmark greeting card guy, I think," Ryan smiled. "How about you? You give, and you give, to all those around you, even when you have little yourself," Ryan prodded.

"These are my people. My friends, my congregation, my community. We are supposed to take care of each other," Allison was offhand in her response.

"Yeah, but isn't it like what they say on the airplane, you have to give yourself oxygen before caring for the person next to you?" Ryan pressed.

Allison scowled, "You're one to talk. Didn't you say do the right thing, and the rest will fall into place? I am just doing the right thing; praying everything will fall into place."

Ryan nodded his head and quietly replied, "It will. You have an amazing spirit. People are drawn to you. Your heart is absolutely in the right place."

"The heart doesn't pay the bills," Allison scoffed and winced at how bitter her outburst was, surprising herself with her words. "I'm sorry, I don't know where that came from."

Ryan's face softened, "It's okay. You've had your hands full these past few weeks."

"Past few months…years," Allison admitted. "I love the store. I can't say it has exactly gone as planned."

"What does?" Ryan scoffed.

Allison wrinkled her nose, "Not sure. God's plan, maybe."

"That would be the only one," Ryan smiled.

"Are you having fun?" he asked. "With the store, I mean."

"Yes."

"Do you work hard? Good to the people in your store?"

"Yes, ...and, yes," Allison sighed.

"Then, you are doing great."

Allison's head drooped. Her eyes began to water.

Ryan cocked his head in concern, "What? What is it?"

"I...the store is in its last couple of days. I have until Christmas Eve to catch up on two month's rent. I can't do that. It's over," Allison admitted. "I'm sorry. Not much of a date, huh?"

Ryan reached across and touched her hands, which were folded on the table in front of her. "It has been a beautiful date."

"You're ridiculously sweet. Perhaps a poor judge of character. Not sure I'd follow your stock advice either, believing in my store so much," Allison offered a weak smile.

"I believe in all good things. Even if they might come to an end someday. All things do, eventually," Ryan retorted.

Allison shook her head, "You really are sweet. Thank you so much, for everything."

"My pleasure, Ms. Tancredi," Ryan said. Glancing at his watch, "I should walk you home...or to your car, I mean."

Allison twisted her lips, "I suppose."

"Could be a big day tomorrow," Ryan said.

"Every day seems to be," Allison laughed. Standing up, she held out her arm. "Sir."

Ryan nodded in acceptance and took her arm in his, "Madam."

Laughing, they sauntered out onto the sidewalk. Glancing up at the overlook, they could just make out the shape of the cross looming high over the town.

Ryan sunk into the wingback chair within the warm confines of the parlor. With the fire glow and the twinkling lights of the Christmas tree as the backdrop, Ryan racked his brain. He knew there had to be a solution for Allison. While a number of marketing ideas rattle through his head, none would have near the impact needed to stave off the impending end to her store.

He hardly noticed as Charlie came in, setting a tray of tea between them.

"You look pensive," the man said, pouring them tea.

Ryan startled slightly, "Oh, hi, Charlie."

"What's on your mind?"

"Trying to figure something out," Ryan admitted.

"Hmm. Sounds intriguing. Care to bend my ear?" Charlie asked, settling back into his chair.

Ryan studied his cup of tea and then looked across at Charlie. "Kind of like the Nativity, I want to find a way to reach out to others, to draw them in. For a good cause, not quite at the real Nativity level, but for reasons good enough," he explained.

"This cause in Twin Springs?"

"Yes, sir. It is."

Scratching his chin, Charlie inquired, "Wouldn't have anything to do with the lovely Ms. Tancredi?"

"Could be," Ryan grinned sheepishly.

"Tall order. She is marked for a quick dismissal I hear," Charlie warned.

"She is."

"Have any ideas?" Charlie asked, pouring a little more tea.

Wincing, Ryan replied, "Not really. There has got to be something that I can do."

"If it is meant to be," Charlie sipped from his cup. "Readers reacted to the Nativity article pretty well."

"They did. It's still getting hits. So is the "War on Christmas" article," Ryan agreed.

Charlie nodded, "Ah, that was a good one. Painted our town's little debate pretty well."

Ryan grinned, "I wanted to make the title "Mayor Cancels Christmas", but settled for "Town Ignites Over War on Christmas".

"Sure, Ms. Faslee was less than impressed."

"She fired me," Ryan admitted.

Chuckling, Charlie noted, "Yeah, that seems about right. Yet, you're still here."

"Story's not over. In fact, I think it has just begun."

Charlie looked impressed. "Offer stands. If Lizzie dumped you, you are more than welcome to stay, as our guest."

"I can pay...," Ryan began to protest.

"Nonsense. Merilee wouldn't hear of it...neither would I. Consider us friends," Charlie extended.

"I do."

"Good. I think Pastor Dave would have words with us if we did any different. He seems to like you," Charlie shared.

"I take both my new friendships as an honor," Ryan said in earnest.

"We haven't solved your dilemma," Charlie reminded.

Ryan cocked his head, "You know, we may just have."

Frowning, Charlie asked, "Oh?"

A little smile creased Ryan's lips, "I think we did."

Scratching his head, Charlie tried sorting through their conversation for a clue. "Ok, if you say so. Let me know if there is anything we can do to help."

"I will."

"Well, good night Mr. Talley. I wish you luck in your endeavor," Charlie said, getting up from his chair.

Ryan looked hard at the innkeeper, "If I am staying here as a friend..."

"Right," Charlie chuckled. "Good evening, Ryan."

"Goodnight, Charlie," Ryan replied.

Settling back, deep in thought, his wheels raced as a plan formed in his head. Pulling out his note pad, he began scratching away a "To Do" list to launch the next day.

Twenty One

Ryan woke to a beautiful day. Streaks of light darted into his room, making bright slashes on the walls and bed. He wondered if anyone had noticed the cross on the hill yet. He hoped Lizzie's crew would be so busy preparing for the new investor and enforcing their new council mandates. They would go through the day oblivious to it.

Not having time to worry about Lizzie and her fury, he jumped out of bed and got ready. He had a lot of pieces to put into motion for his plan to work. Grabbing his phone, he began dialing his contacts for the help that he needed.

After half a dozen calls and a frenzy of messages, he headed out to keep tabs on the committee's efforts. He laughed to himself as he moved down the sidewalk, prepared for a chilly reception inside City Hall.

Upon his first blush with Lizzie, he quickly found his suspicions to be on point. Lizzie froze for a moment when she saw him, offered a scowl with the raise of her eyebrow, and went on with her work. Catching her between doling out instructions to her people, Ryan boldly saddled up to her.

Bending down to try and get in her line of sight, he said, "You, know. I'm not your enemy."

Lizzie tried to walk around him, but Ryan was too agile. "I thought I fired you yesterday."

"Pretty sure you did," Ryan admitted.

"Then, why are you here?" Lizzie snapped. Stopping and looking directly at him.

"Because the story is still alive."

"What story, Ryan? The one where you made a fool in front of me in front of the Council…in front of the whole town?" Lizzie spat.

A small contingent to make their way past the two stopped and abruptly walked away, leaving the pair a wide berth.

"Lizzie, nobody was made a fool. There are those in this town that oppose a "scrubbing" of all things Christmas, all things religion," Ryan argued.

Lizzie huffed, "I can't let a few stuck in the past minds keep the town from moving ahead."

"That's just it. It isn't a few. It is a great majority," Ryan pressed.

"I don't have time for this," Lizzie looked at her watch to drive the point.

"If you don't have the backing from the majority, you will eventually fail. Would you rather have that open discussion in front of your friends, your community…or would you rather have that conversation at a later date with your investors? That is unless they take over, and no one who cares about this town has any say at all anymore," Ryan cautioned.

"What a bunch of nonsense," Eric spat. Overhearing the two arguing, he came to Lizzie's side.

"I'm sorry, did someone say the word 'money'?" Ryan retorted.

"Come on, Lizzie, we have big people work to do," Eric sneered, guiding Lizzie by the arm.

Lizzie stared at Ryan blankly as she allowed Eric to lead her away. Ryan chewed his lip, leaving them to their work. At least he could see by the scurrying of committee members that their plates were full in preparations for Eric's investor.

Walking through the town hall, Ryan slipped away from the workers and stole into the Mayor's office. Jonas Faslee was just hanging up the phone. Rubbing his face, he didn't see the reporter standing in front of his desk right away. When he did notice someone standing over him, he jumped slightly.

"Land sakes, man! You nearly gave me a heart attack," the mayor said, clutching his chest.

"Sorry about that. I wanted to see how you were holding up," Ryan said.

The mayor studied him for a minute. "Well, my daughter has been in a fuss since the town meeting…you caused quite a stir."

"Oh? I didn't intend…"

"Of course, you did. My phone has been ringing off the hook. Fury over the town's decision to appeal to our new investor has been exhausting, to say the least. Even Pastor Dave has called several times to discuss the matter," the mayor said, rubbing his head as if it ached.

"You do realize, the town would have been in a furor anyways. This is kind of a big deal," Ryan said.

The mayor frowned. "It doesn't need to be. It is just a temporary order."

"Come on, Mayor Faslee. You know as well as I do this is a slippery slope. Bad enough when the people of Twin Springs are leading the charge. What do you think happens when the new, high power money-backed troop comes crashing in? Making concessions that go against the town charter, your history…America's history…it leads to change that you had better want, because it won't stop there," Ryan warned.

Mayor Faslee groaned, rubbing his head even more intensely.

"Tell me," Ryan pressed, "Is this what you want?

The mayor sighed, looked out his window, and allowed the question to saturate his brain. "The town needs change, Mr. Talley. I don't know how long we will be a town if we don't do something."

"What about the people who voted you into office. Your neighbors. Pastor Dave. What do they all think?" Ryan asked.

Faslee maintained his gaze out of the window, staring at the morning sun dancing off the hills in the distance. "They probably don't realize how dour things are. I don't want to start a panic. Take your friend, Ms. Tancredi. Sweet girl, her business is dead. The salon next door is dead. Three other shops won't last the first quarter of next year. Their families will need an income."

"Who decides where that income comes from? The municipal government? A small committee fitting the town to their ideals? Some outside firm, who has it all sketched out in a spreadsheet?" Ryan argued.

"Better a begrudging income than none at all," Faslee countered, turning back to face the reporter. "Come on, Talley. What would you have me do? Allow the town to wither along with those shops out there? People will leave, they'll have to leave. Twin Springs won't exist, and some big investors will steamroll through anyways. This way, at least some people in town maintain a say in her future."

"If you had your choice…"

"I'm not sure I do," the mayor said, his voice soaked in fatigue and even a bit of sadness.

"Have faith, sir. Do the right thing, and things will fall into place," Ryan countered.

"Sounds like you've been talking to Pastor Magdalen."

"No," Ryan replied evenly, "Just the man Pastor Magdalen has been talking to."

Faslee nodded in understanding. Placing his hands in front of his face, he seemed deep in thought for a minute. "My daughter fired you after the town meeting, didn't she?"

"Ohhh yeah."

The mayor twisted his lips before he spoke, "I have a proposal for you."

"I'm listening."

"I like the way you think. You rationalize and then deliver responses that are honest and difficult to argue. I could use your balance in my ear," Faslee offered.

Ryan mulled the mayor's request. "What exactly are you asking?"

"How about I hire you on as my special counsel," Faslee suggested and then excitedly cautioned, "Just, uh, keep this between you and me. Lizzie would…"

Ryan smiled, "Yes, she would."

"It's settled then," the mayor said.

"Glad to help," Ryan replied and then thought of the spectacle he and Allison had created up on the hill. "There's one thing…"

Faslee looked up, "Yes?"

Shaking his head, Ryan replied, "Nothing. I'll let you know what the pulse of the town is."

"Thank you, Ryan. Glad to have had you around the past few weeks."

Ryan turned and placed a hand on the doorjamb, "Glad to have been here, sir."

Eric and Lizzie walked the town. City Hall had been scoured for any religious references. Entire plaques that had stood for a century or more had been pried off of walls. The last subtle remnants of Christmas references had been taken down. The halls seemed a bit sterile, but they were "safe" from any possible offense to even the most agnostic.

They were pleased that many of the shop owners had complied with the latest rounds of ordinance initiatives. The temporary injunction allowed for fines to be levied for those who did not follow suit. Lizzie and Eric noted each business that ignored the City Council's ban.

Reviewing their list, Lizzie read, "The hardware store- Jenkins is kind of old school. I'm not too surprised. The coffee shop kind of met the demands, we can let them pass. Allison and the deli. What are we going to do with those two?"

Eric laughed, "The little gift shop? We will own that in a few days. She is in the building that the investors want. We can work that into the conversation as part of the changes we are helping Twin Springs make."

"What about the deli?"

Eric bit his lip, "That is a tougher nut to crack. He owns his building. We have to let him die from attrition. We can just try to hasten that."

"How do we do that?" Lizzie asked.

"Well, we take away his street front parking. Make it for official city vehicles only, or the health spa's valet. He owns the building and an easement out front, not the road. We can raise his utility fees, audit him for coding, sandwich him between the businesses we are bringing in. He won't fit in anymore and hopefully sell. It might take a while, but I think we can single him out as a harmless anomaly. Not like anyone we bring in is going to buy from his store, really," the property developer stated.

As they looked across the street, the Nativity parked in front of the easement separating the deli from the building Allison was in. The gift shop stood out with Santa Clauses, lit Christmas trees, and a large porcelain manger scene set just inside one of the large ship windows.

Eric sighed, "That is a bit bold, isn't it?"

"I don't know what we can do about it," Lizzie argued.

"I have an idea," Eric said. "Come on." Leading Lizzie across the street, he strode directly to Allison's shop. Pushing through the front door, he scanned the shop. Spying Allison, he flashed his most potent smile and walked straight to her. Lizzie followed quietly in tow.

"Ms. Tancredi, Eric Farnham, I represent the owners of the building," he said, holding his hand out to her.

Allison cautiously accepted his handshake and replied, "I know who you are, Mr. Farnham." Glancing at Lizzie, she felt like some very anvil shoe was going to drop down on her at any moment.

"It has been my misfortune to have to extend all of those creditor letters to you. Must be very hard for you," Eric said. Spying Candace and

Maddie, he added, "And for your staff and their families."

Allison studied the man warily, "The shop has had better seasons. The town's initiatives have not exactly made it any easier."

"The heavyweight of growing pains can be stifling," Eric nodded, his voice dripping in empathetic honey. "Look, the reality is, the store is done. In three days, we take it over, and your season is done."

Allison's eyes darted to Candace, and Maddie, who had stopped to watch the conversation take place and replied, "I am afraid that appears to be the case."

Eric grinned, "What if that didn't have to be? I could extend your lease, at no cost to you until the end of the month. Maybe even a week or two in January to claim all of those clearance deals some find so enticing. Give your staff's families a better holiday, give you a chance to leave the store with a little seed money for your next venture."

"O-kaay," Allison cooed reluctantly.

"All we ask of you is to take down the Nativity. Maybe tone down your window displays just a bit. You can holiday it up within the interior of the store, heck, you can hold mass...or whatever it is you do in here," Eric said, his eyebrows raised, "What do you say? Do we have a deal?"

Allison chewed the bottom of her lip as she thought about the offer and the implications. She glanced at Lizzie, who was nearly squirming in glee from her partner's negotiating prowess. She thought of Candace and Maddie. She thought of how she was going to pay her house rent in January, a problem she hadn't wanted to think about it.

Watching her hesitance, Eric upped the offer, "How about just for today? You can put it all back tomorrow and keep it up until December 26th. Ms. Tancredi, most commercial landlords send you packing, but…it is Christmas."

Maddie rolled her eyes as the developer flashed a ridiculously toothy smile at her boss.

Allison's lips quivered, "O…Okay." Subconsciously, she bowed her head as if she had just struck a deal with the devil.

"Great!" Eric beamed. "I trust you can make the necessary changes in say… the next hour and a half?"

Allison sighed, "Yes. We'll take care of it."

"Good. I will place the necessary calls and put your eviction on hold," Eric said and spun away. "You have done the town a wonderful service."

Lizzie, who had remained strangely silent, offered a weak smile and turned to follow Eric out of the store.

The gift shop hung in a strange heavy silence after Eric and Lizzie left. Allison could barely look at her friends.

"Allie, you can't give in to them, can you?" Maddie asked.

"What else can I do? You guys can't work for free. I don't have a job. When the store closes in two days, I will have nothing. I won't be able to make my rent, my car payment," Allison replied, her voice pleading.

"I'm sorry, Allie. I didn't realize..." Maddie said.

Allison turned away, her head in her hands, she broke down in tears behind the check stand.

Candace started to speak, but she had no idea what to say. Looking at Maddie for answers, her friend just shrugged.

"It's okay, Allie. We'll help you," Maddie said.

Nodding, Candace walked over to the window with the porcelain manger scene and began moving the pieces to a shelf at the back of the store, which had been left bare by an artist who reclaimed their items earlier in the week.

Maddie began removing the evergreen garland and strung lights that hung in the windows. The gift shop, like the rest of Twin Springs, would succumb to the cleansing of Christmas. It didn't feel right. Maddie felt awful, but she knew it was a fraction compared to what Allison must have been feeling. Silently, she went about her work to make the shop in compliance.

The afternoon sun gleaming off the hills framed City Hall at the end of Main Street in dramatic fashion. Lizzie wished her investor was there now to see the spectacle that made Twin Springs so beautiful. She admired her compatriot, who had taken her arm and was proudly escorting her back to City Hall to make the final preparations for their visit. They would arrive not long before sunset, and they would have to survey the proposed sites quickly before light failed them completely.

"You are very smooth," Lizzie beamed.

Eric flashed a smug grin, "Are you kidding? I make multi-million dollar negotiations every day. That twit was putty in my hands."

"I'll admit, I was a little surprised with that offer. It seemed a bit generous. Are you really going to let her stay?" Lizzie asked.

Eric choked, "Of course not. I can't do that anyway. I promised the ownership group that I would clean the businesses out that didn't pay. There is no way she can make rent by the 24th. She'll be out that afternoon."

"I see. Nice ploy then."

"Sure. By the time she realizes it, the investor will have come. We'll have inked the deal, and the future of Twin Springs will be in good hands...our hands."

Twenty Two

Candace and Maddie had carefully deconstructed the window décor and placed some of the few remaining artists' displays in the two front windows. The Christmas trees in the front of the gift shop had all been wrangled back behind the check stand. It felt like the day after New Year's when they would normally put the decoration away until the next season. Knowing that Christmas was a few days away just made them feel weird. The store felt like it had been stripped bare.

"Looks like the Grinch has come through," Candace said, looking sadly at the front of the store.

"She has," Maddie said coolly.

Allison finished cleaning, hauled her ladder out of the back of the shop, and made her way outside. She had been numbly complying with the city's orders. She felt hollow, broken, and defeated.

The funny thing was, she felt more defeated now than when she knew her store was closing in three days. She couldn't figure out why she felt that way.

Setting the ladder against the building, she began dismantling the Nativity. With a heavy heart, she set the life-size figures of the wise men against the wall so she could get to the rest of the scene.

The door to Haverstein's deli opened, and the shopkeeper walked up to Allison. "My dear, is something wrong?"

Allison related her agreement with Eric and Lizzie as part of a stay of execution.

"You are sure you want to do this?" Haverstein asked.

"I'm sure I don't want to do this, but I am equally sure I really don't have a choice," Allison relented.

"I see," the deli owner said softly. "My dear, there is always a choice."

Allison put down the figure she was holding, "I wish I did. I'm just not so sure."

"If this is the way, this is the way. Let me take my latkes out, and I'll come and help you," Haverstein declared.

"You don't have to do that," Allison pleaded.

"I know," Haverstein grinned, "It is my choice."

Allison couldn't help but allow a chuckle to breakthrough her melancholy as she watched the infectiously positive man disappear into her store. Sighing, she lofted the wise man back into her arms and carried him over the wall with the other two.

Sadly, she picked the baby Jesus delicately out of his manger. She looked at the little plastic baby in her arms. How an innocent baby could make such alarm. Could make people protest in ire. Demand removal of any signs of him.

She took a moment dejectedly surveying the scene. Her shop looked empty, forlorn, void of character. Her gaze moved down Main Street, following it all the way to City Hall. The town of Twin Springs had been stripped to sterility - cold, uninviting, without heart. Her town, her community, her country was slipping away. She was helping.

Turning to her Nativity, she looked up at the star that who's trial to place at the peak kicked off the season so dramatically. It made her think of Ryan. Suddenly, she looked up to the hills. The setting afternoon sun caught the cross, splaying its shadow across the hillside, extending toward town like an outstretched hand. The shadow felt like it was driving the cross into her heart. Not in a sinister fashion, but in more of a beseeching way, imploring her to reconsider.

All at once, she was awash in sadness, anger at herself, and then confident defiance. She looked at baby Jesus in her arms and placed him back in his crude, straw bed.

"No," she cursed to herself. "No. I won't do it!"

She hadn't realized Mr. Haverstein had reappeared and watched her brief soliloquy. Simply smiling, he held up his hand, "You made the right choice." Without another word, he retreated to his deli, allowing her to make amends to herself.

After reassembling the Nativity, she burst into the store. "Back! Put it all back! I don't care what the rest of the world does. Christmas is staying at my store!"

Despite having gone through the effort of stripping it all down and reconfiguring the window displays, Candace and Maddie were happy to do it all over again.

"That's my girl!" Maddie declared.

Candace just smiled and instantly went to work, removing the window displays to make room for the porcelain manger and Christmas trees out front.

Their guests were due to arrive any minute, and everything was perfect. Lizzie looked around City Hall. Everything was spotless. New modern décor replaced the old pictures, memorials and plaques that had previously adorned the building and the grounds.

Her friends Tiffany and Annabeth, stood by her side. Each was immaculately dressed, pearl strands slung around their necks, the nails freshly manicured. Eric was impeccably attired and looked ready for action.

"This is it," Lizzie beamed.

"We're ready," Eric nodded confidently. His cellphone buzzed in his pocket. Pulling it out, he said, "I should check this, could be them."

Pressing the button, he answered the phone. After a few moments, he replied, "I see. That is very unfortunate, Ms. Tancredi. I offered you a very, very attractive deal. I am at a loss why you would even consider reneging on it. This will reflect extremely poorly on your situation. I am afraid immediate legal action will have to be imposed. If you make it until Christmas Eve, you will be lucky. Yes, I am very disappointed. What…"

Eric slowly lowered the phone and closed the call. Sliding the phone back into his pocket, he looked at the expectant and already fuming Lizzie. "It seems as though the gift shop is not in the order as we would have liked."

Lizzie looked like she would shoot flames from her eyes, "What about your superior negotiating. Putty in your hands, you said!"

"How can you reason with these zealots? That is why their kind is dying. She is finished. She'll be out as soon as I can produce the paperwork," Eric shrugged.

"That doesn't help us today, now does it?" Lizzie snapped.

Eric waved her off and then straightened up as a limousine pulled in front of City Hall, "We'll be fine. It just allows us to impress upon them on we are shaping the future of Twin Springs and how the old- like her- are on their way out."

Pulling themselves together, they donned confident smiles as they walked down the town hall steps to greet their guests. A man in a dark suit scurried out of the car and opened the rear door.

Eric's guest stepped out from the limousine and, followed by her entourage, waited for her hosts to descend to her.

As they approached, their smiles faded, and Lizzie's eyes lifted from Eric and shot past, over his head. "What on earth is that?"

Ryan felt like a sniper, positioned up on the hillside, overlooking the entire town of Twin Springs. Binoculars against his face, he waited for the car to arrive. He could hardly contain himself as he watched the limousine pull up at the base of the City Hall steps. He watched Lizzie, and her arrogant gang descended to meet their false savior. Through the powerful lenses, he could see the smiles pasted on the committee's faces.

With his free hand, he reached down to the box he was squatting next to. Flipping the switch, he was suddenly bathed in light. High above him, the mast of the cross sang through the early evening sky like a visual chorus. It called down to the town, screaming, "I am here. We are here. He is here. And we are all here to stay".

Through the glasses, he saw the troop freeze, nearly stumbling down the steps as their gazes were drawn from their precious investor to the hills above town. Directly above one of the two sites proposed by the town to the investor, was the mighty cross, ablaze in lights, standing defiant, a protective vigil over the town.

He read Lizzie's lips, watched her struggle to compose herself. Wrangling her scowl back to the painted-on smile, she strode, hand outstretched to greet her guest. He watched as Eric shot an angry look up towards the hill.

"Merry Christmas Twin Springs," Ryan muttered and sealed the lid on the plastic tote holding the battery and timer switches.

Lizzie tried to pry her eyes off of the brilliant cross hung above the head of the investor and the entire town. She forced a calm smile and approached the resort developer with as much grace as she could muster.

The investor could sense something was off and eyed Lizzie and her companions with a slight air of suspicion before accepting her welcome. Instinctively, Lizzie guided her away from the cross and led her towards Town Hall.

Eric stuttered, trying himself to levee the correct action. Unfortunately, he knew in the failing light. They had little choice but to press on. Glancing at Lizzie, he attempted to redirect her with his eyes. Lizzie resisted, forcing him to be more blatant, "I'm afraid our reception will have to wait until our site visits are over."

"Maybe we should take the back way, it is really lovely," Lizzie offered weakly.

The investor looked impatient and huffed, "Really, Ms. Faslee. I have no time for tours. I merely want to assess the locations and send my designers out for their review. Mr. Farnham is asking for a healthy financial obligation, and I must personally approve. Your little town is...quaint. I understand your plans, and I am sure one of my properties would undoubtedly make them a reality, but only under my say."

Lizzie looked like a child who had just been scolded, "Yes, of course."

Reluctantly, she turned around and faced the whole of Twin Springs downtown. The cross a gleaming presence in the hills above the town was impossible to miss.

The investor stopped in her tracks, Eric and Lizzie nearly colliding with her backside. "Oh dear," she gasped, clutching her chest as if she had just discovered a slain body. "My, how puritanical. Is that monstrosity always…ablaze like that?"

Lizzie stammered, "Some prank, surely maintenance will have it removed by morning."

"So, where is this first piece of property?" the investor asked.

"Uhm, just at the base of the base of that hill," Eric pointed wearily at the bottom of the overlook.

"I see," they sneered disapprovingly. "I'll have my driver follow one of your people then?"

Eric nodded eagerly, "Yes, ma'am."

"Alright. You two come with me, you can narrate our journey, and you can regale me as to why your town is worthy of a signature resort," the investor commanded. Eric and Lizzie trailed her into the back of the limousine while Annabeth followed Tiffany to her car.

"The town is clean at least, I suppose," the investor commented as they pulled away from the front of City Hall. "You did a decent effort on your Art Walk thing. I have an artist you should talk to. His work may be a bit too forward for your little town, but it may be the type of change you need around here."

"We already have a major part of the downtown landscape ready for a major renovation. The building on the left, is slated for a Hadid inspired rebuild," Eric pointed out of the side window, forgetting momentarily about his earlier ruse failing.

The investor stared out of the window, frowning. Looking toward the Nativity, she asked, "Was that building vandalized? And what on earth was that shop with the gaudy décor?"

"A mere cog in the transformation of Twin Springs," Eric assured. "We have removed her lease, and she will be gone well before the New Year."

The investor scowled, "Is this the sort of culture that is pervasive here? And the hovel next door, is that going away too?"

"The deli? Harmless really. It is quite consistent with the ethnic flavors of Manhattan," Eric informed.

"There is a reason there are no Hildebrand resorts in New York," the investor snapped. Tapping a button near her seat, she called out, "Henry, I believe I have seen quite enough."

The vehicle slowed and wheeled a U-turn in the middle of Main Street. Desperate, Eric burst into a flurry of rationale, "Twin Springs is on the verge of evolution, a rebirth. And you, your fabulous Hildebrand Resort, will be the cornerstone. You can shape the town in the mold of your liking, especially if you are among the first."

The investor stared at Eric, her expression unwavering. "I could build a resort in the desert, and a beautiful, refined oasis city would blossom outside of its walls. But this, this is pushing through a culture of simple, backward beliefs. I have no time for such complications."

"Twin Springs needs the touch, the wisdom of someone of your impeccable design and forward-thinking," Lizzie pleaded.

"Yes. Yes, I would say it does," the investor snarled. "So does Cleveland, but I am not going to put my name on it."

The car stopped in front of City Hall. "Good evening," the investor said, looking at the door nearest to Lizzie.

Eric paused, but the stone face of the investor told him this was a battle lost. Stepping out of the limousine, the developer watched the long black car pull away. He scowled down Main Street, despising the mysterious cross and the simpleton girl who owned that stupid gift shop. He shook his head, feeling dizzy at the massive amount of money, his money that just drove down the street and out of this crummy little town.

Lizzie was silent, her blood too beyond its boiling point. "It's all that Allison's fault."

"Perhaps," Eric said blankly. "Truth is, the investor is right. This town needs a more thorough cleansing."

"It is one investor. There will be others," Lizzie said.

Eric shot Lizzie a cold look. "You don't get it. Hildebrand is like the sun in the solar system of wealthy investors. If she laid down her resort here, others would flock in overnight."

Seeing Lizzie's faith falter, Eric reassured, "You know, you're right. Just the battle, not the war. We will press on. Clear out the riff-raff and bring in more investors."

Lizzie nodded, feeling exhausted suddenly.

"Come on, let's get a hot cup of coffee or something," Eric put his arm around Lizzie. He knew he had to have her to continue his raising the value of the town and selling off its pieces as richly as he could coax from its investors.

Ryan knew the cross would raise the stakes even higher with Lizzie and her group. Before he had even flipped the switch to light up the cross, he had already written a draft for a follow-up article on the town's "war over Christmas". Pastor Magdelan had offered to defend the cross, tying it up with court documents preventing the city from removing it on religious rights grounds. It was a losing case, but winning was irrelevant. The process would let it stand until after the holidays.

Protests on either side had already begun. When Ryan arrived at City Hall, the building had a different energy. It wasn't just the Transformation Committee. A few reporters milled about, people Ryan had seen at church added to the mix. Lizzie's committee seemed to have swollen as well. New faces scurried along with Lizzie and her friends.

Lizzie glared at Ryan as he entered. He tossed back a charming smile as if she had just welcomed him with a friendly "good morning". Ignoring him, she turned her back and focused on her group. Eric Farnham seemed to have had command of the committee.

Mayor Faslee saw Ryan and waved him over furiously. Ducking down the hall, Ryan followed him to the mayor's office. "The town is in an uproar. Did you see the cross up on the hill?"

Ryan studied the mayor for a moment and nodded, "I saw it."

"This whole town versus Christmas, town versus religion thing has exploded."

"It seems. What's your take on all of this?" Ryan asked.

The mayor shrugged, "To be honest, I don't really mind it. I certainly don't have a problem with people decorating. The cross kind of looks cool up there. But then there's the other side. People want the government to remain agnostic. That big resort developer pulled out of her deal. Lizzie blames the cross…and your friend Allison."

"Did you meet her?" Ryan asked. "Seemed kind of like a crank."

Faslee couldn't help but let out a chuckle. "I guess I kind of thought the same."

The mayor leaned in, "But as for me, this is a PR nightmare. What do I do?"

Ryan looked thoughtful. "For the most part, I'd stay out of it. That's just the thing, issues on morality, culture…religion- they aren't for the government to decide anything. The government is the voice of the people. What do your people say?"

"I don't know. Lizzie and her group are on one side, the rest of the town is on the other. It's hard to hear the real voice. Do I need to hold some kind of vote on it?" Faslee asked.

"Not in a formal sense, no. Trust me, in the end, the town will let you know where they stand. Frankly, if you align with one side or the other, you are doomed. You, Mr. Mayor, play Switzerland on this one," Ryan suggested.

The mayor looked unsure of Ryan's direction. "The town is going to explode in the meantime. Lizzie is going to explode. I'm honestly not sure which is worse," though very serious, the mayor couldn't resist laughing at the notion of daughter's ire.

"Hang in there. I can put a quote in for you as being the voice of the people. You go to church. You adhere strictly to the laws of the land. At the end of the day, you will uphold your town's wishes," Ryan said.

"Ooh, that's good. Thanks."

"I'll keep you in the loop," Ryan said. Turning to leave, he paused and addressed the mayor, "You know, it's likely to get worse before it gets better."

"Afraid of that," the mayor nodded.

Eric pulled Lizzie aside. Looking up and down the hallway to ensure they were alone, he whispered intently, "I have something in the works. It will deter any investor visits for the next week, but it will also finally force the non-compliant shop owners' hands."

"Oh?" Lizzie grinned. "What is it?"

"I think I'll leave you in the dark on that one. No need to make you complicit in the details," Eric said. "But, it should make shopping along Main Street…a little bit difficult for the next few days."

Just then, Tommy Trulia burst into City Hall. The maintenance man darted into the mayor's office. Soon after, Tommy Trulia scurried back out with a paper in his hands, and his cellphone stuck to his head.

"What's going on?" Lizzie asked.

"During an inspection on the building that the investment group is buying, we found a pipe burst under the street. We're going to have to close off Main until we get it repaired. It will probably take a few days. Terrible timing with the holidays coming!" Tommy shared before returning to his phone call.

Lizzie shot Eric a shrewd look. Shrugging, the real estate broker grinned and walked away.

"Are you serious?" Allison sighed with her hands on her hips, "For how long?"

Tommy shook his head, "I'm sorry, Allison. We have to bring concrete cutters in, rip a swath from one side of the street to the other. I don't know...couple days?"

Allison dropped her head, "That will take us all the way to Christmas Eve!"

"We'll go as fast as we can, I promise."

"Thanks, Tommy," Allison said.

As he left, Allison turned to Candace and Maddie, "Well, that should just about do it."

"Oh, Allie," Candace cooed, giving into the imminence of the situation.

"Might as well start calling in the artists to pick up their stuff, cut the final commissions," Allison said. "No harm in keeping the doors open with their stuff here, though, with Main closed, I don't expect much."

"I'll make the calls," Candace offered.

"Maybe the workers will need to buy Christmas gifts," Maddie hoped weakly.

Allison smiled at her friend. The season's news has been rough the whole way. This latest had barely marred her. "Once all the air is already out of the balloon, another hole in it won't make a difference."

"You have been hanging around writer boy way too much," Maddie said.

"Yeah," Candace laughed, "You can both go into business together, making fortune cookie messages."

"Better leave the positive ones to him," Maddie teased.

Allison retaliated, tossing a soft-stuffed snowball at her from a bucket on the counter. Socked in the forehead by the toy, Maddie stuck her tongue out at her friend.

Twenty Three

R yan submitted a pair of articles and left the bed and breakfast to report to Mayor Faslee. As he turned the corner onto Main Street, he found the road closed and line cut through the center of the road, almost directly in front of Allison's shop. Curious, he made his way to the gift shop. As he reached the door, a pair of artists emerged, each had their arms full of their crafts, griping about having hauled it all three blocks away.

Holding the door open for them, he ducked inside the shop. He found the ladies spreading out the thinning displays. "Now what is going on?" Ryan asked.

Maddie looked over at him and put down the handmade ornaments she was sorting. "I'll give you one guess."

Allison rolled her eyes, "Oh, come on. You think Lizzie had a hand in centuries-old pipes having issues in the cold weather?"

Understanding, Ryan nodded. "Might be more likely than you think. It probably wasn't Lizzie, but her partner in crime, Eric Farnham. He arranged the inspection of the building for the new buyers. Let me guess. They said the work would take until roughly the 26th to complete?"

Allison stared blankly at Ryan and wrinkled her nose, "Well…yes, actually."

"The pipes may have needed some work, but the timing I have no doubt, was aimed directly at you," Ryan sighed.

"Retaliation for me not removing my decoration and the Nativity," Allison assumed.

"Probably," Ryan nodded.

"Nice work on the cross," Maddie said. "I heard that chased away one of their investors."

"Their biggest," Ryan concurred.

Candace chirped in, "I think it's pretty."

"Yeah," Allison nodded, "It is."

"There is something powerful with it calmly presiding down on us," Maddie added.

"Well, it will be there until the city gets the circuit judge to set a date," Ryan said.

Allison looked at the writer, "Ryan, I wanted to tell you, I appreciate everything you have done for me…for the store. But I think the bell has finally tolled."

Ryan studied Allison for a moment and then her employees, a mischievous gleam in his eye.

Glancing at his wrist, "It's still the season of miracles according to my watch."

"I'd say a bus pulling up outside would be a miracle that might save the store for a day or two, but that can't even happen now," Allison remarked, nodding toward the street.

"Hmm...that does make it a bit more challenging. I think that is what makes faith so powerful. Even when the chips are down, and you can't see a way, that is when our faith sees its biggest test," Ryan said.

"You are an interesting man," Allison said, admiring his perseverance.

Excusing himself, he left for his follow up with Faslee.

"I like him," Candace piped up.

Maddie and Allison turned to their friend.

"He reminds me of Allie, before the store struggled," Candace shrugged.

Allison stared out the window, watching Ryan walk away, contemplating her friend's words.

The knocking on the door frame made Mayor Faslee nearly jump. "Oh, Ryan," Faslee raised his eyebrows and sighed.

Grinning, Ryan inquired, "That good of a day, huh?"

"It's been a doozy. I guess it wasn't enough to have my own daughter in one ear, half the town in the other, warring over the town's history, Christianity, Christmas decorations, and the Constitution. Now I have every business owner on

Main Street up in arms over the road closure," the mayor related.

"That's a handful," Ryan agreed. "Have you developed accommodations for the businesses?"

Faslee frowned, "What do you mean?"

"Well," Ryan explained, "Their customers are struggling to reach the businesses on Main, provide access, parking...heck, take a page out of Lizzie's book and provide valet."

"Hmmm. That's not bad. We could use the stretch right as you come into town as a big parking area, make the side streets more accessible and amenable to parking..." the mayor rubbed his chin.

A shrewd look crossed Ryan's face, "I remember a Christmas tree farm not too far from here. They had these two carriages with draught horses. They would just loop the parking lot to the tree areas carrying families around the farm. Make the misfortune of shutting down Main into a charming, seasonal feature."

Mayor Faslee snapped his fingers, "I like it! You're talking about Murphy Farms. I went to school with Johnston Murphy. I bet he'd do it for me."

"Send the word out to the businesses. Have them post it on their websites. The inconvenience becomes a draw," Ryan added. "Now, about the war. You're going to have to choose a side. A publisher of mine once told me, let my readers know where I stood. I was afraid, knowing I would lose some. I did. But those I kept, were even more vested in me. My numbers actually grew because people knew where I stood."

"Which half do I choose?"

Ryan grinned, "I'd say the right half."

Faslee stared blankly down the hall. Ryan understood what was running through the mayor's mind – his daughter.

"There's another flaw in your thinking," Ryan informed the mayor.

"Oh?"

"The battle isn't between two halves of the town. What you are hearing is a tiny vocal minority. The funny thing is, if pressed, half of that vocal minority doesn't believe in what they are saying," Ryan replied.

Faslee looked confused.

"It's popular to come down on all things American, conservative, religious. There's big money, mass media. Trends are fleeting. Genuine, solid core beliefs are lasting," Ryan said, preparing to leave the office. "I don't think you really need to struggle to figure out where you stand."

Ryan was feverishly scribbling notes in his pad when Charlie entered the parlor. "You sure are hard at work," the hotelier said, settling into the chair opposite of the writer.

Looking up, Ryan smiled, "Been a busy few days."

"Our little town is front-page news," Charlie said, spinning a paper down on the little table between them. "Not often is Twin Springs the talk in the city."

"That's just scraping the surface. The article hit national top 10 digital news in the past hour," Ryan acknowledged.

"The picture of Twin Springs with the cross lit in the background is impressive," Charlie said.

"Symbolic within a symbol. Unfortunately, the fight isn't Twin Springs' alone. We are seeing an attack on Christmas around the country. Christmas trees are remanded holiday trees, 'Happy Holidays' is called instead of 'Merry Christmas' with the exception of a rebellious few. Schools are forbidden to put on performances, color Santa Clauses or make paper wreaths," Ryan replied.

"I still remember doing that stuff as a kid. Good memories..." Charlie drifted off for a moment.

Ryan nodded, "A big part of my childhood, too. We didn't all do that. My friend drew things for Hanukkah instead. Those are all taboo. It's okay to learn about and celebrate other cultures now, just not those who belong to the evil majority."

"Maybe articles like this will make an impact."

"I hope so. I am a little surprised they got picked up, even more, that they put it on the front page," Ryan said humbly.

"There was another article here. Not quite front page with the town war over Christmas, but pretty impactful in and of itself," Charlie said.

Ryan jumped in his seat. "They ran it!" Snatching the paper from the table, he flipped through rapidly until he found the small article with the photo of the manger. His grin could not be suppressed.

"Does Ms. Tancredi know about this?"

Ryan shook his head, "No. It's part of a larger surprise."

"That what you have been so hard at work on?" Charlie mused.

"It is. Not sure what effect it will have, really," Ryan said.

"All you can do is try," Charlie offered.

Twenty Four

R yan woke early and headed directly for Main Street. He couldn't help but get a little excited when he heard bells jingling in the distance. Mayor Faslee's connection must have come through. Making the long loop from the Byrd's Nest, he found himself at the edge of town.

The city crews had plowed a wide swath for parking where the highway dumped into Main Street. Just past the construction barriers, two teams of horses were attached to carriages. Ryan watched the horses being brushed by their handlers. They shuddered and stamped their feet as though they couldn't wait to get going.

The coach driver noticed Ryan approaching and shrugged, "They love their job."

"Johnston Murphy," the man released his hand, which had been stroking the side of the massive horse's neck. "This is Frank, and the one alongside is Myrrh."

"Glad you could come out, I'm Ryan Talley." Ryan extended his hand to shake the farmer's.

"Jonas Faslee mentioned you. Kinda caught up in the town fracas?"

"Don't stir the pot, the truth will never rise to the surface," Ryan grinned.

"Well said," Johnston nodded. "Just about to take the boys on the first loop to get them acclimated, want to come?"

Ryan noticed a little hatchback navigating the parking area the town had set up. "Mind if we wait for one more passenger?"

Seeing Allison lumber out of her car, pulling a hat over her hastily brushed hair, the carriage driver acknowledged, "Not a bit."

"Ryan?" Allison called as she collected her bearings. "What's going on?"

"The town needed a solution to its main thorough fair being closed, solution delivered."

Allison looked suspicious, "You did this?"

"Merely planted the idea. Mayor Faslee and the good farmer Johnston Murphy are the ones who graciously pulled it off," Ryan informed.

Tipping his hat as he helped Allison into the carriage, Murphy welcomed her, "Ms. Tancredi. My wife loves your store."

"Thank you," Allison said, still trying to fully comprehend the scene.

Ryan snuggled in next to her. "Shall we?"

Allison shook her head in admiration for what this visitor had brought to her town. "This is nice. I like it."

With a light tap on the reigns, the pair of draught horses began to steadily pull, charting a course, they and their farm mates would follow the rest of the day.

Gentle snow danced and sparkled all around them as the bells jingled and hooves crunched along the snow. The streets were quiet, with shop owners just arriving for the day, only the coffee shop open for business so early in the morning.

"It seems so peaceful this way. No cars rumbling through, the street covered in snow, just the soft jingle of the sleigh. I think maybe we should keep it this way," Allison cooed.

"Something to be said for simpler times," Ryan agreed.

When the carriage stopped in front of the gift shop, Allison was hesitant to get out. The peacefulness of the morning streets, the gallant company, the classic spirit of the horse-drawn carriage – it was easily the sweetest part of what had been a very taxing holiday. Still, the wagon paused at her door, and the driver turning expectantly towards his passengers, she felt urged to surrender her seat.

Ryan hopped out first. Holding out his hand, he helped Allison down. Exchanging a nod with the farmer, the jingle of sleigh bells once again took chorus in the air.

As the carriage continued with its maiden voyage, Allison spun to face Ryan. "Thank you. For everything you have done."

"I haven't done anything," Ryan protested modestly.

"Yes. Yes, you have," Allison responded in earnest. The air between them hung awkwardly for a moment. Allison twisted uncomfortably and suggested, "Come in for a fairly average cup of coffee?"

"Average would be better than half the cups of coffees I have ever had," Ryan conceded. "I accept."

Turning the key, Allison pushed into the gift shop. "You know, if Lizzie was behind the street closure, this is a going to be another giant thorn in her side."

"I know. What can she say? The farmer is a friend of her dad's, and he came at his bequest," Ryan shrugged.

Allison wrinkled her nose, "I think that will only make it worse."

"Maybe that's the point. The world around her, her world, is not in agreement with her," Ryan acknowledged.

"Think that will work?"

"Probably not. At least, not a first. Who knows after that?" Ryan guessed.

Pouring coffee grounds into the filter, Allison called over her shoulder, "How about her dad? You seem to have the mayor under your guidance."

"I think he is lost somewhere in the middle. He has good solid ideals. The town is in trouble, and the Transformation Committee made some valid points. The direction and implementation are just counter to the culture of the town, and he knows it. He just doesn't have any other ideas either," Ryan replied.

"And he hopes the new blood will reassure re-election in case the town loses confidence in him if things don't improve," Allison understood.

"Pretty much."

"Then how did you get his ear?" Allison prodded.

"I just appealed to the man I thought I saw inside of him. I could tell that he cared for the town. While he did face time for the transformation, he didn't carry it as he did when he would talk about the legacy of Twin Springs," Ryan said.

Allison handed him a cup of coffee. "I see. You sure about that?"

Ryan sipped his cup thoughtfully. "Yeah. I think so."

"Well, here's to those with a little Christmas left in their hearts," Allison said, clinking her mug against Ryan's.

"I think there are far more than you think," Ryan answered, holding his coffee mug in the air.

"Oh my gosh! Did you see this?" Candace asked, flopping a paper on the checkout stand in front of Allison.

Maddie looked up from her work at the sound of the paper smacking against the counter.

Allison hesitantly picked the paper from the counter and read the front page. "The War on Christmas" in small suburb Twin Springs had captured the attention of the media around the state and the nation. "Hmmm. Our little town has made front-page news," Allison remarked.

"And by Ryan Talley, no less," Candace beamed. "But that's not all. Flip to page four."

Allison rustled the paper until she found the interior page. "Teacher's Union is threatening a strike in the city school district."

"After that," Candace instructed.

"Nativity Weathers Storm", Allison read. "The rustic manger scene, a long-standing tradition, maintains its annual vigil outside of the Humble Beginnings Gift Shop in the recently beleaguered town of Twin Springs.

The centerpiece of a smoldering feud in the town over Christmas and any reference to the holiday celebrated by over ninety-six percent of the population has come under fire from members of that ninety-six percent on behalf of the four percent who have yet to identify or complain themselves.

Allison Tancredi, who, along with her grandfather, handcrafted the structure and enlisted local artists to create the beautifully faithful recreation of the scene in Bethlehem, has displayed her manger in front of her store for years. Only this season, the commemoration has come under fire as the town struggles to bring in new `investors who propose to revitalize the town, but also alter its two-century long heritage.

The Humble Beginning Gift Shop has served the community by celebrating local artisans and craftsmen while serving families throughout the region. Ms. Tancredi shares that the pressures imposed on her since displaying the Nativity scene have crippled her business, and she fears this year may be her shop's last. Despite the adversity, Tancredi has refused the city's assistance in return for dismantling the Nativity.

At one point, the city even resorted to confiscating the scene. Somehow, during the night, the Nativity found its way back to its site along Main Street. On display now, the Nativity can be seen between the gift shop and Haverstein's Deli at 426 Main Street. It stands a defiant gem in a rough sea of societal growing pains."

"You're famous-ish!" Candace squealed.

"Man, that article is a few weeks too late," Maddie said. "It was nice, but what good is it going to do now?"

Allison looked thoughtful, "My story has been told. Maybe others who have wavered on taking their Nativity, their cross, their tree down will know they aren't alone."

"And know that you stood up and lost your...," Maddie started and stopped, horrified at the implication she was about to make.

Allison surprised her and laughed, "It's true. But you know, I would rather remain true to myself and my beliefs and fail than bend to those who would have me change."

"Funny," Candace scoffed. "I thought that is what America was all about."

"Used to be," Allison answered softly.

"Know what? I'm glad I was here with you this year Allie," Maddie declared.

"Me too!" Candace joined.

Allison swelled as she accepted the praise from her friends. "Thanks, guys, that means a lot."

The sound of sleigh bells ringing in the air brought joy to Ryan's ears. It gave him a little bounce in his step. He noticed others had a bit more cheer when they greeted those they passed.

All but Eric Farnham and Lizzie Faslee. Ryan ran into the pair standing on the step of Town Hall, staring at the festive turnabout on Main Street. Lizzie glared at Ryan, knowing he had a hand in this new development.

Ryan grinned at the duo, "Kind of festive, isn't it?" Walking past, he skipped his way up the steps and into the building.

Faslee was just finishing a call when Ryan stuck his head in. For the first time in days, the mayor looked calm and happy. "The carriages are a huge hit. The business owners have been calling all morning. They love it."

"It's nice. I think you might have to work out a deal to have them here every year," Ryan suggested.

"Maybe," the mayor agreed. "I think Lizzie and Eric are a little miffed. Kind of threw a wrench in their little plan for revenge on Ms. Tancredi's shop."

"Not much they can say, nothing overtly religious about a horse-drawn carriage, even if some of us conjure Christmas scenes in our heads anyway," Ryan conceded.

"I read the articles. Thank you, I think," the mayor sighed.

"Everything in there was factual," Ryan defended.

Faslee nodded, "I saw that. Kind of made me wonder how we got to this point."

Shrugging, Ryan answered, "People are scared. Our world is in a time of uncertainty. Some feel this dictates change. Sometimes they're right. Sometimes they're not. Those who want change see historical values, the church, and even family values as roadblocks to change."

The mayor rubbed his eyes. "I'm glad you're with us, Talley."

"Pleasure to be here, sir. Just for transparency, I, uh…I'm not quite done with my efforts," Ryan admitted.

"Oh?"

"I have one more little thing planned to bring light to the issue. A call for those who are willing to stop and see what is happening. Not just here in Twin Springs, but around the country. From there, we'll see what happens."

The mayor raised an eyebrow, "Don't suppose you're going to share with me what this plan is, are you?"

Ryan smiled wide, "No. To be honest, not sure it will have any impact. Just kind of came to mind, and I thought I would see how it played out."

"Alright. I guess I will see what you have cooked up along with everyone else," the mayor said.

"Thanks. I better get going, I have a few more things to get into place." Ryan made his exit and left the town hall building.

Out on Main Street, the downtown area had noticeably more activity than any time Ryan could remember. The horse-drawn carriages made their loops around the cordoned off the thoroughfare. Johnston Murphy had more horses brought down, as well as drivers to give the teams regular breaks throughout the day.

Even Allison's shop had a steady flow of shoppers circulating through bags anchored on arms as they left the store. In the center of Main Street, the gash carved into the road was void of activity; the construction crew had to halt their efforts to wait for a replacement part that wasn't to arrive until after the holiday.

In the meantime, the construction crew had broken into a mad snowman building competition hiding the unsightly construction area. Dozens of snowmen, a couple donned with hard hats, and safety vests dotted either side of the pit. Nearby shop owners donated wares to the crew to dress up the additional snow people. From his vantage, Ryan could see one wearing a coffee shop apron, another a smock from the hardware store, and a snow pastor was reading from a bible to a bride and groom complete with gown donated from the bridal shop.

Whatever spirit had been sucked from town seemed to be slowly seeping back into place. To Ryan, it felt wonderful. It felt like home, even though he was far from his own. As he drank in the sights of Twin Springs, he reasoned, this is what the town was supposed to be. This was the town's draw. It's legacy.

Surprised, he felt a hand on his shoulder. Turning, he saw the grinning face of Jonas Faslee. "Hard to believe. We are considering a move away from all of this," the mayor whispered hoarsely.

"That would be a shame. This is beautiful – aesthetically and spiritually. Look at your community," Ryan said.

"How, how do we keep this?" Faslee asked.

"There are two sides to that one. Side one is standing up directly for what you, the town believe in. The other is more subtle," Ryan shared. "Here's a couple of examples. I did some marketing for a conservation group. Everything they said resonated with their current membership, but the "green" stance caused the casual supporters to shy away. I rewrote their pieces that linked their message to corporate executives – a base they thought they were on opposite sides. They did realize the common ground they shared, providing them their ear."

"I wrote a series of articles for a radio station a while back. They were a Christian station that wanted to expand their base of listeners. The articles were laced with the values that they held but refrained from being overt. This got people to listen. It led them to the opportunity to hear His message in that manner the station could share."

The mayor nodded, "I hear you. The same can be applied to politics. We spend so much energy declaring our side. We don't give any attention to where we agree."

"Exactly. It doesn't have to be a fight. It isn't one side of Twin Springs or the other that will win. It is the whole of the mutual of Twin Springs that will," Ryan said.

"You'd make a terrible politician, Ryan," Mayor Faslee warned. "You make too much sense."

Ryan looked amused, "You know, I think I'll take that as a compliment."

"As it was intended."

Ryan stood at the door for over a minute, letting shoppers come and go from the gift shop, arms laden with shopping bags and boxes. While not crowded, the store was certainly busy. Maddie and Candace scurried around, helping customers while Allison was putting the finishing touches on a gift-wrapped box.

Handing it across the counter, she looked up and saw Ryan. She gave a little smile and a quick

wink before accepting another item to ring up.
Maddie brought a customer over and booted
Allison out of the way, freeing the shop owner a
moment.

"Hi," she said, her cheeks flushed.

"Nice to see the store full of life," Ryan said.

Looking around at her guests, she nodded,
"It's wonderful."

"The whole town is this way," Ryan
reported.

"Who's doing was that?" Allison probed.

Ryan shrugged, his hands in his pockets,
"The mayor's?"

"I don't think so," Allison rolled her eyes,
then she got excited. "Have you seen Main Street?"

"Winter Wonderland…hey, might have to
use that for the next piece," Ryan snapped.

"It's so cool. The girls and I each built one
during slower spots," Allison said.

"I'll have to try and guess which one's
yours," Ryan said. "Hey, do you have access to the
roof by any chance?"

Allison looked at him, warily, "I suppose,
why?"

Ryan scratched the back of his neck and
glanced away, "No reason. I might need to…go up
there for a moment, if I can."

"Okay, I guess," Allison shrugged. With a
final suspicious glance, she fished her keys out of
her pocket, "I trust you…I think." Slipping a large
silver key off of the chain, she handed it to the
writer.

Grinning, Ryan held the key up, "It's in good hands."

"I hope so," Allison smiled back. "Well, it's a good problem to have, but we're pretty busy. I should get back to work."

"Carry on," Ryan tucked the key carefully in his pocket.

Waving to Candace and Maddie, Ryan made his exit, back onto the streets. With darkness overtaking the evening sky, the snowman town in the center of Main Street was even more lifelike and charming. Through the soft lighting of the street lamps, he felt like he was in a Christmas cartoon with snowpeople frolicking all around the town.

Ryan gave a nod as Johnston Murphy drove by with a carriage full of travelers. Heading down the sidewalk, Ryan made his way to the end of the block and turned. Following the rear of the line of buildings, he found a van waiting for him, just as he requested.

A man hopped out and met him, directly behind Allison's shop. "I'm not sure the town needs any help, it looks like business is good," the man said.

"Thanks for meeting me, Matt," Ryan said, greeting his friend. "Today is good, but it is the tip of the iceberg, both from a message standpoint as well as helping the businesses down here."

"Well, you wanted dramatic. I think this will do it," Matt said, walking to the rear of the van. Removing a pair of latches, the rear doors swung open. Sliding out a long crate, the man set it on the ground.

"This is going to be cool...I think," Ryan said.

"One way to find out," Matt said with a grin.

"The university know you took this?"

Matt looked at his friend, "No one really uses it anymore. Not with satellites and drones and spotter planes. This is like sticking your finger in the air and giving a forecast." With a jerk of a nozzle, the crate came to life. Out of it crawled a twisting, twirling latex mass, snaking its way to life. "It will hold up to 15 pounds and climb to 60,000 feet if you let it, but the FAA would be paying you a visit then. The line I have attached to the carabineer will hold it steady under their threshold."

"I can't thank you enough," Ryan patted his friend on the shoulder.

"I read the articles. I know what you're trying to do here. I think you're doing a good thing. I'm glad to help."

"Wow, this thing is massive," Ryan stared at the giant weather balloon, nearly at its full flight size.

"Yeah, she's a big one. We used it to carry equipment, sensors, cameras...stuff like that. Should hold the rig you want just fine," Matt assured. "That's it. Why don't you go to where you need to be? I'll control it from down here. There's a gaff just inside the van. You can use it to hook the line."

Reaching in, Ryan found the pole with the hook on the end. "I'll see you from above."

With the key Allison gave him, Ryan unlocked the service stairs at the back of the building and climbed his way up to the roof. As he had hoped, there were several cleats used by maintenance workers scattered around the rooftop. Finding one towards the edge of the store, nearly directly above the Nativity, he ran to the rear of the roof.

Rising slowly above the roofline was the tip of the enormous balloon. Climbing its way up until it was overhead, Ryan reached out with the gaff and reeled the line in. With a firm grip, he slid the heavy-duty line to the cleat he had spied. Allowing the line to play out and the balloon to rise high into the air, Ryan found the end with the carabineer and clicked into place. The balloon was so high, it faded out of view in the night sky.

Footsteps crunching behind him told him his friend Matt had come up to help him. "Want a hand?"

"Sure," Ryan said. "I can't believe it. I can't even see it up there."

"We used this one at night. It is a little more discreet, fewer UFO sightings near the university. There is a little red light on the very top, not that any aircraft should be that low, if they are, they've got other problems," Matt laughed.

Ryan lifted a thirty-foot tall PVC pipe structure, "This is it."

"Holy cow, man. You weren't kidding. Alright. I set carabineers at intervals. We can attach it to them. It'll spin a bit, but I have a feeling that

will just add to your effect," Matt reeled the line
back in until he found the top carabineer. Leaning
the top of the piping down, he slid the open end of
the carabineer into an eyehook screwed into the top.

Bleeding the line out, the structure rose until
it was at head height. Finding the matching eyehook
and carabineer, they clicked those two into place.
Slowly, they let gravity loft the structure into the air
until it floated somewhere in the night sky well
above them.

"Hope this works," Ryan said nervously as
he switched on a flashlight and searched the top of
the building.

"There, by that air conditioning unit," Matt
called, pointing to the center of the roof.

Jogging over, Ryan flipped open the cover
found the receptacle. "Here goes!"

Suddenly, the night sky was bathed in
brilliant light. High above them, a giant star shone,
its long elegant tail a beacon for the town of Twin
Springs. Directly below the star, was the Nativity.

Ryan stared up at his creation, awed at the
spectacle. He was suddenly surprised by the
welling of emotion that began to overtake him. He
felt his eyes water as he choked. Less for what the
moment was then, but for the wonderment of what
that actual star on the other side of the world must
have looked like. He suddenly felt humble and
almost embarrassed to have tried to even consider
its recreation.

"Man, that's beautiful!" Matt said, clamping
his hand down on Ryan's shoulder.

"It's not...too false an attempt at..." Ryan began.

"Shut up, Ryan. Are your intentions good?" Matt scolded.

"Yes."

"Are you doing it in reverence or in mocking?"

"Reverence, of course," Ryan replied.

"Then, you are fine. You don't think the big guy doesn't appreciate what you are trying to do here? We're his instruments. Tonight, right here. You and me, man," Matt said, grinning as he admired their work.

"Alright," Ryan conceded, still a little unsure.

"Check it out," Matt said, switching his gaze to the street below.

The crowd of snowmen had been joined by hundreds of people in the street. The horse carriages stopped. Shoppers and diners poured out of stores and restaurants, all eyes on the sky. Children pointed to their parents. Couples hugged as they took in the sight. This giant star, shining bright in the sky. The Nativity, with a sweet, amazing baby bundled under in its wake.

"Is that Gabriel?" a child's voice rang through the night, breaking the silenced hush that had fallen over Main Street.

It took Matt and Ryan a moment to realize the child was pointing at them. "Ooh, the jig's up. Better go." Matt led the way down off of the roof and down the maintenance stairs.

"Treat you to coffee or dinner?" Ryan asked.

"Maybe when I come back to pick it up," Matt replied, "I'm meeting Clarice for dinner in town. Her folks have the kids tonight."

"Thanks again."

"Keep doing good things, brother," Matt said, hopping in his van and pulling away.

As Ryan walked around the corner, back onto Main Street, he felt almost sheepish. He watched as the flow began to return to normal. Ryan couldn't mistake the smiles. The people loved it. Seeing it above the store, above the Nativity for the first time, Ryan had to admit. It was pretty amazing.

"Your handiwork, I take it," Mr. Haverstein said. "I like it."

"Thank you," Ryan replied humbly.

"Oh, there's the girl. Looks like she's coming out," Haverstein nudged Ryan forward.

Ryan hesitated, staying with the crowd as Allison was led out of her shop by Maddie and Candace. She could see all eyes were on her and the Nativity. When they were out far enough, mingling with the snowpeople of Main Street, she turned.

Allison's eyes widened, her mouth dropped, and she covered it with her hands. She stared at the star overhead and then followed the trail of light down to its faintest point, right where the top of her Nativity scene began. She took in a deep breath as she drank in the picture before her.

When she finally turned, she caught sight of Ryan. Without a sound escaping her lips, she mouthed, "This you?"

Ryan chewed his lip, trying to interpret her mood. Reluctantly he nodded his head. She started towards him. He moved towards her. "Are you crazy?" Allison's voice a hoarse whisper as they met.

"Yeah, probably...a little," Ryan smirked.

"It's stunning. It's beautiful," Allison said.

"It's the Nativity. A call to the faithful," Ryan whispered back.

Allison stared at Ryan, watching the star twinkle in his eyes against the backdrop snowpeople. "You are a remarkable man."

"I don't know about that."

"I do," Allison said. Leaning up on her tiptoes, she kissed Ryan quickly on the lips.

Stunned, he watched her slowly land back on her heels. "I'm just a trouble maker in a sweet little town. You are the amazing one. Standing tall through adversity, weathering your values tested and ready for the fight. That's remarkable."

"You are trouble, yes. But I'm not sure how many times I would have folded if you had not been here, encouraging me," Allison said, then her eyes spoke of confusion, "Why? Why would you do all of this for me?"

For a moment, Main Street was empty. It was just Ryan and Allison. Her warm eyes staring into his. Each holding the sparkle of the star shine.

"I only partly know. I know this beautiful woman who captivated me with her spirit. Calm, welcoming even in the face of grueling struggles and unpleasant people. I know the town, sweet in its simplicity, fighting to maintain its identity. I know along the way, having my heart flutter every time I neared your store, every time I saw you. I know I found myself thinking about you each day when I awoke. Wanting to make your life better, somehow," Ryan said.

"The part I don't know, at least not completely…why I am compelled to be here. Why I am driven to Twin Springs, to you."

"Whatever it is…I'm very glad you are here," Allison replied.

The two locked eyes, Ryan felt his cheeks glow. Realizing they were, in fact, not alone, but surrounded with hundreds of people, of the flesh and snow varieties, Ryan wrapped his arms around her. "You have a store full of people," he said.

Allison turned and saw that she did indeed have a mass of customers. "I should probably go. Care to meet me later?"

"Nothing I would rather do," Ryan replied and let her go. Watching her disappear into the crowd and into her shop, he studied the Nativity. It was sweet, quaint. He chewed his lip for a moment and nodded to himself. A final step in the plan was beginning to take shape in his head.

Ryan holed up at the bed and breakfast, stealing a few quiet minutes to complete his articles for the day. Just as he hit "send" on the second article, Charlie Byrd sauntered up next to him.

"Quite the day downtown," the innkeeper said.

Nodding, Ryan answered, "Yes. I loved the snow people collection. Great to see the town having so much fun."

"It's been a while since the people of Twin Springs have come together and just had fun," Charlie said. With a spry look, Charlie grinned, "And an amazing Christmas star has heralded our little town. That your handy work?"

Ryan shrugged, "Needed to light the way."

"You are something else. I like having you around. You're good for this town."

"You know," Ryan looked at Charlie, "I think the town is good for me."

"So, what's next," Charlie leaned forward with interest.

Ryan chewed his lip for a moment. "My work is nearly done. I have a few…enhancements to add. But the rest…the rest is out of my hands."

"Anything I can do to help?"

"How are you at heralding?" Ryan asked, his eyes alight with mischief.

Charlie studied the writer, "Heralding?"

"Yeah, rally the troops. Hail the masses. Assemble your people," Ryan elucidated.

"I see," Charlie chuckled at Ryan's exuberance. "I will see what I can do."

"Perfect!"

Twenty Five

By the time Ryan had returned to Main Street, the town had become more crowded. Shoppers bobbed in and out of stores and restaurants. Families gathered with friends in what was now an impromptu town snow park. Ryan laughed to himself, wondering if Lizzie and her friends might suggest outlawing snowmen next.

Just within the interior of the barricades, Ryan noticed a camera crew panning the scene of downtown Twin Springs. A light flashed on, and a reporter stood in front, the field of snow people, the Nativity, and the bright star as her backdrop.

Out of the corner of his eye, Ryan recognized a newspaper local interest writer from the city. He was unable to suppress a smile. His simple plan was unfolding better than he could have hoped. The final piece would be tomorrow. For now, he was content to watch the town celebrate together. This was their night.

As the newscasters completed their reports, families with children began to head home. New visitors took the horse carriage back to the parking area. One by one, the shops started to close up, the gleaming star still shining high in the sky.

Allison glanced outside her window as she flipped her "open" sign to "see you soon". She smiled, catching Ryan staring absently at the scene. His contentment was evident, even from that distance.

Opening the door, Allison called out, "Hey. Why don't you come in from the cold for a bit?"

Ryan shook himself back to the present. Seeing Allison grinning at him from the door, light snowflakes sparkling in the light from the street lamps, her shop, and the star, she looked like an angel amidst a dance of falling stars. It wasn't just the snow. Her affect had changed. A peace had come over her for the first time since he had met her.

"I could warm-up," he agreed and got up from the snow-covered construction barrier he had been leaning against.

"It's been quite the night," Allison proclaimed, locking the door behind them.

"Glad to hear it," Ryan congratulated.

Candace and Maddie were in the background doing their closing duties, but each paused to chorus a cheery 'hello' to him.

Allison's eyes danced, "I at least get to close down being able to pay my staff for their hard work this season."

"That is good news," Ryan said.

Allison placed her hand on his, "Thank you so much. For all of this."

"Genuinely my pleasure," the writer assured.

"Mind staying for me to lock up?" Allison asked.

Ryan shrugged casually, "Sure."

A knock on the door caught everyone's attention. Farmer Murphy was rapping gently against the glass. Allison opened the door.

"Afraid it's the last ride of the evening," Murphy warned.

Allison instantly whipped around, "Candace and Maddie. You two get out of here. I'll get the rest."

"But..." Candace started to protest.

"Seriously, I've got it. Ryan will walk me to my car, right?" Allison insisted with Ryan nodding his assurance.

"Alright," Maddie acquiesced.

Gathering their things, Candace and Maddie hurried to the door.

"Thanks again, Johnston," Ryan said.

"It was fun. I think my team loved it. Gonna be back twice as strong tomorrow," the farmer assured.

"You guys are amazing," Ryan said.

Murphy beamed, "Happy to give a little gift to the town. Besides, Faslee's going to owe me big. See you tomorrow."

"Goodnight," Ryan waved.

Allison locked the door again. "It will just take me a few minutes. Actually kind of nice to have a little work to do at closing, for once."

"Anything I can do to help?" Ryan asked, glancing around the store. Several shelves were bare.

Crinkling her nose, Allison had wanted to tell him 'no', but she could tell he was antsy. "Alright, how about you just kind of spread stuff out- fill in the gaps and open spaces."

Ryan nodded and started tackling a shelf of angel figurines. Over her counting, Allison watched him carefully moving the pieces around. He would set them down, step back, study the shelf, make a tweak, and repeat the process for each. The sight made Allison smile to herself. Looking down, she realized she lost count and had to start over, but she didn't mind.

In silence, the two worked, Christmas music softly serenading them as they did so. By the time Allison had wrapped up her bank deposit, Ryan had made sure that no shelf was left bare. The store certainly was sparse, but more in the spirit of a gallery showcasing exceptional items as opposed to the knickknacks and local fare that dominated the gift store.

"Well, I guess I won't have much to move. That's a good thing," Allison said cheerily.

"You seem to be taking all of this well," Ryan said.

Allison looked at him, undaunted, "You mean the final day of my store being open? I guess you were right. It feels better to have gone out fighting."

"It was a gallant fight," Ryan smiled. "Final round tomorrow."

Allison shrugged, "It was a fun way to go out."

Allison grabbed her coat and her purse, "Shall we?"

Clicking off the lights, she looked back before pushing the door open. Ryan felt like she was taking her shop in for the final time.

The outside air was cold. Instantly, their breath was visible as little puffs of mist. "Brr." Allison shook, leaning into her escort.

Ryan wrapped his arm around her shoulders and pulled her close as they walked. The brilliance of the star still hung above them. Around Main Street, a few people still lingered. One couple was busy adding their snow people to the mix. They laughed and giggled as they admired each other's work. Across the way, another couple stared up at the star over Allison's shop.

"It is pretty impressive," Allison admitted.

"I like how the light shines down on the Nativity," Ryan said.

"Wonder if the city is going to cut the power to it tonight."

"Nah, I have an inside connection," Ryan boasted.

"You always do," Allison laughed. Turning to him, she looked very serious. "You have had a wonderful effect on this town. On me."

Ryan squeezed her tighter, "I don't know about that. I'm just a trouble maker."

Allison choked another laugh, "That you are. A good kind of trouble, though."

"I'm glad you think so."

"I do."

As they reached the end of Main Street, where the impromptu parking lot had been constructed by the snowplows, Allison stopped suddenly. Turning, she leaned against the traffic barrier, which had been strung with evergreen garland sometime during the day.

Main Street was beautiful. Snowflakes drifted lightly through the air. The gas-style lamps flickered along the street, which was dotted with playful snow people. In the center of it all, highlighted by the star hanging a hundred feet over the town, was the Nativity. From a distance, it looked even more real. Allison could picture a line of people waiting to offer their praise to the child in its shelter. She was proud of her Nativity. Though its time had come to an end, she was proud of her store too.

Despite her strongest intentions, tears made their way to the surface and seeped from her eyes. Slowly, they snaked their way down her cheeks. Embarrassed, she sniffed and wiped them away. "I'm sorry."

"Don't be. It's okay. You did good," Ryan consoled.

"I'm not even crying because of the shop, don't get me wrong, that stinks...it's just so beautiful. I can't believe what you have done for me. I still don't understand why."

Ryan licked his lips, which were dry in the cold night air. He stared at the star over the town before he looked at Allison and answered, "Because of you. You have such a good heart. Like what you just said, you aren't upset because of what you are about to lose. You are happy for what you see."

"I'm blessed, store, or no store," Allison conceded. "I'm blessed because...of you."

She blinked new tears away, looking directly into Ryan's eyes. With a hand on each of his shoulders, she raised herself on her tiptoes. Slowly, her face inched closer to his. Their breath intermixed, their warmth tied into one. Finally, their lips met. Allison squeezed her eyes shut, feeling Twin Springs spin around her. It felt like the star was now focused on them, but she didn't care because it felt like they were alone. For that moment, the entire town was theirs.

Pulling away, she looked down at her feet. Her hands still on his chest. She breathed softly, content to drink in the moment.

"You okay?" Ryan asked softly.

Opening her eyes, she tilted her head up to look into his. "Yes," she nodded. "This is probably the nicest anyone has ever been to me."

"I don't believe that," Ryan scoffed.

Allison was firm and direct in her response, "It's true."

"Well, then you need some better friends," Ryan replied, shaking off the compliment that melted his insides. Noticing Allison's shiver, he nodded towards her car. "We should probably get you home."

"What about you? I can drive you," Allison offered.

Grinning, Ryan shook his head. "It's not that far to the Byrd's Nest. Besides, I want to say goodbye to all my new friends," he motioned towards the street full of snow people.

"You're something else," Allison laughed.

"See you tomorrow?" Ryan asked.

"Of course," Allison gushed. "You are beholden to me for Christmas Eve service. Pastor Dave said that."

"Beholden, huh?' Ryan grinned. "I don't think I mind that so much."

"Sure, you don't want a ride?" Allison pressed.

"You drive safe. I'll see you tomorrow," Ryan said.

"It's a date!" Allison's faced dropped when she realized what she said.

Ryan nodded, a wry smile drawing on his face. "It's a date."

The two shared a moment. Wonder and hope and admiration bubbled from within and poured out through their gaze. With great reluctance, Ryan pulled himself away. "Goodnight, Allison."

"Goodnight Ryan." With equal reluctance, Allison closed her car door and started it up while Ryan swept away the snow with his gloved hand.

Through the frosty windshield, Ryan waved goodbye and watched Allison drive away. His heart swelled, watching her taillights disappear into the night. Lifting his head, he saw the giant cross that stood above the town. A light flurry hazed the white lights, giving the scene an even more ethereal look.

Turning towards town, the view was no less impressive. From the field of snowmen, the Nativity lit by the enormous star, and the overall beauty of town mixed with the thoughts of Allison, he felt as though he could nearly burst. As calm as he tried to appear to his new friends in Twin Springs, he was actually a little overwhelmed with the entire experience.

He had never expected to be so drawn to the town when he was given the assignment, to begin with. Yet, here he was. Completely smitten with the city- and of course, her inhabitants.

Twenty Six

The morning before Christmas Eve
came with a gentle snowfall. When
Ryan left the warm sanctuary of the
Byrd's Nest, he thought the weather couldn't have
been more perfect. The sun had barely offered its
gauzy light through the thick layer of clouds, but
the town of Twin Springs was already surging with
activity.

The city workers had carved out an even
bigger parking area outside of Main Street. Farmer
Murphy had returned with two additional teams of
horses and a few special additions he brought for
Ryan. More 'random acts of Christmas' had made
their way into town overnight. Every traffic
barricade was now adorned with red bows
accenting the evergreen garland placed the day
before. Every door along Main Street had been
graced with a wreath. Haverstein's deli had one

specially decorated with a Star of David and blue bows instead of the red ones attached to the others.

The site at the end of the street coaxed a chuckle from Ryan. The town tree had been re-decorated. Bows, popcorn garland, and a myriad of random ornaments had been placed on nearly every bow of the tree. It was inelegant, yet strangely beautiful, standing tall in front of City Hall.

Farmer Murphy saw Ryan and waved him over. "Where would you like Ewing and Yoty?"

"Let me guess, Ewing is the lamb, and Yoty is the donkey?" Ryan asked.

"Yep," Murphy grinned. "Donkey Yoty."

Ryan laughed. "Can you make them comfortable by The Nativity?"

"Sure. They both love people. I brought their favorite alfalfa; they'll be great all day."

"Thanks again."

"No problem," the farmer said cheerily and gave instructions to his son while he finished preparing one of the carriages for the day's passengers.

Ryan's phone buzzed in his pocket. Reading the message, he hesitated. He wanted to wait for Allison to come in for the day, but he relented to the request. Trudging through the snow-covered sidewalk, the city crews were just clearing, he made his way to City Hall.

Mayor Faslee met him at the door and escorted the writer to his office. "Have you seen the town?"

"Yes," Ryan replied warily, not sure where the mayor was going with the question.

"Now we have a new problem on our hands," Faslee said.

"Oh?"

"I have been flooded with calls. The town is raving about Main Street- even that stunt you pulled. Well, most of the town. I had a few complaints and demands to take it down forcibly. None more fervent than my own daughter," the mayor shared.

Ryan couldn't resist a chuckle, "Yeah, I bet."

"Johnston has agreed to double the carriage rides and bring a relief team of draught horses."

"I caught up with him on the way in," Ryan nodded.

"We have to pick our battles on this one. Business is up on Main Street. Way up. That's good, regardless of what Eric and Lizzie say. The tree, though. That is directly in the face of the temporary order," the mayor said.

Ryan laughed, "That one was not me. I like it, though. I wish I had thought of it."

Faslee looked confused, "What do you mean?"

"The tree, the wreaths, decorating the barricades...the snow people- that was the town, not me," Ryan replied.

"I see," Faslee put his fingers to his lips.

"Makes dealing with the tree a bit tougher, doesn't it?" Ryan said.

The mayor stared at Ryan for a moment, mulling the situation. "Yes. Yes, it does. Any idea who did it?"

Ryan shook his head. "Mysteriously decorated in the night. I would say simply from "the town"."

The mayor sighed, tapping his pencil on his desk.

"I do have an idea," Ryan said. "You get front in center on this. Look at the town. It was thriving yesterday and not just for business, but as a community."

"It was nice," Faslee admitted.

"Go with it. Run with it. I'll find ways to help you capitalize on it."

"Alright," Faslee agreed. Invigorated, Faslee repeated with more enthusiasm, "Alright."

"I'll be in touch," Ryan said.

Turning to leave, he nearly ran headlong into Lizzie. Flanked by Eric Farnham, she stood in the doorway steaming. "You!" she snarled. "You have turned our town into a circus! We are in danger of losing the second investor because of you. That horrific star made the news all the way to New York City. New York! He is not happy with his new building lit up like Rudolph!"

Turning to her father, she spat, "What is up with the tree? Have you completely lost respect in this town? A city order demanded against decorating the tree!"

"Lizzie, the town is reacting. Business was booming yesterday. They loved it," Faslee protested.

Eric cut in, "Sir, if I may. The antics have provided a temporary boon, but they won't survive the sudden drop off. I'm glad your constituents had a good day. In fact, I…we can use that with our investors- showing them the marketplace is out there if we have the right draw for them. But really, what are we going to do in January, wrangle in clowns?"

"I think that is a little much," Faslee argued.

"Think about your next re-election. When the next few months see economic collapse, you think warm, and fuzzies over a few snowmen are going to carry you? Or is a mayor with a real economic plan going to carry the town?" Farnham challenged.

The words had an impact on the mayor. He looked up at his daughter, the developer, and then Ryan.

"Which town do you want to be mayor of?" Ryan asked.

"You won't have to worry about that if we don't fix things now," Eric warned.

"I'm not so sure this is a town that is need of fixing if you ask me, Farnham," Ryan retorted. Ryan excused himself and ignored the glares from Lizzie and Eric as he left.

Ryan was surprised when he left City Hall. Twin Springs was already bustling. The horse carriages were in full swing bringing passengers around the circuit. Among the traffic, Ryan noticed more news vehicles pouring in. The articles and last night's media activity were having more of an impact than he had expected.

Waiting for a moment, he allowed Lizzie to storm out with Eric, each crossly, spouting commands into their cellphones. With the pair scampering off to do who knows what, Ryan had several things he needed to set in motion himself, but first, he knew how to help the mayor.

Rushing back inside town hall, he burst back into the mayor's office. "Fix your hair and straighten your tie Jonas, your national audience awaits," Ryan announced.

"What?" the mayor gasped.

"Four news crews are parked just outside of Main Street. Two from the city, one from the capitol and one from CNN."

"Hmm. Wonder which message they are trying to get across, the winter wonderland of Twin Springs or the improper mingling of government and religion," Faslee mused.

"I believe they are here for your story. Have you figured out what that story is?" Ryan asked pointedly. "You probably have twenty minutes or so. I'll route them to the front steps. From there, they can capture the entire town. You can be there to speak to them."

Without another word, Ryan spun and left the mayor's office. Hustling, he jogged down the step of City Hall and out onto Main Street. Passing the gifts shop, he waved to Allison, who was opening the doors for a slew of customers.

Near The Nativity, he met Pastor Dave. There he was assembling the final stage of Ryan's project. Allison's figures had been removed and stored in the back of Haverstein's shop. In their place, living forms of Joseph, Mary, and the Wise Men basked in the grace of the still analog baby Jesus. As much as they wanted, they couldn't keep a baby in the cold. That thought gave Ryan a deeper appreciation for the real Nativity in Bethlehem.

"We're all set, Ryan!" Pastor Dave beamed.

"I can't thank you enough," Ryan addressed the pastor first and then his actors.

"Are you kidding? Year after year, we do this same presentation in our church, to do it out here, for the town, for the world...it's long overdue," Pastor Dave assured.

"Well, we have lunch set up for you at the restaurant across the street or Haverstein's and unlimited coffee and cocoa at the coffee shop," Ryan promised.

"This will be great. We have five sets of volunteers that will rotate throughout the day," Pastor Dave informed the writer. Then grabbing Ryan by the arm, the pastor stopped him from running off. "You are doing a great thing for this town."

Ryan was speechless. His face humble. He simply accepted the pastor's praise. For fear of becoming emotional, simply nodded and ran off to welcome the television crews and the rest of the press.

The TV trucks had to drive around town to the backside of City Hall, while the paper, digital, and radio media elected to march straight through town, taking in the experience themselves en route to the town hall. Ryan moved ahead of them, wanting to observe the mayor's reception.

As he approached the end of Main Street, he was horrified to see Lizzie and Eric supervising Tommy, cutting down the tree, ornaments, and all that stood just outside of City Hall. It landed with a crash of limbs and shattered ornaments. Several other employees quickly began cleaning up the site, hauling the tree away just as the TV crews had pulled up on the adjacent street.

Ryan froze, awestruck and in total disbelief of the hardened brashness of Lizzie and Eric. To be fair, Eric's part didn't really surprise him all that much, but Lizzie, he felt this was beyond her willingness.

She looked up when she saw him. At first, she looked guilty, like a child caught by their parents, hurt by the disapproval. With a pat on the shoulder from Eric, she quickly returned a stoic affect. "It was a violation of city ordinance. If it stayed, it would have diminished Father's authority."

"Really, Lizzie. This is the message you want to send. This is the town you want? You do realize, it was the town that decorated that tree. I learned at the coffee shop, most of the town either came out to help decorate or donated a family ornament for it. It was the town's tree. Not Eric's, not mine, not even your father's. People like him will trash this town just as he encouraged you to trash that tree," Ryan scolded, nodding towards Farnham. "I wonder how many of the news media caught that."

The reporters were just filing onto the steps. Faslee's receptionist greeted them as he descended the steps to join them. His face drew to horror as he witnessed the stump outside, just beyond the steps. His shock landed on his daughter briefly before adeptly pushing it aside and offering a smiling welcome to the press.

Ryan stayed just long enough to hear Faslee's direction with the interview. "Our world has gotten complicated- a pool of so many wonderful cultures, their own history melding with our history, together making our country as wonderful and rich as it is. What I have learned this Christmas, watching my town...the responsibility of culture is not divined by the government, but by her people. When they are respectful of one another, wish each other happiness in whatever language, religious reference, or tradition, it is a beautiful thing. Here in Twin Springs, we represent what our country was built on- the freedom to be yourself and express yourself in whatever loving manner that may be. Notice the wild scene of snow people – I'm pretty sure I have seen a snow priest, a snow rabbi, a snow angst-ridden teenager...I think it was anyway. They all seemed to get along. At first glance, it may seem like chaos. When you look at it. Really look at it, it is beautiful. I invite you all to explore Main Street. Fall in love with the town just as I love it."

With that quote, the reporters disbanded. A few cameramen stayed to capture the town from that viewpoint. Ryan shook his head as he passed the town stump. A few fragments of shattered ornaments remained. He casually drew his phone out of his pocket and snapped a photo of the decoration fragments lying on the ground for his own article.

Twin Springs was growing busier by the minute. Farmer Murphy was running three carriages in a constant loop and was preparing a fourth. People milled in and out of shops, despite being so close to the actual holiday, they were pleasantly laden with packages. Many merely came and admired the field of snow people or the Nativity.

Then something else caught Ryan's eye. In one of the few remaining open spaces on Main Street, a crowd had gathered and began packing snow. People filed in from the side streets toting wheelbarrows of more snow. He paused to watch and understand what they were doing. After a few minutes, their design of snow began to take shape. Layer by layer, they were defiantly crafting a new town tree out of snow. Whether they watched the debacle perpetrated by Lizzie and Eric, or they simply recognized its absence, nearly a dozen had gathered to erect a new tree in its place.

As more realized what they were doing, the group grew larger, as did the tree. Before long, it was in place, nearly as tall as the original. Families walked in strings of garland and began wrapping it around the tree. The hardware store took notice and donated garden stakes to help hold things tight to the snow.

Allison walked out with a box full of ornaments and handed it to one of the craftsmen. She smiled at Ryan as she hurried back to her shop. There were so many things Ryan had witnessed and cataloged since he first visited Twin Springs that made his heart swell. This one ranked up near the top. Seeing a simple gesture grow into a coordinated effort, nearly the entire town pitching in, celebrating, sharing. He hadn't a single reservation about the direction Twin Springs wanted to be, if he had, it would have been erased at that very moment.

Main Street Twin Springs had turned into a giant town Christmas party. Visitors who began to stream in by the masses from all directions were delighted to witness the heart of the town. As the roads leading into Twin Springs began to become congested, volunteers started walking the line, delivering candy canes and cups of cocoa.

A radio station from the city took notice from their own reports and cut into their planned Christmas Eve broadcast for a special Twin Springs traffic program. Field reporters walked with the volunteers and talked to the people who had trekked to the tiny town.

Soon helicopters circled overheard, capturing the scene for television broadcasts. Ryan's phone began to explode with incoming messages. More than half were bold reports that the scene in Twin Springs had gone viral. Every major television network was reporting on the mass exodus to visit the Nativity.

Ryan's eyes welled up with tears. Overcome by the absolute magnitude and power of the event in Twin Springs, he began to articulate what Christmas in Twin Springs was beginning to mean to the rest of the country. Reports of widespread – 'RACing' – Random Acts of Christmas were breaking out all across the country.

Ryan even got a text from Charlie Byrd that the Twin Springs visitor's bureau was being swamped with inquiries. One thing centered him. Pausing to watch the Nativity was the one thing that drew him back to focus. Pastor Dave's second shift had taken over. The scene was incredible. Mary and Joseph held the wonder that any parent would in the presence of their newborn child. He couldn't even imagine what that must have been like to fathom that their son, lying in that little wooden animal trough, was the king of kings. The Wise Men kneeled with their offerings. Royalty mixed with this humble family in the inauspicious shelter and its natural occupants, the donkey and the lamb.

A store nearby pushed a large television screen toward the window. Ryan watched the newscast, the shot obviously from one of the helicopters circling overhead. Starting with the cross on the hill, the cameraman panned to the star high above where he stood. Focusing in, the report captured the Nativity. Beyond the actors, a growing crowd came to take in the scene. Behind them, as the camera pulled back, the line grew, snaking its way down Main Street, beyond the makeshift parking area, and as the camera continued to zoom out- an endless line heading towards the city.

Another camera angle, starting from the Nativity itself, showed the back end of the line of traffic. In the distance, the beckoning star. Ryan shook his head. It was a monument well beyond his expectations. He had hoped to shake Twin Springs. He realized Twin Springs was shaking the nation.

Twenty Seven

When Ryan walked past the gift shop, he realized how incredibly busy they were. His stomach growling, he checked his watch. It was well beyond lunchtime. He could tell by the frenzy inside. There was no way Allison and crew would have time to break for themselves.

Ducking into Haverstein's, he waited in a line that twisted all the way to the door. Mr. Haverstein and his staff looked pleasantly exhausted. Several items were crossed off the big chalkboard behind their heads. By the time Ryan got to the counter, he saw Haverstein and smiled.

The weary deli owner feigned being cross with him. "This was all your fault. It isn't even a holiday for me tomorrow."

"Hey, you are a willing accomplice. The Nativity is on your property," Ryan reported.

"Ah, yes. I did agree to that, didn't I?"
Haverstein sighed. Finally, he broke a smile, "It's a
good thing you did."

"Thank you."

"This place will never be the same," the deli
owner added.

"Even better, maybe it will stay exactly the
same," Ryan said.

"Very true, my friend, very true," Haverstein
eyed Ryan approvingly. "What can I get you?"

"Four of anything you have left," Ryan
requested.

Nodding Haverstein acknowledged, "For the
ladies next door and yourself?"

"Yes, sir."

"Very good. I'll have you ready in a few
minutes."

Ryan started to withdraw his wallet.
Haverstein shook him off. "Oh, no. I got it. If it
weren't for you, the store would be dead today. You
made me a lot of money!"

Ryan didn't have a chance to argue. The
friendly older man had shuffled off to personally
care for his order.

The crowd was impressive. Yet, everyone
seemed so cheery. The snow tree was fully
decorated and had become a beautiful spectacle
itself. The shiny balls that been staked into its
snowy boughs were a beautiful accent to the white.
The evergreen garland seemed oddly appropriate
for the "tree".

Sliding into the gift shop, he paused. A local artist had an entourage carting loads of goods back into the store to restock some of the empty shelves.

Through the crowd, he found Allison behind the check stand. Seeing Ryan with a bag from Haverstein's, she shrugged apologetically. Ryan understood. Given the volume of shoppers, there was no way any of them could take a break. Ryan thought for a moment.

As he edged closer to the counter, he said, "How about I relieve each of you one at a time. On the floor, of course...I wouldn't trust me with the register. I'm a writer- words versus numbers."

Allison thought for a moment. Her girls had been working hard all day. They could probably stand for a little refueling. "Ok. Start with Maddie. She got here right after me. She is helping people look for things, suggest gifts, carry stuff...things like that."

Nodding, Ryan waded his way towards the back of the store. Seeing her find a box and give it to a woman holding a star ornament, he raised the bag. "Need a break? Boss filled me in on the duties. I'll fill in the best I can."

Maddie hesitated, but her stomach had been growling for the past hour. "Yeah, sounds good. Thank you."

Ryan handed her the bag, "Haverstein said he knew what you all liked."

Her eyes widened, "That's awesome. I'm starving."

Ryan started to turn and find a customer that needed assistance. Maddie's hand on his back caused him to pause. Maddie looked at him and said softly, "You are terrific. Allie and Twin Springs...all of us are lucky to have you."

"Merry Christmas, Maddie." He watched her disappear into Allison's office and found a woman admiring one of the porcelain nativity sets and set off to help her.

By the time it was Allison's turn to take a break, Candace and Maddie insisted they could handle the store for a little bit and coaxed a couple of artists who were stocking the shelves to stay and help.

"Come on. I bet you haven't eaten all day either," Allison said, tugging Ryan by the arm. "Mind if we take our food outside? I have heard incredible things. I wanted to see it for myself."

Seeing the live version of the Nativity with such a big audience and an even longer line milling through, Allison gasped. "That's amazing! Who...you?"

Ryan shrugged, "Pastor Dave and I."

"Wow. You even have a donkey. He's kind of cute," Allison squealed.

She whipped around toward City Hall, pulling a sandwich out of the bag. "Is it true about the town tree?"

"Saw it crash down right in front of me. Moments before the TV crews got there," Ryan nodded.

"Unbelievable."

"Faslee did a good job, I think," Ryan said.

"If he did a good job, that must mean Lizzie is beside herself," Allison said between bites. "And the snow tree. Look at it. It's beautiful!"

"You have an amazing town here," Ryan said.

Allison put her sandwich down and looked at Ryan. "We might have lost it if it wasn't for you."

"Nah," Ryan brushed her off, "They would have come around eventually."

Shaking her head, Allison said, "I'm not so sure."

"You should see the news reports. It has gone viral all over the country. You can see the star from the city," Ryan said proudly.

"Really? That's awesome," Allison beamed, glancing at the giant light hanging above the town. Sighing, she said, "I would rather stay here with you, but I better get back."

"You going to be too exhausted after work?" Ryan wrinkled his nose.

Allison laughed, "You aren't going to get away from me that easily. Besides, I think after all of this, I could use some time to unwind..."

"I bet," Ryan nodded.

"How about you swing by at closing?" Allison suggested.

"See you then," Ryan agreed and watched her disappear back into the shop.

Main Street was packed with families. Some out for an early dinner or holiday treat, others finishing last-minute shopping in the festive ambiance. Most were just there to visit and see for themselves what the talk about Twin Springs was all about. The Nativity was the primary draw. With the crowd in support and the line of people trekking to see, it was a faithful recreation with the live re-enactment of the Nativity.

For the first time in months, Allison was glad to do the day's final account. The shelves were nearly bare. She, Candace, and Maddie were exhausted. But, it was by a comfortable margin, her best day ever. The day's receipts would have matched an entire holiday month from years past.

Finishing up the last tally, Allison grinned, her checkbook in hand, returned to the sales floor. Candace and Maddie were putting the final touches on gift wrapping job for a family that had bought nearly half of what was left in the store. They were a sweet family, the parents helping the children find gifts for a children's charity.

Right on time, Ryan pushed through the front door. A sight for weary eyes, Allison broke into a grin. Even when Eric Farnham snuck in immediately behind Ryan, Allison's affect was undaunted.

Holding up a check, she called, "I have something for you. November, December and even January."

Eric looked stunned at Allison's statement. Eric took the check, frowning as he studied it. "I see. Uhm...I don't believe I need January's. Ms.

Tancredi, it's after five o'clock. The deadline is passed. There is nothing I can do. The new building owner was very clear…excuse me."

The broker stepped away and answered his phone. The family looked on as they waited for their packages. Ryan stood by, biting his lip.

"Nice job today," he consoled Allison.

"Yeah," she smiled wearily. "A hair too late, I guess."

One of the children had asked for a green ribbon for her package. "It's Molea's– that's our sponsored child- it's her favorite color," she explained.

While the father had walked away to place a phone call, the mother added, "We adopt a family each Christmas and have the children make all the decisions on what to get them. They love your figurines. They are beautiful."

"Thank you," Allison said, "They're my favorites. Each one has such a powerful message."

Across the room, Eric's face had turned pale. He glared at Ryan. "You just cost me a lot of money." His phone rang again, and he turned his back on Ryan. "Really? Upfront? No kidding." He snapped the phone shut.

"Well, well, well. Easy come, easy go. Easy come again," Eric beamed. "Another buyer was already waiting in the wings. I'm sorry Ms. Tancredi. I will accept this check for the back rent and the penalties. The office will return any remainder once you are vacated. Which I am afraid is still by tomorrow at 5 pm."

The family had gathered their packages. The father stepped forward, "Wait. That seems a bit hostile and unnecessary. You don't have to go anywhere."

Eric was already confused by the string of phone calls, but this man was the pinnacle of a weird evening. "What are you talking about? Who are you?" Eric asked in disgust.

"I'm the man who just bought the building," the man said solidly. Turning to Allison, he said, "Ms. Tancredi, I have read about your recent struggles here. I believe you are a pillar of your community. I commend you for risking everything to stick to your values. After a long, hectic day, you and your staff showed nothing but patience with my family. If you have any issues with paying your rent in the future, I am sure we will be able to work it out."

Allison stood in shock before the man. His daughters giggled behind him. "Uhm, congratulations?"

He laughed. "Merry Christmas."

"Oh," he turned, to Eric Farnham, "The partners at your firm would like to have a word with you."

Eric's head drooped, and he let out a sigh. "I hate this town."

"Good evening Ms. Tancredi," the man said.

"Merry Christmas," Allison called.

"Oh, my goodness!" Candace exclaimed.

"That was crazy!" Maddie said and then teased Ryan, "I guess someone reads your articles."

Allison was still stunned. "I get to stay?"

"That you do," Ryan said. Looking around at the empty shelves, "Might have a little work to do after the holidays."

They all laughed.

"Girls, go home," Allison said. "Oh, take your paychecks and your Christmas bonuses."

She handed her friends checks and gave each of them a hug. "See you at church tomorrow," she told Maddie. "And maybe you?" she nodded hopefully to Candace, receiving a nod.

Candace walked up to Ryan. She studied him for a moment and then gave him a tender hug. "Thank you for being so good to Allie. Merry Christmas."

Ryan's cheeks turned slightly pink as Allison's friends left the shop.

Allison leaned against the counter and blew the hair on her forehead up. "I don't even know where to go from here."

"It seems like you can go just about anywhere, with a little faith," Ryan said softly.

"How about with you," Allison winced, hardly believing those words came out of her mouth.

"No better place I could picture you," Ryan said, holding his hand out to her.

Allison stepped towards him, their hands meeting first. She let Ryan's grasp pull her into him. She laid her head against his heart as he wrapped his arms around her.

Twenty Eight

The spirit of Twin Springs on Christmas Eve was starkly different than it had been nearly a month prior. There was a peace and togetherness. People greeted each other with cheer as they passed on the street. Johnston was assembling his carriage teams for a few more hours work, volunteering to work until noon.

Ewing the sheep and Yoty the donkey were tied up at the Nativity, fresh alfalfa, and other treats as rewards for their performances. A crew of volunteers had replaced Allison's figurines with a fresh set of actors. Pastor Dave had an entire guild at his disposal of people wanting to be a part of the experience.

Knowing virtue of the news coverage, Twin Springs might still be receiving more visitors, and that many shops would be closed for Christmas Eve, Ryan made a suggestion in his final article. It was evident that his suggestion was impactful.

Nearly every new visitor who came to view the display, was carrying a gift. At first, they simply laid them in a covered area within the makeshift stable. It soon became clear that that space would be grossly insufficient.

Ryan was overwhelmed with the response. Thinking that the event would have been nearly drawn to a close, it became clear it was still reaching its pinnacle. What was even more amazing, the visitors were coming armed with things for the town. Gifts for the charity in Ryan's article, decorations for the city, and treats for the actors were pouring in.

The door outside of Allison's shop started to fill up as well. Cards, samples from area artists and craftsmen, presents, and more were piled out front. If there was an ounce of lack of faith in the people of his country before he accepted the assignment in Twin Springs, it had been eviscerated with the experience. Ryan watched humanity at its most neighborly, its most loving.

"What's all this?" Allison asked, handing Ryan a cup of coffee.

"I guess you have a few new fans," Ryan said.

"Are you Allison Tancredi?" a woman asked, her arm draped around a little girl with wisps of red hair snaking beyond the hood of her winter coat.

"I am," Allison admitted.

"My daughter and I have been reading about you. We respect your stand and what it might have cost you. The Nativity is beautiful," the woman said.

The daughter looked up and grinned, holding out a handmade card, "I like your town. It's cool." She flashed a toothy smile.

"She wanted to bring a donation for the charity, but we don't really have much," the mom said meekly.

"You taking the time to visit us is a gift. Thank you very much," Allison said. Admiring the construction paper card, she asked, "Did you make this?"

The redheaded girl nodded.

"It's beautiful," Allison cooed.

"That's your Nativity," the girl pointed on the page, "And that's the star."

"Nice job. You know who put that star up there?" Allison asked as the girl shook her head. "This man. He is the one who wrote all of those articles. He believed in our town when a few us started losing our faith."

The girl's eyes grew wide, "How did you do that?"

"A little Christmas magic," Ryan grinned.

"You're a wonderful writer," the woman said. "You put heart into your stories."

"Thank you. Don't think I would do it if I couldn't find meaning and have fun with it," Ryan replied.

"Well, Merry Christmas," the woman said with her daughter echoing the sentiment.

"Hey, if you have a moment, I have something inside I would like to show you," Allison said.

"Sure," the mother nodded.

Allison led them to the shop and inserted her key into the lock. Stepping over the notes, cards, and gifts piled near the entry, she went into the shop. "I didn't expect all of this," she replied meekly. Flipping on the light, she waved the little girl towards one of her few remaining displays.

"I hope you get to keep your store," the girl said.

"Sally…" the mom scolded.

Allison laughed, "It's alright. I think we might just make it."

Kneeling by the display, she picked up a little wooden manger. It was a very close replica of the one outside. "I would like you to have this."

"Really? It's just like yours," the girl squealed.

"It is," Allison said. "I'll make you a deal. Every year my store is open, if you come visit me at Christmas time, I will give you an item to complete it. You know, like Mary, Joseph, baby Jesus…"

Sally burst in excitement, "Thank you!" Rushing forward, she wrapped her arms around Allison.

Standing up, she addressed the mom, "Have a wonderful Christmas."

"You too. Thank you."

Sally and her mother left the shop, the girl admiring every angle of the wooden manger.

When they were alone, the gift shop densely quiet, in a peaceful kind of way, tears streaked down Allison's cheeks. "How did all of this happen?"

"You. Your resilience. Your faith," Ryan replied.

"No," Allison covered her eyes. "I was going to give up. You did this."

"You weren't going to give up. You just needed a little nudge. A reminder that you weren't alone. I think your whole town needed that," Ryan said, pulling her into his arms.

Tears continued to stream down Allison's face. "You saved us."

"I wrote what I saw. You saved yourselves," Ryan insisted.

Allison gave in and squeezed him tight. The sound of another package being placed outside her door encouraged her to push back. Wiping her tears away, she said, "If you don't mind helping me, I think we have work to do."

"Oh?"

"The store may not be open for business, but I think we may have become a donation spot. The Nativity was getting pretty full," Allison observed.

"Let's do it," Ryan grinned.

Turning on the Christmas music, warming the pot for cocoa and tea, and flipping on the lighted garland, Allison readied the store as she usually did. Ryan pulled some display tables around to use for receiving donations. Gathering

Allison's fan mail, Ryan brought the pile of items at the entry to the check stand.

Putting a sign in the window designating the shop as a donation center for the Nativity, Ryan started to collect the items left under cover of the manger. When he came back into the shop, he found a man standing in front of the table, Ryan had moved into place.

Something about the man was familiar, but Ryan couldn't quite place it. He was carrying a large brown paper wrapped package under his arm.

"Hello," Allison called out.

"Are you Ms. Tancredi?" the man asked.

"I am. Merry Christmas," Allison replied, studying the man, her eyes grew large for a moment, "Are you..."

"Hayden Thomas," the man bowed teasingly.

"I love your work. My mom collected music boxes taken from your paintings. She loved your Christmas collections. I do, too," Allison shared excitedly.

Mr. Thomas chuckled, "I'm flattered. The inspiration for my paintings has always been spiritually fueled. Finding God's work through humanity. That is where I find the light that illuminates my images. I see that light in you."

"Thank you. I don't know I deserve such praise. Ryan is a wonderful writer. Maybe he is a little too good," Allison nodded towards Ryan.

The painter turned towards Ryan, "You are an excellent writer. If you ever write something in need of an illustrated cover, please let me know."

Ryan's jaw dropped, "I may be just so inspired, Mr. Thomas."

"Good. I look forward to that. But call me Hayden."

The painter turned towards Allison again, "Now, other than to meet you, of which has been an honor, I came to ask you for something. I would like your shop to be my official gallery in the region. We were searching for a site in the city, but I think Twin Springs is just the place I was looking for."

Allison was shocked. She looked around the store, its empty shelves and disheveled state from the crazy previous day left her a bit embarrassed.

Hayden smiled, "I understand what your shop has been through, I also can imagine what a magical place it can be. If you are open to it, I would like to give this painting to you. I would be privileged to have you display it here in your shop. We can work out the details of the gallery if you are interested."

"Of course. I would adore being an ambassador for your work," Allison agreed earnestly.

"Ambassador. I like that. Might have to use that in my other galleries," Hayden said. He handed the paper-wrapped package.

Carefully opening the package, Allison began to reveal a picture. Inch by inch, a beautiful painting began to show itself. It was Allison's shop with the

Nativity stationed in front. Both were bathed in golden light from the shining star above. Allison covered her mouth, "It's beautiful!"

"I'm glad you like it. I was a bit nervous," Hayden declared.

"You were nervous?" Allison was incredulous.

Hayden shrugged, "I don't paint specifically for others very often. A terribly humbling experience."

"I don't believe it," Allison gasped.

"Others might call me a master, I never gave myself that title," Hayden said. "If you will excuse me, I have a flight to catch. It's Christmas Eve. I need to be with my family. I'll see you after the New Year?"

"Yes!" Allison exclaimed. "Merry Christmas!"

"Merry Christmas, Ms. Tancredi, Mr. Talley," the painter bowed his head slightly as he exited the shop.

Allison and Ryan stared at each other for a long while. Both were utterly in awe of what just happened. Their moment was broken by the first donation being brought in. They categorized gifts by age and male or female. Allison greeted guests and accepted the packages. Ryan provided cocoa, tea, and candy canes. Often, people brought in gifts and letters for Allison herself.

The pair worked feverishly to keep up with the near-endless procession. They were overwhelmed emotionally, as well as physically. Spiritually, they more than fulfilled and charged.

Pastor Dave made a visit to the shop. He was blown away by the mass of donation that had poured in.

"I hope your charity can handle all of this," Ryan grinned.

Pastor Dave let out a soft whistle, "We will make a lot of folks who do not have very much, very happy." He cocked his head, "Is that a Hayden Thomas?"

"It is," Allison beamed.

"It's stunning," the pastor admired.

"He just stopped in. He wants my shop to be a gallery of his," Allison reported.

"He couldn't have picked a better site," Pastor Dave said. "Well, I have a Christmas Eve service to prepare for. I trust I will see you both there?"

"Wouldn't miss it," they both chorused.

As the day wore on, they had nearly filled the gift shop with donated items. Occasionally an artist would wander in, requesting to have their item in her shop or apologizing for having removed their items earlier in the season.

Members from the media had streamed in. Most captured images of the shop, Ryan and Allison, and the pile of donations. Several asked questions or requested full interviews. One even offered Ryan a job with their publication.

Throughout the day, Allison and Ryan rejoiced in the generosity of the people who came in. They were continually humbled by the attention they received. Together the pair grew more proud of their work, their town, and the people. The two grew closer with each other, sharing their good work.

A man backed into the shop, his arms laden with packages. Ambling up to the receiving table, his head bobbed above the packages.

"Mayor Faslee, Merry Christmas," Ryan called.

"How is the king and queen of Twin Springs doing on this fine day?" the mayor asked. "Like it or not, you two are the talk of the town. Oh, here. I brought gifts for every age group I could think of." The mayor plunked his armload of packages onto the table.

"If there is anything you two need, please know my office is at your disposal," Faslee said. Whipping his head around, he frowned, "Is that a..."

"Yes, a Hayden Thomas," Ryan answered.

"It's exquisite. I haven't seen a rendering of our town so beautiful...save for when Mrs. Faslee was still around. She did some beautiful paintings of Twin Springs," the mayor declared.

Oblivious of the line forming behind him, Faslee addressed Allison and Ryan, "You have done a wonderful thing for our town. For me. You have reminded us who we are. What we are about. We were about to lose ourselves, but thankfully, you two have saved us. I genuinely believe that. Twin Springs is grateful to you two. I am reversing all of our ridiculous decisions effective immediately. I just wanted you two to know."

"Thank you, Mayor Faslee. I have always respected you and the work you do for the town," Allison said.

"I'm sorry for the pain we have caused you," Faslee said, his head bowed.

"I know you, and even Lizzie meant well..." Allison began.

"Lizzie," the mayor nodded. "Impetuous, that one. She took her mother's passing very poorly. She resented coming back here, yet I know something anchored her here. I think she has been misdirected."

"That first investor. The resort they were planning was right on top of the spot that Lizzie said her mother used to bring her to," Ryan declared.

The mayor sighed, "I didn't know that. Did Lizzie...."

"I don't think she knew that was the plan. Took a little digging," Ryan assured.

"I see."

Ryan piped in, "You know, I have an idea. Her Art Walk idea was a good one. It just had the wrong medium. She told me about her mother's work. I have seen from the artisans bringing things into the shop there is amazing local talent indicative of the spirit of Twin Springs. That is what people

really want to see. That is what would make the Art
Walk an amazing success. Lizzie's success."

"I like that," Faslee snapped his fingers.

"And you're right. Thank you so much. You two are
terrific. See you at church tonight!"

The mayor scampered out, only then
realizing the sizable audience that had assembled
behind him. The entry had become crowded with
visitors toting gifts for donations. They didn't seem
to mind. Likely privy to the stories of the town, they
seemed pleased with his pronouncement. A few
even offered applause for the mayor's statement.

Twenty Nine

Allison and Ryan were joined by the Byrd's and several of the inn's guests as they left the bed and breakfast for Christmas Eve service. "You two sure have made a splash on our quiet little town," Merilee Byrd mentioned. "The Byrd's Nest is on a waiting list all next year."

"It's been quite the holiday," Allison admitted.

As they walked through the light falling snow, the group grew larger and larger as residents joined them on their trek to church. Ryan and Allison walked arm in arm, receiving lavish praise by those who added to their party.

The church entry was packed as people milled in for service. Ushers met visitors at the door and helped them find seating, which was rapidly in short supply. Mayor Faslee and Lizzie were on the church steps when the group that started at the bed

and breakfast arrived. Lizzie cast them a hurt look
and spun her head away. The mayor offered a shrug
as Ryan and Allison approached.

"Hi, Lizzie. Merry Christmas," Ryan said
simply.

"Hello, Ryan...Allison. Merry Christmas,"
Lizzie replied flatly.

"Lizzie...," Ryan started.

Lizzie cut him off. "We really don't need to
do any of that right now." Spinning, she motioned
for the usher to help them find a seat. The mayor
nodded a hello to each and followed his daughter.

Allison squeezed Ryan's hand as if to
encourage him to be at peace with Lizzie.

From the steps, the church symphony was in
ethereal harmony with the worship team band.
Christmas carols were brought to life welcoming
people to the service. Through the music, as Ryan
and Allison climbed the steps, they were given a
hero's welcome by the town. Their cheeks glowed
under the praise. Bowing their heads, they merely
offered a "Merry Christmas" in return.

Every seat taken, the back of the church was
remanded to standing room only, several layers
deep. Pastor Dave looked out the congregation
while the song crescendoed. It was obvious how
moved he was at the participation.

Ryan held Allison's hand tightly. He, too,
was moved by the experience. He was
overwhelmed to watch all of the people, the new
friends that he had met with their families all
gathered. Peaceful, united, joyous. As he watched

the band, when his eyes caught contact with another's, they smiled, waved or nodded at him. Allison smiled at the recognition she felt he rightfully received.

As the song ended, all at once, the church fell into complete silence. Pastor Dave bowed his head for a moment. Initially in reverence for the blessing of his town, the people that filled his church. Beginning his prayer, he acknowledged the One he was truly in reverence for- Jesus, the little baby they had spent nearly a month celebrating.

When his prayer had ended, the band and the symphony softly played a melody in the background. Occasional echoes cooed in from the choir. Pastor Dave swallowed hard and addressed the audience.

"Christmas means so many things to so many people. Church, God…the world around us. We have deep passion, motives, curiosity. We have good intentions, occasionally matched with good implementation, often not. None of us are truly righteous, certainly not as much as we think or would like to be.

Individually, we are humble. We lift our heads when we celebrate, when we plead. We bow our heads when we are prayerful, when we plead. We try and follow a path. God provides us direction, but rarely the blueprint. We are humble.

When I looked upon the Nativity in town. The much simpler one outside our own church, I was reminded just how humble we really are. God delivered us his son in the most insignificant of ways. As one of us, not even as proudly as we typically arrive on earth. He came to us in a food trough, in a stable. His mother, father, and a few common animals his welcome to our world. Humble, yet so wonderful.

Then the people came. Following that star so bright in the sky. The people came. Ordinary people, like us, perhaps. Kings came. Wise men. Each, as powerful and rich or as weak and poor as they may have been, they came. Humble. They looked upon the baby. They looked upon each other. They prayed. Everything greater than themselves.

We celebrate Christmas, and we make a grand display of it. Lights on our trees, our houses…weather balloons suspended hundreds of feet in our sky. We fret over the right gifts to give. We occasionally hope a little too much about the gifts we may receive. The true celebration isn't the decoration, the gifts, the trees. It is what those things represent, what they honor. The humble baby, lying in the manger. Our gift."

Pastor Dave paused for a moment, taking his time to scan the audience before he concluded. "Our town is beautiful. Our town is both humble and proud. Not proud of its economy, its buildings, its real estate. Proud of its people. Humble, caring, loving people. Humble alone, greater together.

When I watched people from miles away come to gather, following a star- if a bit contrived- I couldn't help but to be humbled. Coming to our town. They didn't come here to see a show, a display, a really cool street full of snow people. They came here to see us, God's children. To watch us come together at our finest. Doing His work.

I stopped by to visit Allison Tancredi at her gift shop today. Her empty gift shop. It was devoid of items to sell, but amazingly full of gifts for people they have never met, likely will never meet. As a pastor of a church for thirty-plus years, I have rarely been reminded so vividly of how humble we are alone, how amazing we are together.

While the travelers who visited and the gifts that were brought in were not for the King of kings, this has been the most inspiring Christmas of my lifetime. I witnessed God's hand using our community as an instrument. Maybe you felt it. Maybe you didn't. Maybe you heard him whispering in our ear. Maybe you didn't. I promise you. He was here. He is here.

People came to this country to be free to worship. We grew a strong nation in His guidance, in our faith as our foundation. We didn't turn away others of different faiths. We didn't force them to change or come to church. We did try and lead them to church, by our actions. By our example. By the love and charity that we exhibit.

Twin Springs, in a bit of a Christmas miracle, has reminded the nation, perhaps the world, what it means to share the joy of Christmas. Our tidings of goodwill, peace on earth toward all men.

Let's pray and sing a little praise, shall we?" The pastor bowed his head and prayed. The congregation sang together. They doused the lights and lit candles together as they sang. Ryan and Allison exchanged glances, smiling at each other. Across the way, Ryan could see Lizzie, watery eyes catching the reflection from the candles' flame.

When Pastor Dave released them and wished them a safe and Merry Christmas, the crowd began to slowly trickle out in the night. As Ryan and Allison funneled towards the door, they found themselves wedged in with the Faslees. Ryan could tell Lizzie's makeup had run slightly and tried to give her space. As they descended the steps, Lizzie reached out for them.

"Hey…guys," Lizzie called. Allison and Ryan walked over to her. Stepping out of the flow of traffic and offering the occasional "Merry Christmas" to those who passed, they studied one another.

Lizzie breathed deep, "I…I'm not really good at this." All at once, it poured out of here, mixed with choked tears, "I'm sorry. I'm so, so sorry." Dropping her head at the ground, she stared at her feet. Allison rushed in and gave her a big hug, both women dripping tears on the ground.

"I didn't want to come back. I was frustrated. I thought the town needed…" Lizzie sputtered.

"Lizzie, it's okay," Allison consoled.

Lizzie sniffed, knocking away another tear with her gloved hand. She looked at Ryan with kind eyes, "Daddy told me about your idea with the Art Walk. I think it is beautiful. Mom would have liked that. I would like that. He also told me what would have happened if the first investment had gone through…" Lizzie looked away for a moment. Breathing deep, she turned back, "Thank you."

"You are most definitely welcome," Ryan said.

"Uh oh," Mayor Faslee warned abruptly.

Footsteps crunched through the snow. A panting Eric Farnham rushed up, ignoring the others, addressed Lizzie specifically. "I got a new job…and a new investor. We can still do this."

Lizzie sighed and glanced at the others, "I don't think so, Eric."

The broker frowned, catching her glance. "What do they know?" he demanded.

Lizzie straightened up. She looked slowly from her father to Allison, the Byrd's to the owner of the coffee shop, all streaming out of the church. "About Twin Springs? Everything."

Eric's frown turned into a scowl. He started to huff, but Lizzie cut him off.

"Eric, I think you are done here. Twin Springs will never be your town," Lizzie said, a look of relief washing over her. "Now, if you'll excuse me, it's Christmas Eve. A time to be with your friends and family, not making business deals. Goodbye, Eric."

Lizzie draped an arm around Allison and another around her father, "The Byrd's still do their Christmas Eve service party?"

Charlie Byrd thrust an egg nog into Ryan's hand as he entered the bed and breakfast. With his free arm, he slung a hug around the writer, "Merry Christmas, Ryan."

"Merry Christmas, Charlie," Ryan echoed.

"You've saved the town, now what?" Charlie prodded.

"Hmm," Ryan rubbed his chin. "You know, I was kind of thinking of starting a magazine here. There are wonderful stories to tell."

"I like that. Sign me up," Charlie said. "Give you a free room for a monthly ad."

"Deal!" Ryan announced, shaking the innkeeper's hand.

Merilee Byrd joined the two, "What are you hens cackling about? Charlie, are you giving away rooms again?"

Charlie teasingly hushed his wife, "Trust me, honey, we're getting the better of the deal."

Catching a look from across the room between Allison and Ryan, Merilee shook her head, "I think they are getting the better of the deal. Couldn't happen to a nicer pair."

Charlie laughed and nodded. Ryan pretended not to hear, but his grin gave his true thoughts away.

Pastor Dave walked up, egg nog in hand. "You know, I book up pretty quickly. Now that we are on the map, probably not going to have too many Saturday's open on my schedule," the pastor teased Ryan and Allison.

Ryan blushed, "Thank you, sir. I will be sure to keep that in mind."

"Dave, you're as bad as Merilee. Give these kids at least another month or two before you start pressuring them," Charlie grinned.

"Okay, okay," Ryan waved them off. He smiled at Allison.

"They are right. You two make an amazing couple," Lizzie Faslee offered. Hoisting her mug, "To you two, bringing sanity, hope back to Twin Springs."

Sharing her toast, the three hugged as Charlie and Merilee Byrd began a Christmas carol around their piano.

An egg nog or two later and the Christmas Eve party began to break up, families heading for their homes their own stockings to hang and presents to sort under their trees.

"Walk me home?" Allison whispered in Ryan's ear.

"Of course," Ryan said. Taking her by the hand, they said their goodbyes and holiday greetings to the remaining revelers.

Slowly, they walked arm in arm down the snow-packed street. Another band of flurries drifted down on them, their way well-lit by Ryan's star. "I'm going to miss that star," he said.

"I think my store is going to miss it," Allison giggled.

"Are you kidding? You are famous now. And you are the exclusive Thomas Hayden gallery in the region," Ryan lauded.

Allison squeezed his arm in delight, "I know! It's amazing. It's all so amazing."

"Very well deserved," Ryan praised.

Allison gave him a correcting glance, "Now you're kidding me. Pretty sure I was going belly up and throwing in the towel when you came in."

"Did you take the Nativity down when they demanded you do it?" Ryan pressed.

"No," Allison conceded.

"That was the precipice. That was the snowflake that started the avalanche. That was all you," Ryan corrected.

"Fine. It only became worldwide news because of you," Allison added.

Ryan looked thoughtful for a moment. "Alright, I might have contributed to that," he laughed.

"One last stroll down Main Street?" Allison asked.

"Absolutely."

For the first time in days, Main Street was silent. The frolicking snowpeople vigilant in their own silent celebration. The Nativity, under the bright star. Its motionless figures put back in place, speaking volumes in their silence. Both Ryan and Allison couldn't resist their hearts fluttering with how much that scene meant to them. To the town and who knows who was affected beyond that. An incredible experience merely meant to commemorate another incredible experience.

Allison curled into Ryan's chest. She could feel his heartbeat, slow and steady, to a fast flutter.

She felt her heart match his. The breaths in rhythm, her chest rising and falling with his. Under the watchful light of the cross high up on the hill, they kissed. A deep, meaningful, loving kiss under the Christmas star.